PRAIS

I knew Heartmender was a winner when, after reading mountains of other books, this was the one I kept thinking about.

— S. C. MEGALE, NEXT GENERATION INDIE
BOOK AWARDS

V. Romas Burton's *Heartmender* pumps new blood into the classic good-versus-evil paradigm by way of the classic Seven Deadly Sins.

— LOREHAVEN MAGAZINE

This is a perfect combination of fairy-tale and Christian fantasy that I absolutely adore.

— M. H., AMAZON

Though Addie's story is only fictional, her journey testifies to us that there are forces of light and darkness around us. That we can choose to be "mended" by someone greater than us and who loves and cares for us.

— LAURA, BARNES & NOBLE

This is one of the best allegories I've ever read.

We feel, taste, smell all the different challenges faced with great description.

It was frightening and beautiful, a tale of the war between good and evil and our parts in the fight.

Highly recommended for those who love light romance, action/adventure, sibling stories, christian allegory that's done in a very relatable, not overbearing/heavy handed way.

Narnia meets Dante's Inferno.

Addie is a flawed yet dynamic character I couldn't help but root for.

A deliciously dark world sprinkled with Hope.

I read it breathlessly racing along as fast as the main character did.

I devoured the new world created by the author.

The artistry is hauntingly surreal yet truthful for its depiction of a young woman who must overcome the trials of life that blindside so many of us.

This has been one of the greatest books I've had the pleasure of reading this year.

A very unique take on the seven deadly sins, and the choices we all face throughout our lives.

Decim

Re.

Patet
Ocean

Shalley Mou

Wintertide

The Market

Barracks

HEARTMENDER

HEARTMENDER #1

V. ROMAS BURTON

Quill & Flame

Map by Adam Gray

To my wonderful family, loving husband, and amazing friends. Without all of you, this wouldn't have been possible.

"[E]very time you make a choice, you are turning the central part of you, the part of you that chooses, into something a little different than it was before. And taking your life as a whole, with all your innumerable choices, all your life long you are slowly turning this central thing into a heavenly creature or a hellish creature[.]"

–C. S. Lewis, *Mere Christianity*

PROLOGUE

he dark, twisted trees arched high above my head, casting shadows all around me. Sweat beaded at my brow. I took my steps cautiously, knowing what was coming next. Every time I tried to outrun it, I failed.

Agonizing screams erupted through the forest around me, sending a shock through my spine as my feet sprinted across the dirt ground. Branch after branch cut into my skin as I pumped my legs harder, running toward the screams. My arms stung, but I kept running faster. With each step, the shrieks grew louder and more desperate, ending at the mouth of a cave. The screams beckoned me in, pleading for my help.

A wild heartbeat rang in my ears, but not in my chest. Where was it coming from?

A scream bellowed louder than the others. I had to do something. Gathering my last ounce of courage, I stepped inside the cave.

As soon as I entered the cave, the ground hardened beneath my feet, shifting from the soft soil into something solid and unmoving. The dim light around me extinguished. The heartbeat continued to palpitate. As the cave darkened, the screams ceased.

The heartbeat quieted as well, and I reached down to the earth. A hard, smooth object weighed heavily in my palm, chilling my fingers. As soon as I closed my fingers around it, a blinding light appeared, igniting the space around me. The blood drained from my face as I stared at the object in my hand.

A black heart.

The light reappeared, growing brighter and revealing piles of black hearts surrounding me. I screamed and dropped the heart. As I turned to escape, the piles of black hearts grew, trapping me within the cave. The more I struggled, the more they consumed me. I cried out but knew no one would come.

The hearts constricted around me, squeezing the air out of my lungs. As they buried me, my head about to be encased, the hearts stopped moving, and a chilling voice said, "Don't worry, little Addie, your time is coming."

CHAPTER 1

I bolted from the house, slamming the door shut as I raced to catch up with Lyle. The warmth of the morning danced across my skin as my dress swished with each step.

"Lyle, wait!" I panted with excitement. It was time for Heart Reign, and I couldn't wait.

There were always countless trades to choose from at the annual Heart Reign festival, many of which we had just learned about from Headmaster Clive. From wealth and beauty to social standing and the latest fashions, you could trade your heart for *anything*. Headmaster Clive had explained that some of the vendors, being citizens of Barracks, were always the same: old man Chank with his youthful potions, Lady Truosh with her class caste system, and, as always, Lord Farmount, looking for a new wife.

"Hurry up, Addie," Lyle huffed, sterner than he usually

was. I frowned but brushed it off as nothing more than nerves.

"Coming!" I skipped to catch up to his long strides. "Are you excited?" I grinned up at him.

He glanced down at me with the ice blue eyes we shared before adjusting the spectacles he wore in front of them. "You seem to be."

I pushed a lock of my dark curls out of my face, allowing the breeze to twirl it. "I'm just excited to see if what everyone says is true."

Only eleven, I had spent the previous weeks begging Lyle to let me go with him to Heart Reign. I had heard so many stories of how the vendors would pull out their best tricks when they came to the festival to attract Traders to their booths. There were beautiful colors of fabric and flags surrounding each display, enticing Reigners, those who had already traded their hearts at previous festivals, to take a closer look. Some held mouth-watering foods that made the mind go numb to anything but their rich, delicious flavor. Other displays glittered and sparkled like stars in the night sky. No one could withstand their beauty, and all were instantly entranced. I had read about the interesting trades previous Reigners had made and the even more interesting people they had met. I couldn't wait for my own Heart Reign to do the same.

Unfortunately, since the first Heart Reign of Barracks, the only individuals allowed to attend the festival were those of the age of eighteen or those who had already traded their hearts. Everyone knew that by the time most children in Barracks had reached adulthood, their hearts were shrunken, gray, dead, or dying. Once a child was of age, their heart was so shriveled and gray, it would only kill them if it stayed within their chest. At least, that was what the vendors had insisted and was the reason why the people didn't mind trading their hearts to begin with. After all, what good was a dead heart?

Lyle and I both knew the rules, but Governor Willow hardly ever enforced them. And, since Lyle was my guardian, he agreed to let me come.

The brilliant colors of the tents and booths gleamed against the light of the risen sun. My eyes widened with awe as we came upon the gated entrance.

"Lyle Tye?" the guard seated behind a tall table asked in a monotone voice, his cheek resting on his fist as a green quill dangled from his fingers. His hooded eyes glanced down at the large book of names before looking at us again with an apathetic sigh.

I stood on my tiptoes and strained my neck to see around him and into Heart Reign, but the table was too high. Lyle's hand grabbed my shoulder and shoved me behind him.

"Yes," he said, shielding me.

The guard let out a lethargic sigh. "Has your heart already been extracted?"

Lyle hesitated. "Yes."

5

The man waved to two other guards monitoring the entrance with another sigh. "Very well, proceed."

The guards simultaneously placed their hands on the shining handles and opened the large, iron gate that was installed each year for Heart Reign. I latched onto Lyle's shirt as we walked through, holding my breath until we passed. If the guards noticed me, they didn't care.

Once we had walked far enough from the entrance, I released Lyle's shirt, my mouth falling open at the scene before me. The stories I had heard were true.

A huge smile enveloped my face as the vibrant colors of the flags above the displays waved in the breeze. Each of the vendors called out to whoever passed by, trying to entice them to trade. The giant clocktower stood tall in the center, decorated with the different flags of the twelve lands of Decim.

"Come on, Addie," Lyle said gruffly as he pushed me past a large-nosed woman selling self-adjusting dresses.

I frowned again, pushing a lock of stray hair behind my ear. Lyle usually wasn't this forceful. Could he really be that nervous about trading his heart?

"This is so fun," I told him with a smile before reaching out to take the cherry donut he had traded a fuzz-covered stone from the desert land of Obesque for. Not all the vendors at Heart Reign required a heart for trade; some were satisfied with exotic objects from the other northern lands in Decim.

I watched all the people laughing with one another as

they traded their hearts to better their lives before I bit into the flaky crust of the pastry. A small glob of red jelly dripped out, and I quickly lapped it up with my tongue. I looked back at Lyle, expecting to hear him laugh at my charade, but he didn't. Instead, he looked distant, uninterested in everything around him. While others freely traded their hearts for the first thing they saw, Lyle gripped his tightly in his pocket.

"What's wrong? Are you not having fun?" The donut felt like a rock in the pit of my stomach as he gave me a weak, unconvincing smile.

"Nothing, Addie. Just thinking." He quickly withdrew his hand from his pocket, allowing a crumpled piece of paper to peek out from between his fingertips.

"Thinking about what?" My eyes scanned his clutched hand, then his face. It was strange for Lyle to keep something from me. He had always been honest, and his secrecy ignited a flame of curiosity and concern within me.

I waited for an answer when the clock tower in the center of the market rung loudly. Everything stilled until a cloud of black smoke appeared a few feet away. A woman holding a vase of flowers screamed, releasing the arrangement to shatter on the ground. Those around her didn't notice the mess, their eyes too focused on the charcoal mist swirling in the air. Soft whispers emerged from the townspeople, but they were silenced as the smoke cleared, revealing a vendor no one had ever seen.

Dressed in black slacks and a crisp white shirt, a burly man stood in front of the white birch trees of Wintertide Forest. A bright blood-red door stood on his right, and a bright blood-red door stood on his left. Grinning through his pale, smooth skin, the Vendor revealed perfectly chiseled teeth that entranced the growing crowd before him.

Lyle and I watched as the crowds left the other displays, flocking toward the strange new Vendor. I studied the man as an uneasy feeling sprouted within my chest. Looking back at Lyle, I began to ask if he felt the same, but there was something in his eyes that silenced me and provoked the uneasy feeling to grow.

Stretching his arms out, the Vendor caressed the arched frames of each door. He leaned forward, allowing his dark, straight hair to roll over his shoulders.

"Are you brave enough?" he questioned in a deep tone, silencing the chittering crowd. His eyes were a black abyss, masking any existence of pupils. They scanned over the crowd, as if reading the hearts of every person standing before him. "Are you brave enough," he repeated, "to choose without knowing your choice? To take a leap of faith and trust your judgment, whatever the consequence?"

As if in a trance, Lyle was drawn toward the crowd, dropping the piece of paper on the ground before leaving me without a second glance. I quickly finished the last of my donut, wiping the excess crumbs on my dress before I scooped up the crumpled paper and ran after him. Something strange was going on, and my heart didn't like it.

Lyle pushed and shoved the other Traders, his dark curls disappearing into the crowd as he made his way to the front. I jumped, trying to find him, but the plume of a man's hat obscured my view. Grunting, I crouched and crawled through the crowd. Thankfully, I was small enough to weave around their legs, and I caught up to Lyle right as the Vendor spotted him. Hungry eyes stared at my brother, ready for a feast. The uneasiness that had been building within me grew into fear, slithering through my veins as I stood next to Lyle.

The Vendor removed his hands from the doors and walked the perimeter of the crowd, causing them to gape at his beauty. He clasped his hands behind his back, accentuating his muscular chest, and grinned at the crowd until he singled out one person.

"You. Young man." A long, pale finger pointed at Lyle. "Do you think you're brave enough to choose?"

The fear in my heart slightly subsided, knowing that Lyle had never been easily fooled. Every decision he made, every step he took, was always thoroughly planned out. He would research and research until he mastered a subject completely. I had nothing to worry about. Lyle wouldn't be swayed by this new Vendor and his unknown trades.

"Choose what?" Lyle asked as he pushed up the bridge

of his squared spectacles, a gesture he had performed for as long as I could remember.

Fear barreled into my heart. Lyle didn't refute the stranger. The air around me began to thicken as I stared, dumbfounded, at my older brother. What was happening? Didn't anyone feel the same fear about this strange Vendor as I did?

The laugh that erupted from the Vendor's mouth sent painful chills ricocheting up my spine.

"A door, of course!" He flicked one of his hands back, gesturing toward the two doors.

Lyle gave the man a skeptical look, his eyes darting between the two doors before they locked onto the grinning Vendor. "What's behind them?"

For the second time, the Vendor let out a horrid laugh, throwing his head back for emphasis. The crowd, as if they knew what he was talking about, chuckled along with him.

My skin crawled again, and I knew I had to get Lyle out of there. Something wasn't right. The way the Traders were transfixed by this Vendor was odd. Though the displays at Heart Reign were tantalizing, I had never heard of one Vendor captivating every person in attendance.

I reached out and grabbed Lyle's hand, slightly tugging it to signal I wanted to go.

"What fun would it be if I told you?" The Vendor flashed his shining grin again.

Lyle didn't speak but took a step forward, releasing my hand. My heart cried out, feeling his touch disappear. I didn't know what came over me, but the force of the pain and fear in my heart caused me to lurch forward and grab his hand again.

"Don't!"

We were in full view of every person attending Heart Reign. The laughter had ceased, and the glares and sneers of the people I had grown up with beat down on me as I grasped my brother's hand.

The Vendor took an easy breath and relaxed his broad shoulders, allowing a smirk to stretch upon his lush lips as he peered down at me. My heart tightened with dread before it plummeted to my stomach. His gaze felt as if he knew every horrible thing I had ever said, every nasty comment I had ever thought, all in one glance. What was worse was that his grin grew wider, his eyes hungrier.

"Who is this?" he asked with a cocked head and a look that froze my limbs.

"Addie, let go." Lyle forcefully ripped his hand from my own. The condemning snickers from the crowd swirled around my ears. A large knot formed in my throat, and I tried to swallow it down.

"Lyle, you can't go," I whispered. Tears burned in my eyes. I didn't know what I was doing or why I was doing it. I only knew that this Vendor was bad, and Lyle couldn't believe what he said.

"Addie." Lyle glared down at me, increasing the pounding in my heart. "Everyone chooses something."

"You don't have to choose this," I sobbed, not caring about the growing murmurs of the audience and the enjoyment of the Vendor as he watched our debate.

"I'm going," he said with finality before squaring his shoulders and walking toward the door on the right.

Pity-filled words of, "That poor young man," and "What a burden it must be to care for a needy child" slithered through the air, branding into my heart. A burden. Is that what Lyle thought I was?

"What a brave young man!" the Vendor exclaimed as my world began to crack. "Let's give him a round of applause!"

The crowd threw their hands together, goading Lyle to continue his trade into the unknown. My heart cried out again, but my body remained frozen in disbelief.

The new Vendor, knowing I had lost the fight for Lyle's heart, locked eyes with me and grinned, confirming my thoughts of his ill-intent.

"Now, young man, before you choose a door, you must make your trade." The Vendor reached out his pale hand toward Lyle. A heart for an unknown choice.

Terror built upon the fear in my heart as Lyle nodded, reached into his pocket, and placed his extracted gray heart into the Vendor's palm. As soon as it landed on the deathly white fingertips, the heart vanished into a cloud of smoke. The crowd gasped in amazement, clinging to every moment of the Vendor's show.

"No need to worry, my good people of Barracks! This young man has just made the best trade of his life! A round of applause one more time, please!" The false grin shined upon the deceitful Vendor's face once more.

My heart cried out again, begging me to stop Lyle. But I couldn't. I was a defenseless child, a burden weighing him down. My fists clenched at my sides, the worn edges of Lyle's paper rubbing against my skin. I opened my palm and smoothed out the wrinkles, praying there was an answer inside. But as I read the script I had only seen in old letters written by my father, my heart stopped.

Take care of her.

The paper fell from my hands as my eyes shot up to see Lyle's shoulders rise and fall one last time before he chose the door on the right. Placing his hand on the knob, he paused, and my heart prayed he would look back. But the door swung inward, and he walked over the threshold.

The crowd paused, their anticipation rising. And then it happened. The door slammed shut, sealing Lyle in, never to be seen again.

The crowd stood in awe before they jumped at the chance to trade their hearts for the mysterious choice given by the Vendor's magical doors.

My eyes darted side to side, my lungs constricting as

the fools of Heart Reign closed in, pushing their extracted hearts toward the Vendor. Tears sped down my cheeks as my chest heaved. I had to escape.

I shoved through the lively mass, retreat the only thing on my mind, when a dark presence surrounded me. Bumps raised on my bare arms as a frigid, thick aura swirled over my being. The chaos of Heart Reign slowed, as if time itself had stopped. Although I ran to flee, I traveled nowhere. I stood paralyzed, wrapping my arms around my waist for protection when, only inches away from my ear, the Vendor whispered, "Don't worry, little Addie, your time will come."

CHAPTER 2

SEVEN YEARS LATER

"I don't understand," I said with a frown as I read through the article written in this week's *Barracks Conversation*. I could almost hear the peppiness of the woman's voice as I scanned the words. Why must I be subjected to this torture every year?

"What's there to get?" Silas asked in his usual indifferent manner as he kept his cool brown eyes focused on his own copy. "Lila Crosswater found something worth her heart, so she traded it. Everyone does it, Addie."

"That doesn't mean it's right," I mumbled under my breath. I felt his apathetic stare boring into my skull as I folded the paper and dropped it on the ground. I pulled my knees into my chest and looked out the ice-covered window of my home. It was one of the many houses suffering through the icy wrath that had arrived with Schism Breaker seven years ago. Before him, Barracks was a land of warmth and growth; now it was nothing but a frozen prison.

"Everyone has to choose something, Addie. You know that."

I didn't respond, allowing the crackling of the fireplace to fill the silence.

Silas cleared his throat before reading aloud from the list of vendors for this year's Heart Reign aloud. I shot him a death glare, already knowing who to expect. But, as usual, Silas didn't react. Only a few years older than me, he was always steady and unwavering, never having a rash thought or emotion. I couldn't say the same for myself.

Peering again through the window, I ran my chilled fingers through my dark hair. It was almost long enough to be used for a valuable trade, but I was torn between cutting or keeping it. I had been planning to get a new pair of boots or even some books. Books weren't too common in Barracks, but I hoped there would be a few. It would be nice to get lost in a few stories other than the ones plaguing the newspaper.

But Nana had also said that my hair made me look so much like my mother. I could keep it long to have something to remind me of her. I had only a few trinkets that were hers and my father's before they died.

The words written on the note from seven years ago beamed across my mind before Silas began reading about Governor Willow. The governor's husky, lethargic voice filled my mind as Silas recounted Governor Willow's story about the power his heart trade had given him, which had allowed him to become the governor of Barracks for what seemed like decades.

I narrowed my eyes at the glass. Governor Willow. There was always something about him that didn't sit right with me after Schism came to Barracks. I had never gone to the market again after that day, desiring to isolate myself within my home rather than confront the false happiness of the people infecting the streets with their judgmental comments. But since Lyle had disappeared, I had kept up with the wealthy governor's actions through *The Barracks Conversation*, which Silas would bring to me after his work with Gladio. The vendor uprising a few years back had certainly been a scandal, but after they required each Trader to be personally escorted by one of Governor Willow's armed men, the vendors' complaints had died down. I wondered why all the fuss had begun in the first place.

Twirling a piece of hair around my finger, I peered through a small hole in the ice. Local merchants were beginning to set up their tents and displays for this year's Heart Reign. The fear in my gray heart hardened. It was finally here.

"Are you finished daydreaming?" Silas asked in his monotonous manner, causing the stone in my chest to soften. It had been doing that a lot lately in Silas's company.

"I'm sure I didn't miss much," I mumbled, forming my

shield of disinterest toward all things related to Heart Reign.

"You did," he replied, nonchalantly. "Lord Farmount is predicted to get two women at Heart Reign this year."

I turned and looked at Silas, his angular face an austere mask as I allowed my short legs to unfold to the ground. "Honestly, I don't really care what Lord Farmount does in his spare time." The wealthy lord had taken after his father in preying on young female Traders. But at least his father had the decency to marry them. Frankly, Lord Farmount's use of women's hearts was disgusting, and I was glad I had hidden inside my home for the last seven years.

Silas gave me a strange look as he cocked his head. If I didn't know any better, I could have sworn I detected a small smirk cross those straight lips. But when I gave him a questioning glance, he stood, placed his newspaper on the chair, and strode into the kitchen.

I let out a sigh. When Silas first came into my life, I was on the brink of destruction. I had lost my best friend and the only person who cared about me. I had hidden myself in my house, locking away all feelings of hope or life. Nothing had mattered. It had been days since I had eaten or showered when Silas first knocked on my door. I never answered it, instead staying rolled in the safety of my quilt. But every day after that, a knock would sound at my door at the same time. Eventually, loneliness, curiosity, and annoyance overcame me and, one day, I unlocked the door before running up the stairs and locking myself in my room, thus beginning the tentative relationship we had today.

Although I had locked Silas out of the house the first few times he knocked on my door or locked myself in my room when I did allow him in, he had continued to come without fail. When I wouldn't let him in, he would leave small meals on the front porch. I would ignore them, too depressed to acknowledge my own self wasting away. When I would let him in, I would retreat to my room, so he would leave food in the kitchen. The mere notion that it was there, filling my home with salivating scents, would encourage me to creep down the stairs and feast.

I had always thought it strange how he would come in and out without saying a word, providing me with food, fixing the shutters that had blown off in the latest snowstorm, and cleaning my neglected home. I was the pariah of Barracks, ridiculed and condemned for trying to prevent Lyle from the "best trade of his life." Why would anyone choose to help me? At the time, I wanted to be left to die.

But as I got older and realized loneliness and depression would consume me whole like it almost had before, I tried to engage Silas in conversation. He would never talk much, and his emotions never wavered from the same blank face. But one thing was true: he was always there for me, just like he promised Lyle.

The wind howled outside, and I looked back through the window to see a piece of purple material flying through the air as the local merchants ran about to retrieve it. So much hype and preparation for such a terrible thing.

The sound of a wooden box creaking open brought my attention to the small table standing across the room. A knot formed in my throat as I watched Silas place each wooden chess piece on the scratched board. Though some were broken and falling apart, they still held precious memories.

"I thought you would like to play in memory of Lyle," he said, keeping his back turned to me.

I studied the black sweater stretching across Silas's shoulders, realizing he was trying to divert my attention from the Heart Reign preparations outside. I hated the festival and what it stood for so much that I had become obsessed with my contempt. I knew he was right, and Lyle was gone. But a small hope still lay within my heart, and I prayed that wasn't true.

Standing, I joined Silas at the table, welcoming the distraction from the events outside. I settled into a chair, enjoying the familiarity of the wooden chess pieces within my fingertips as I straightened each one into position.

We were long engaged in battle when a knock sounded at the door, and I jumped in my seat. We both stared at the door, then at each other. Long before Lyle traded his heart, people stopped visiting our home. They were afraid of being cursed, like Nana. And when Lyle disappeared, it only got worse. The unwanted advice and slanderous words of the other citizens of Barracks still rattled through my mind.

As if it were a rite of passage, every year a new group of Traders would come by, throwing more than words at my home. I hated how many times Silas had to repair the broken windows from the rocks and chunks of ice. The worst year was four years after Lyle had disappeared. The Traders for that year came with fiery torches, ready to wipe my actions from Barracks' history. They decided the leper of Barracks needed to be taught a lesson about the glories of Heart Reign for good. Thankfully, Governor Willow stopped them before too much damage was done. But I'll never forget the hate they spewed toward me.

The knock sounded again with more force. I looked back at Silas, knowing it was too early for this year's Traders to visit. His lips thinned into a line before he nodded. I stood and swallowed, bracing myself for the condemning words. Grasping the cool metal knob, I turned it and eased the door open. Silas's warm presence behind me gave me some comfort, but not enough for what stood before me: one of Lord Farmount's liaisons, dressed in a fine scarlet cloak that touched the ground as he bowed deeply. I stood paralyzed. What would Lord Farmount want with me?

"Adelaide Tye?" he questioned as he stood tall once more. He had a long face with a long nose, and his eyes were hooded, glazed with boredom, like he had been on an errand such as this many times before.

"Yes?" I answered, gripping the door handle until my knuckles turned white.

He didn't seem to notice my discomfort. The man sighed and held out a golden envelope that shined brighter than the sun had in years. I stared at it until the liaison cleared his throat, making me jump before snatching the letter out of his hand. He bowed deeply again, turned, and stalked down the stone path.

Closing the door, I kept my eyes on the envelope, unable to believe Lord Farmount would want me to join his collection of women.

I was still trying to decide whether or not to open it when Silas calmly took the golden paper out of my hand and ripped it in two before walking to the kitchen. The hinges of the wood fire stove squeaked as the door opened. The squeak didn't sound again until a few moments later when Silas returned, the envelope nowhere in sight.

I stared down at my empty hands until a surge of annoyance built within me. I jerked my head toward Silas and snapped, "Why did you do that?"

"I'm doing you a favor," he replied, his strong shoulders lifting slightly.

I looked at him, unsure of how to proceed. Steady Silas wasn't acting steady.

"I could've at least read it," I said, feeling unusually curious about the lord's letter. Being at home kept me safe from the evils of Barracks but also created boredom for my active mind.

Silas's lips pressed into a flat line as he crossed his arms in front of his chest. "You're going to waste your heart to be a part of Lord Farmount's harem?" The fibers of his sweater tightened as he sucked in a deep breath, as if trying to calm himself.

I stared at him, trying to decide whether or not to continue the conversation. Silas had always been there for me when no one else was. But the tense stance he was holding and the unexpected fiery look in his eyes were feeding the fears that had grown in my heart years ago.

"No." I kept my eyes fixed on him, not breaking contact as I took a step back, distancing myself from him.

Silas's stance relaxed slightly before he uncrossed his arms and nodded. Though there was still tension between his shoulders, he walked over to the table and began putting away the chess pieces. The old feelings of loneliness sprouted in my heart as I watched him slowly place each piece within the wooden box. It was easier, wasn't it, to trade your heart and lose your emotions?

A dark cloud passed over my heart as I pulled myself up the stairs, silently closing my bedroom door before crawling into bed. I had come so far since that time seven years ago. It saddened me to realize I was still just as alone as I had always been.

Eventually, I pulled myself out of bed, remembering everything I had planned for tomorrow. It took all my strength, but I yanked myself from bed and walked down the stairs, finding everything cleaned and tidied.

Guilt weighed heavily upon my heart as I spied Silas through the window. The outline of his golden waves faded as he trudged down the snowy stone path, away from me. Why was he so persistent with helping me if he didn't really care? Didn't he see I was a lost cause, a depressed and worthless burden to anyone who entered my life?

Yet part of me wished he would stay; having Silas around made me feel safe and secure. But I understood that he wanted to have time away from the leper named Adelaide Tye.

I balled my hand into a fist, hating what Schism and his doors had done to me. Fear controlled my every moment. Every day, his cursed blood-red doors invaded my thoughts.

Relaxing my fingers, I watched the blond locks fully fade into the browns of the community housing. Because Silas wasn't born in Barracks, he had to live in a house with other nonnative citizens. If a family had been born in Barracks and had lived here for at least three generations, they were given their own house and property. Silas had mentioned that it was the only way Governor Willow could keep people from leaving, and he was partially right. *The Barracks Conversation* had published the agreement that was made by the governor after people had started fleeing into the Shalley Mountains toward the other lands of Decim to avoid Barracks' icy wrath. It had worked, to a point. People still traded with one another at the market, but it was nowhere near the thriving society it had once been.

I turned around, pressing my back against the wooden door. My family had lived in Barracks for generations, so our house had been ours for decades. I was thankful for that. Otherwise, who knew what would've happened to me after Lyle's disappearance? Since Nana decided to move out and Lyle disappeared, I inherited the house.

"Nana!" I said aloud, sliding to the floor. I ran my hands through my hair. I had completely forgotten that Silas and I were going to visit her later tonight. Dread filled my heart. I never ventured from the house without Silas.

I looked at Lyle's old metal clock on the wall. There was still time. Maybe Silas would come back. I hoped he would.

CHAPTER 3

The hands on the clock moved half past the hour, and Silas still hadn't returned. I stood from my crouched position on the floor. If I was going to complete my plan for Heart Reign, I had to leave the house alone, and going to see Nana was the best way to prepare.

Pushing myself across the creaking wood, I reached for my tattered wool cloak and mittens, simultaneously blocking out the memories of the comments from the horrid people outside.

Worthless, they had chided. *Burden.*

And one more added on the end: *Don't worry, little Addie, your time will come.*

I shuddered, closing my eyes as I tightened my grasp on the cloak before I pulled the hood over my long curls. It would be fine. I could do this.

When I opened the door, the crisp air slapped me in the face, penetrating my nose as I took in a deep breath. My body froze, reacting in shock to the icy chill that had come with Schism.

Glancing around, I placed one foot out the door, trying to subdue the images of laughing faces and pointing fingers. No one was here. I inhaled and fully left the doorway, balling my hands into fists, determined to leave the house I had condemned myself to.

The wooden step creaked as I placed my foot down. I took another step, welcoming another creak until I had made it successfully down the stairs. A small ball of hope sprouted in my heart until I looked up at the abyss of night, and it reminded me of the dark eyes of Schism.

Lyle was the first of many to disappear through his blood-red doors. Whether Traders chose the left or right door, no one knew what had happened to those who crossed through. Although loved ones vanished, no one reacted as I had.

Even though I had locked myself away, I had kept up with the following Heart Reigns. More and more people desired to trade their hearts away for an unknown choice, and more and more people disappeared. With each choice, the town grew colder. With each heart traded, emptiness overtook those who remained.

As I took a step toward Nana's, I saw the top of blond waves peaking from the edge of the path. Relief washed over me as Silas came into view. Fluttering danced in my chest, and I couldn't help but smile. He had come back.

I stood at the beginning of the snow-covered stone path, waiting for his arrival as the bitter wind howled.

"You left the house," he said, his impassive eyes studying my descent from the front steps.

I nodded quickly, clutching my cloak around my neck. The beating of my heart had increased with his arrival, bringing warmth to my cheeks.

"Good," he replied, his breath creating a cloud of white mist in the air. He hesitated, studying me once more before turning back toward the path. "We're going to be late."

He walked down the path to the snowy trail that led to Nana's as I stepped in stride next to him. I clasped my hands in front of me, lacing my fingers together and squeezing. Silas had shown me the trick of transferring my fear to my fingers when I had first had nightmares about Schism.

Glancing over, I watched Silas stare straight ahead, his eyes never diverting from the trail before us. Ever since I'd known him, he'd been Steady Silas, never wavering from his dull, blank personality.

"I apologize," he said. I sucked in a breath. His eyes stayed fixed on the path. "About earlier."

I let out the air slowly. "It's okay."

"It's not your fault." He paused. "About Lyle."

The knot in my throat formed again, and I squeezed my hands tightly, not trusting myself to answer. Tears stung the corner of my eyes as the lonely years without Lyle played through my mind. All the birthdays and holidays he wasn't there for. The empty chair at our table, convincing me he would never return. I blinked in amazement, allowing a tear to fall as I slowly reached up to catch it. Most people had used up all their tears by the time they were eighteen. Once it was their year to trade their hearts, Traders would begin detaching from deep emotion, leaving only superficial nonsense in their hearts. Many said it made the Extraction easier.

A cold wind froze the teardrop to the tip of my mitten as Silas continued walking. After a few steps, he turned.

"Addie."

I glanced up to see him staring down at me. A breath of air escaped from his lips, swirling into another white puff of warmth in the bitter cold night. My heart leapt as the cloud brushed against my cool cheek.

"You know why everyone loves Schism."

I waited for him to continue, wanting to hear someone other than myself say what we all knew was true.

"Since childhood, we've been taught that the only way to live is to surrender our hearts. Even though Schism takes hearts, who knows what trading for an unknown choice really means? Do those people get their hearts back? Is an oasis on the other side of those doors? We don't know." He paused and turned away. "But you and I both know that every year, Traders think it's worth the risk of trading for an unknown choice. Lyle thought so, too. He wanted to trade for a choice, and he got it." Silas glanced at me over his shoulder. "What you do with your heart is your own choice."

I paused for a moment, not knowing if Silas knew what I had planned. But after his austere face turned away, I replied, "I know." I let the tear fall off my mitten to the icy ground. "I try to tell myself that, but I'm not too convincing. Especially now."

Heart Reign always resurrected the memories of Lyle in terrorizing force. I would wake up screaming in the middle of the night, drenched in sweat from the nightmare that Schism was coming for me next. It wasn't until I had gone days without rest that Silas noticed the sleepless nights in my eyes. From then on, he offered to sleep downstairs on the couch. It would always give me comfort knowing he was there, but the nightmares never ceased.

"You're stronger than you think," he said before trudging down the snowy trail.

I blinked a few times, my steps feeling lighter as I followed his footsteps in the snow.

The welcoming orange lights of Nana's oil lamps glowed like stars. I blew out a sigh of relief as I rushed past Silas, only relaxing at the sound of the wheezing wooden steps.

I looked up to see Nana bundled in her ragged sweater and seated in her rickety wheelchair. The sight of her made my heart heavy with sadness as I remembered the heartache she had endured.

When my mother and father had died, leaving Lyle and me alone, Nana could barely stand. By various trades of old heirlooms, we were able to get her a wooden wheelchair and help her move into the house she was raised in. Once Lyle disappeared, Nana took a turn for the worse. Her white hair fell from her scalp in chunks, and her arms could barely work to move her wheelchair.

When Nana had moved back into her childhood home, the emptiness in her life caused her to never leave the front porch. From the market, the townspeople could see her cemented to her chair, staring off into the distance. They began to use her as a lesson to those who would soon trade at Heart Reign, explaining that trading your heart for love was frivolous and ignorant, leading only to a cursed and lonely life.

Whenever we came to visit, Nana made certain she took good care of Silas. He was the reason these visits had begun. The first few times Silas suggested it, I barricaded myself in my room, not wanting to leave the safety of my home.

But when I discovered he had been going by himself, I decided to try. I began with small steps toward my front door, Silas leading the way. Many times, the result was the same: the words and images of that day would plague my mind, and I would retreat back to my room. Eventually, I had made it down the steps with Silas guiding me.

But tomorrow was different. Tomorrow, I couldn't have Silas guiding my way. I had to stand on my own.

CHAPTER 4

*T*he groaning of the wood beneath Silas's feet refocused my thoughts as Nana slowly reached an arm toward me. Her skin was dull and her hand shook, so I moved closer and gave her a tight hug. Her body felt so cold. I blamed it on the weather.

"It's past seven," Nana noted, slowly patting my arms still wrapped around her.

I quickly removed them, swallowing the realization of similarities between myself and the aging woman. Isolated, depressed, alone.

She looked toward Silas with a resolute stare. "I thought seven o'clock was the time we agreed on, Silas. It's almost eight."

"Yes, I apologize, Nana," Silas replied from the top of the steps.

"My food has been getting cold for almost thirty

minutes," Nana said, her tone as even and emotionless as Silas's. "You'll be lucky to get some."

I gave a slight smirk at Nana's sassiness, but as I looked at their blank faces, it quickly vanished. We could all speak fine, but that's all we ever did. There was no smiling, no laughter, and no happiness. It was another curse cast by Heart Reign and the Extraction.

Straightening, I cleared my throat and wrapped an arm around Nana's frail shoulders. "I think we can let it pass this time, right, Nana?" I looked back at Silas with a small smile. He blinked twice and cocked his head, the corner of his lip twitching slightly before he looked at Nana.

Nana stared back at Silas before turning her chair around. "I suppose."

"Thank you, Nana," Silas said, sliding a look at me.

"Well, hurry along. Unlike you two, I'm starving." Nana didn't give us another glance as she wheeled herself toward the door. Silas reached over and opened it in two steps while I waited for Nana to go through.

By the time Silas and I entered the house and hung up our cloaks, Nana had already wheeled herself into the kitchen and positioned herself at the head of the rectangular table. Once Silas and I sat on either side of her, she thanked the Heavens for our food, and we dove in. I wasn't sure how she did it, but Nana's food was always divine. The chicken was incredibly moist with gravy oozing out as I took a bite. The vegetables were cooked to perfection, making me want more, even though I was stuffed.

"I tried to get your favorite donuts, Addie," Nana said with a grimace. "But it seems they were all out at the bakery. I hope raspberry tarts will do." Her eyes dimmed more than usual at the mention of the pastries.

"That's okay, Nana. I like raspberry tarts just as much." I grabbed a tart and began munching on its crispy crust.

"Tomorrow's the big day," Nana said in a more serious tone than I liked.

I paused, not knowing whether to reveal my plan or not.

Silas's fork paused on his plate as well as he waited for my response.

The topic of my trade at Heart Reign had been taboo up to this point. Neither Nana nor Silas had brought it up, so I didn't, either.

Since childhood, I had been trained and prepared for Heart Reign. I knew of all the vendors, what they sold, and what they wanted in return. But that was where the problem lay. There was only one vendor I wanted to face, and I wasn't going to give him what he wanted.

"Yes, it is," I said, placing my tart to the side of my plate, unwilling to lift my eyes from it. I swallowed before knitting my fingers beneath the table. When I finally looked up, I found Silas staring at me.

"Have you decided what your trade will be?" Nana asked as if she was commenting on the weather.

Silas's hand tightened around his fork as his eyes drilled into me. Sweat began to build on my forehead as my heart rattled inside my chest, the veins of my fear squeezing it tightly. If they knew, they would try to stop me. But if they stopped me, my small hope would die altogether.

Silas's eyes continued to pierce my own, like they could see exactly what was hidden in my heart.

"I've thought about it some," I said finally, not even convincing myself.

"That's good," Nana said indifferently as she lifted a potato to her mouth. "But you won't know what your heart is worth until your Extraction tomorrow."

Past Traders had escaped Heart Reign by not showing up for their Extractions. Many of them believed in the Mender, a man who could mend and purify their dying, gray hearts. It was a small belief, but it was growing enough that Governor Willow enacted the Extraction law: every citizen of Barracks must have their heart extracted on the day of their Heart Reign. Any opposition will lead to death and their forcibly extracted heart being traded by another citizen.

My vision blurred at the edges. I didn't know how to respond.

Just then, a fork slammed on the table, causing me to shriek and jump from my chair. When my racing heart settled, I watched in bewilderment as Silas mumbled an apology and left the table, slamming the door on his way out.

Nana let out a small sigh.

I didn't respond, still overcome with surprise at Silas's response. Steady Silas just threw a utensil as if he were having a temper tantrum. He had always said that everyone had a right to choose what they wanted to trade their heart for. What had changed? Did it have something to do with his Heart Reign?

I extended my stiff fingers to allow the blood to rush back in. *What had Silas traded his heart for?*

I was thankful for his outburst because I didn't have to lie to the only two people I cared for. I was going to miss them, but they would be better without me.

"I'm going to go talk to him," I said, slowly rising from the table.

"All my cooking, gone to waste," Nana mumbled as she rolled toward the sink to wash up.

I shuffled to the old door. Swallowing, I opened it, forcing myself to release my fear of the unknown. I had just left my own house an hour before. I needed the practice if my plan for tomorrow was going to succeed.

Squeezing my hands together, I took the first step out. Cold air pierced my sweater, freezing my skin to the bone. I wrapped my arms around my waist and breathed deeply before taking slow, steady steps toward the stairs.

I looked around, praying to the Heavens that Silas was near. My teeth chattered from the cold as I found him leaning against the trunk of a withered plum tree whose days of bearing succulent delights were long over. With his arms folded over his chest, Silas kept his eyes fixed on the night sky.

My arms tightened around my waist as I crept down each step. The wood moaned beneath my feet until I made it to the icy ground. Pausing, I gave myself a victory smile. Twice in one day, I had controlled my fear.

Sucking in another breath, I stared into the void. The walk to Silas stretched beyond my vision, making it appear farther than I knew it was. Anxiety bubbled in my chest, but I pushed it down and continued on. It wasn't until a throat cleared that I realized I had been keeping my eyes focused on my feet. Forcing them up, I saw Silas standing in front of me. I had begun to think he had walked toward me, but when the tree came into focus, I took a step back.

"I told you, you're stronger than you believe," Silas said in an even manner, keeping his eyes focused on the night sky.

Blinking in confusion, I stared at him before risking a glance over my shoulder and seeing the house behind me. I had done it.

Allowing myself another smile, I turned to Silas. "Are you okay?"

"Yes." His voice was sharp. The warm breath from his curt reply swirled and danced in the moonlight. I didn't know what to make of his tone, so I stood frozen.

"What are you trading your heart for, Addie?"

Chewing my lower lip, I wrapped my arms tighter around myself and looked away. Silas was never so direct. "I haven't decided yet."

He pulled his gaze from the dark clouds and stared straight at me with those brown eyes that knew when I was lying. Letting out a sigh of defeat, he returned to his somber state and said, "Yes, you have."

The air from my lungs dissipated inside my chest. How did he know? Was he going to stop me? My heart beat faster. He couldn't.

"No, I haven't," I answered adamantly, balling my hands into fists. But before he could reply, I turned, retreating through the deep snow as I rushed back to the house.

Throwing the door open, I grabbed my cloak, threw it around my shoulders, and turned back toward the open door. I could explain everything to Nana another time. But now, I needed to leave.

The wind seemed more bitter than it had a few moments ago as it scraped against my face. I swallowed the knot of fear growing in my throat. I would leave by myself. But as I tried to command my legs to move, they stood still, refusing any steps.

Disgust at myself crept into my fluttering heart. Who was I to have hope of saving Lyle when I couldn't even find the courage to leave a house on my own?

CHAPTER 5

"**Y**our heart is a valuable thing," Silas said as he walked up the stairs to Nana's home.

I didn't know how long I had been standing in the doorway, staring into the night, but judging by the pain searing my muscles, I had been clutching the doorknob for a while. I shifted my eyes up to Silas, who stood in front of me, his face blank, as usual.

My stomach squeezed as heat returned to my cheeks. Where was this feeling coming from? My heart was small and gray, like everyone else's. Why was it beginning to feel like it was overflowing with emotion when it should be dead?

I took a deep breath and closed my eyes, feeling the emotion consume every cell of my body. What was happening to me? The fluttering rose from my stomach to my throat as I tried to think of something to say.

"Addie, did you hear what I said?"

The feeling didn't recede when I looked at him. I nodded as my mind wandered back to its previous thoughts on Silas's Heart Reign. He was the same age Lyle would have been, so his Heart Reign had to be the year Schism came, too.

Before I could think of a subtler way to ask, I blurted out, "What did you trade your heart for?"

"May I come inside first?"

I looked at my hand still grasping the knob of the door, my body blocking him from entering the house. Carefully, I peeled each finger from the worn metal, flexing them as I moved out of the way.

Silas entered and closed the door before he turned to me. His lips stretched impossibly thin, and his eyes darkened, but he answered nonetheless. "I don't have a heart."

I crossed my hands over my chest, rocking forward slightly on the balls of my feet. "Of course not. Once you trade it, it's gone."

"No," he said forcefully. "I've never had one. Not that I can remember."

I tilted my head, not understanding. How could someone not have a heart? Everyone had a heart, even if it was dying. I waited a few moments before asking, "How is that possible?"

He ran his hand through his disheveled hair. "The morning of my Extraction, I went to Doctor Magnum, just like everyone else. I went right before Lyle." He paused, drawing in a breath and releasing it before he continued. "When Doctor Magnum began the Extraction, he stopped mid-way through my procedure. I remember the confused look on his face." Silas paused again before striding to Nana's couch. A small table with various trinkets sat on the end. Reaching out, he grabbed a stone carving of a castle.

Studying the small structure, Silas rotated it between his fingers until I asked, "What happened after that?"

His hands stopped, and he placed the castle back on the table. "He called in a nurse and mumbled something I couldn't hear, then sent her away. The next thing I knew, a mask was put over my face, and Doctor Magnum told me to take a deep breath. After that, everything went dark.

"I woke up the next morning and felt a small lump in my pocket. I pulled it out and saw a small gray heart, barely alive." Silas squeezed his hands into fists, staring down at them with a slight furrow in his brow. "I don't know what it was, Addie, but for some reason, I *knew* that heart wasn't mine. And I couldn't live with myself if I traded another person's heart for my own pleasure."

I unfolded my arms and laced my fingers together, not because I was scared, but because I was confused. Doctor Magnum was a renowned heart extractor throughout Barracks. *The Barracks Conversation* had rated him as the number one doctor to see before Heart Reign. He was often flooded with appointments from upcoming Reigners, or so the articles reported. I bit my lower lip, not knowing which story was true.

If what Silas was saying was true, then this had to have happened seven years ago. Had no one else discovered that he didn't have a heart to trade? Clearing my throat, I quietly asked, "What did you do with the heart?"

"I still have it."

I blinked twice, furrowing my brow as I released my grip on my fingers, extending them slowly. "It's still alive?"

He nodded.

"But how?"

Silas let out a sigh. "I don't know. But it's held on for all these years." Turning to me, he repeated, "A heart is a valuable thing. You need to choose wisely what to trade it for."

I nodded, clamping my mouth shut, deciding to keep my plans for Heart Reign to myself.

The sound of Nana's chair wheeling over the uneven floor alerted us before my grandmother entered the room. "Addie, why don't you rest in here for a while?" her level voice suggested. "I need to speak with Silas about something."

I knew Nana had probably heard our conversation or my abrupt near-exit from her home, but I was thankful that she didn't mock me for it. Though we were years apart, we understood each other's reasons for our actions.

Nodding, I retreated to a chair by Nana's broken bookcase, though my curiosity piqued as to why Nana needed to speak to Silas alone. I watched their exit to the kitchen, straining to hear the hushed words. But after a moment of indecipherable whispers, I gave up.

Sinking into the chair, I enjoyed the way the stuffing had been worn over the years from me curling up to read. While Nana didn't have many books, she had more literature than I did. In the days before, when Nana would merely peer out the window into the distance instead of acknowledging or speaking to Silas and me, I would often seek comfort in the stories in her books. Triumphant heroes who diminished evil with a cut of their swords. Magical wizards who could heal with a touch. How nice it would have been to escape to one of those realms instead of the one I was stuck in.

A wave of nostalgia washed over me as I leaned over the arm of the chair to admire the stack of books. They were perfectly organized: large ones at the bottom, ascending to smaller ones.

A small smile came to my lips as I ran my fingertip along the unique bindings of the books. How many times had these stories distracted me from my fears? How many times had I sought love and companionship in their pages when I had none?

The wheels of Nana's chair pulled me from the stack as she entered the room. Her glance was as lifeless as stone as she said, "I know this is a hard time for you, Addie. It's a hard time for all of us." She took in a long breath, her unwavering stare making me uneasy.

Luckily, Silas came through the kitchen doorway,

holding a large red book in his hands. "Just finished up the last of the dishes," he said. He looked at Nana, then to me. "Addie."

I turned toward him. His face, as always, held nothing.

"Are you ready to go?"

Nodding, I glanced at the book. "What's that?"

"That's something for Silas's eyes only," Nana said quickly before positioning herself near the door, ready to say good night.

I cocked my head at the unusual reply but padded over to her and gave her a kiss on the cheek, anyway. "Thank you for tonight. And I'm sorry . . . about everything."

Nana nodded slowly.

I wandered over to Silas, who had already said his good-byes to Nana and was waiting at the door. He clutched the red book tightly in his hand as he gave me my cloak and mittens. Though he bore no emotion, something was off. I started to wonder if it had anything to do with their talk in the kitchen or the book I had never seen before.

Glancing up at him, I gave him a small smile and said, "Thank you for always helping me." I reached out to take the cloak, my hands brushing against his. An electrifying sensation ricocheted up my arm, straight into my chest. I sucked in a sharp breath, hoping my reaction went unnoticed.

But Silas's eyes never wavered as his hand slowly receded. He swallowed and nodded firmly. Before I could say anything else, he turned and opened the door, marching into the bitter night.

Wrapping the wool cloak around my shoulders and pulling on my mittens, I gave Nana a small wave. She nodded quickly and wheeled herself around, fleeing into the safety of her home.

Taking in a breath for good measure, I walked out the door. The cold wind hit me again as I stared out once more into the night sky. Silas's golden hair gleamed in the moonlight as he waited at the bottom of the steps.

I swallowed hard, looking at the long trek before me.

"You can do it," Silas said coolly.

I nodded again, repeating that phrase in my mind as I grasped my hands and walked down the stairs.

Eventually, I made it down the steps and Silas began trekking down the snowy trail. Using him as my guide, I followed each step he took.

We walked through the icy night in silence until we reached the worn steps of my house. Relief overcame me when I saw the cracked white paint and barely attached shingles, and I rushed up the stairs, thankful for the safety of my home. I expected to hear Silas's footsteps follow, but the creaks never came. Halfway over the threshold, I turned around. Silas looked up at me, his eyes heavier than usual.

I tried to muster up a smile, but my words came out with a wobble. "Silas, is everything okay? Are you staying?"

His lips formed into a tight line. "I just want tomorrow to be over with." Before I could react, he turned toward the community housing. "Good night, Addie."

A tightness squeezed my chest, but the fear never came. Instead, the warm feeling I had begun to have around Silas faded, dulling into a layer of disappointment as I watched him disappear into the shadows.

I quickly turned and went inside, locking the door and placing a wooden chair in front of it like I always did when Silas didn't spend the night. My heart, fully calmed since earlier this evening, knew without a doubt that it was safe. Yet, as I looked around at my darkened home, the loneliness that haunted me crept in. Shaking my head, I pushed those thoughts away as I lit every candle and oil lamp I had, extinguishing the shadows.

Satisfied with the light, my eyes began to feel heavy. I knew I needed sleep for tomorrow. I had no idea what would happen. But that's exactly why I couldn't sleep. Taking one of the lit lamps, I walked up the stairs toward Lyle's room. Maybe being in there would bring me some peace before Heart Reign.

The wood squeaked and groaned under my feet as I reached the top of the stairs. Another small lamp sat on a table in the upstairs corridor. Carefully, I used the flame of the one in my hand to light it, causing the hallway to illuminate.

I crept cautiously toward the door adjacent to mine, slightly cracked like Lyle always left it. Taking a deep breath, I pushed it open entirely, allowing the crisp scent of cedar to fill the hallway. Everything was exactly as he had left it seven years ago. Clothes were scattered around the floor, various strange items for trades were stacked in a box next to a pile of books. I had never moved any of them, even when I had reread my own several times and desired something new.

I held the lamp high before I found a candle resting atop one of Lyle's shelves. It was a nub from all the nights when he would stay up late researching. I feared lighting it would cause it to melt completely. Thankfully, my oil lamp cast more than enough light, so I wouldn't have to light Lyle's candle tonight.

Placing one hand on my hip, I studied the room, memorizing every detail of it as I had the day Lyle disappeared. I had convinced myself that if I didn't touch anything, he would come back.

My gaze roamed throughout the piles of things, memories connected to each one. A bundle of light blue fabric caught my eye, and I let out a gasp. Tiptoeing around a mound of socks, I reached out and carefully dislodged the sweater that was buried beneath them. My eyes welled with tears, and I clutched the sweater close. This was Lyle's favorite sweater. After he disappeared, I searched everywhere for it, but couldn't find it. How had it gotten here?

I scanned the room once more, my eyes landing on a familiar stack of papers. Something didn't seem right.

Taking a step closer, I was careful not to disturb a piece of cloth that resembled a wolf from the forest. A thin text, maybe fifty pages long, was covered with Lyle's old scribbled notes. Its length was larger than the paper he had used. I knew I had never seen this before.

Holding my breath, I slung Lyle's sweater around my neck as I carefully nudged the scraps of paper away from the book. The cover was leather, and simple twine bound the yellowed pages together. It looked so frail, as if a single breath would disintegrate it.

Excitement rose in my stomach as I carefully placed the oil lamp on the table and slid the thin text out without disturbing anything else. With my curiosity piqued, I peeled back the tattered cover. An elegant script covered the front page: *Writings and Thoughts by Anna Dilig.* I sucked in a breath. This was Nana's journal.

CHAPTER 6

My fingers squeezed the book. I had always wondered what Nana was like before her Extraction. Thoughts of how this and the sweater had come to Lyle's room when no one had entered it but me flew from my mind as curiosity took over. Carefully, I flipped to the next delicate page and began to read.

"Today was the most wonderful day! I just went down to the market and received a beautiful golden gown. Who would've thought a quick wink and a smile could do so much! I can't wait for Heart Reign. I just know I'll be able to trade my heart for anything I desire."

I blinked at the words. Nana sounded just as disoriented as the woman from the newspaper I had read earlier this morning. But this entry had been written before Schism, when there was still hope in Barracks.

Looking at the fluid, delicate writing, I read the next page.

"Something quite unexpected happened today. Upon my Extraction, I learned I had the purest and brightest heart among anyone! Me! I can hardly believe the luck. Everyone in line was extremely jealous of me, especially Patty Farmount. He has always tried to best me at everything, but this time he came up just a tad too short. Or a tad too dim, I should say! I'm excited to see what trades await at me Heart Reign tomorrow."

My eyes scanned over the passage a second time. A pure heart? So what Headmaster Clive had taught me when I was young was right. Barracks did have an abundance of pure hearts. But that wasn't the case anymore. No one had extracted a bright red heart in years.

Placing my hand in the text so I wouldn't lose my place, I tiptoed from Lyle's room, extending the oil lamp to find my way so I didn't disturb anything else.

Once I crossed the threshold, I carefully placed the door back in the same position it had been in and entered my room.

Reaching for the group of candles I had stacked on my dresser, I grabbed the first one and ignited it. After the flame burst to life, I used it to alight the others and retreated to my bed, placing the oil lamp on the small stool next to it.

After putting Lyle's sweater on the edge of the bed, I nestled under the warm, thick quilt, propping my flat pillow behind my head and opening the journal once more. As I reread the previous passage to make sure I had read Nana's writing correctly, I focused on where she had written about Patty Farmount. Disgust wrapped around my heart. That had to be Patrick Farmount, Lord Farmount's boorish father who had begun the tradition of offering women marriage in exchange for their hearts. I didn't know Nana had grown up with him.

I continued reading.

"Heart Reign was especially exquisite! The colors of the vendors' displays were immaculate, and my golden dress glittered beautifully in the summer sun. What a glorious day! And that's not even the best part! I, Anna Dilig, was able to barter my heart for TWO trades. Everyone scowled at that. No one has ever been able to do it before! I've always wanted to have money of my own, so I chose unending wealth, and, because I could trade once more, I chose beauty. Who doesn't want a pretty face? I'm extremely pleased with my trades!"

I let out a sigh. Nana was just like the others, fooled by the façade of Heart Reign. But I was still curious as to how this exuberant woman transformed into the scarred woman I had too many similarities with. So I read on.

"It has been a few weeks since Heart Reign, and I must say my trades were the best decisions I have ever made. Every day, I receive new beauty potions and garments to adorn myself with. I also have been given a luxurious case of rare jewels, all of which I can trade back at the market for anything I desire!

Though I'm happy with the trades I made, I must be completely honest. Since it was discovered that I received two trades, I have had an unprecedented number of suitors. None, unfortunately, whom I desire. I would never say this aloud, but though the jewels and clothes are beautiful, and the attention is welcoming, none of it feels the same as having my heart did. I feel happy on the outside, but my inside is hollow, as if it's been carved into a hole that only one thing can fill. I'm not sure if this is how everyone else feels, but I wouldn't dare bring it up to anyone, for fear of what they would say."

I placed the journal flat on my lap, staring at the blank wall in front of me. It was true. Once a heart was extracted, your emotions became shallow before fading into nothing. Was Nana the only one who had ever felt this way? Or did everyone else experience and ignore it? I focused on the last sentence, feeling comfort that I wasn't the only one afraid of the ridicule of others. I flipped to the next page.

"Today was a complete disaster! I cannot believe the boorish pig's insolence!"

My brows rose with curiosity.

"I was minding my own business, trying to pick out the perfect tray of cherry donuts for my birthday party, when I overheard Patty haggling with one of the vendors I traded my heart to. The beast was trying to get the vendor to trade MY heart to him! Can you believe it? As if I would actually want that ignorant fool to wrap his sweaty hands around my beautiful, pure heart!"

I pursed my lips, assuming that was when Lord Farmount, Sr. had begun his marriage tradition. I returned to the journal, wondering what Nana had done to him once she found out.

"I wasn't going to stand for that. How dare he! I left the pastry vendor and marched right over to him in a rage. And you wouldn't believe what happened next. A market boy I had never seen before came barreling out from behind the vendor, spilling an entire tray of raspberry tarts down my beautiful lilac skirt. The horror! How would I ever get raspberry filling out of silk? Even though he looked around my age, I was ready to take out my fury at Patty on the market boy. But when he lowered the empty tart tray, it was if I had been struck silly. His eyes—they were like crystals as blue as the seas I had read about. And his hair, like a chestnut tree, thick and wavy. I don't know what happened, but I couldn't speak, I couldn't breathe. I didn't know what to do!

Patty took advantage of my speechlessness and ran toward the handsome market boy, ready to strike him. Luckily, the market boy was too quick and bolted away! He ran so fast, he left Patty in the dust."

Who was this man Nana was talking about? He couldn't be the one she had lost long ago, could he? I ran my fingers over the delicate script. Nana never talked about Paw Paw. Whatever happened was too painful for her to share. Though I never thought he had died, I understood enough to know he wasn't around anymore. But if this man was him, then I was finally discovering who my grandfather was.

"Well, I couldn't let him get away, so I dashed right after

him. I couldn't believe I was so bold! I ran so hard that the thin heels of my boots completely snapped off! By the time I reached the boy, I was a complete and utter mess. My hair had fallen out, there was mud and raspberry tart smeared on my dress, and I was covered in sweat. I'm sure I looked like a disaster.

But that boy looked up at me, and I will never forget it. His blue eyes gazed at me, and he told me I was the most beautiful thing he had ever laid eyes on. An odd thing happened then. I began to feel something strange in the cavity of my chest. It jumped, and I screamed, not expecting the beating of my heart to greet me."

I brought the text closer, scrutinizing the words. Hadn't Nana traded her heart away? How did it come back? This was something I had never heard before. Who was this market boy who had such a power to bring back lost hearts?

"My scream instantly brought the market boy to my aid. He placed his hand on the beating heart in my chest, but I couldn't allow that; I have a reputation to uphold. So I smacked him in the face! And do you know what he did? He grinned and kissed me on the cheek! I was astounded at his boldness. I know he is the man I am going to marry."

Leaning back, I stopped reading, unable to comprehend what had happened. I knew that Nana was married before. I had seen her wedding band on a chain around her neck. She oftened cradled it in her hands when she thought no one was looking. But was the man who had restored her heart her husband? If that was so, where was he now?

"Things have moved quickly, but each time I'm with James, I feel my heart coming back to me more and more. I'm about to burst with happiness! There's not a silk skirt or diamond necklace that could replace how I feel when I'm with him."

So, James must be the market boy who had saved Nana's heart from Lord Farmount's father. And the one who had brought back her pure heart.

"Today was the day my life has changed for the better. James asked me to marry him, and I said YES! A thousand times yes, yes, yes! My returned heart beats ferociously for him now that I feel its life within me once more.

I reread the last sentence a few times, biting my lip as my eyes scanned the text. Had Nana grown her heart back? I've never heard of something like that happening before. How was it possible?

It's quite a strange thing, and it's never happened to anyone before. I didn't even know it was possible until the two vendors I traded my heart to came storming to my front stoop, demanding to get the power of my heart back. How dare they! My heart's power was no longer my own. I have fully given it to James.

They began threatening to take me back to Doctor Magnum's to have another Extraction, but I would never go through that terrible procedure again. Losing the love I have in my heart would kill me."

Doctor Magnum? He really had been extracting hearts for decades. Examining the passage again, I felt my own heart fall to the pit of my stomach. Was the Extraction that terrible? I had never heard negative things about it, but then again, after the procedure, no one talked about what had happened during it. I swallowed, trying to put it out of my brain, and continued reading.

"*They were about to drag me down there when James appeared. He had a strange item in his hand, like an axe, but it had a hook on the adjacent end. James didn't even have to say a word, because when the vendors saw the axe, they let go of my arms and ran away. My savior had rescued me, and we are to be together forever after this very evening!*"

A strange item? More mysteries about Nana's past kept piling up, one after another. I turned the page, my heart racing. But when my eyes moved to the next page, it was blank. I flipped through the pages once more, seeing if I had missed anything, but the entries stopped. Running my hand down the center of the book, I noticed tufts of paper sticking out, as if the next entries had been torn away. I gripped the journal by the binding and gently shook it, hoping the missing pages would fall out. After a few futile shakes, I sighed and set Nana's journal on the ground beside my bed.

My eyes grew heavy. I hadn't realized how late into the night it had become. As I curled under my blanket, my mind filtered through all the information I had learned. Pure hearts, multiple trades, hearts returning. What was the connection? And why didn't anyone discuss it?

My thoughts then drifted to Silas. He had been acting

stranger than usual when we left Nana's, and he was holding onto that red book for dear life. I didn't know what to think of it. And him not having a heart? What did it all mean? But the more I thought, the more tired I felt, and my eyes slowly closed as I drifted off to sleep.

J woke up screaming, streams of tears barreling down my face as I shot up from my bed. I quickly laced my fingers together, squeezing my knuckles until I was sure they would break. The same nightmare had haunted my dreams for the last seven years. Even after I awoke, I could feel the cuts of the branches on my skin and the thumping of my heart in my chest, waiting to explode. The one thing I never forgot were the black hearts. Every time it felt worse, darker, as if the events in the nightmare were becoming more severe with each year that ticked by.

I swallowed before sucking in deep breaths. Black hearts were only known in legends, because one had to be truly evil to create a black heart and gain its uncontrollable power. There was only one legendary figure known to have the power to create them: Ophidian.

My body shuddered, thinking about the snakelike beast from the old tales I had stumbled upon in Nana's books. Headmaster Clive never addressed Ophidian or black hearts in class. When I had asked, a horrific look consumed his features, and I was forced to stay after class and write *Ophidian does not exist. Black hearts are a myth* until I believed it.

But as my nightmare plagued my evening thoughts year after year, I began to wonder if I honestly believed Ophidian didn't exist. The Mender didn't exist, so Ophidian couldn't, either; both were legends passed down from generation to generation to help us escape from the cruel reality staring us in the face.

My heart finally returned to its normal heartbeat, and I unclasped my hands. Thankfully, my lamp hadn't burned out, and my candle was still aflame, reflecting off the light blue fabric of Lyle's sweater. Wiping the sweat from my forehead, I looked over the side of my bed to see the journal still there. I took in a deep breath. Everything was exactly where I had left it.

I burrowed under my quilt once more, knowing the nightmare might be waiting again. But if I was going to succeed at Heart Reign, I had to be able to withstand the darkness, because tomorrow I would face the real thing.

CHAPTER 7

Governor Willow's men came for me before dawn. I half expected it to be Silas when the loud knock sounded at my door, but as I turned the knob, the flutters of my heart vanished. I grabbed my cloak, ready to face the monster who had ruined my life.

The guards were silent, making it easier for me to concentrate on what I needed to do. We reached the market before the sun had fully risen. It was still clouded by a gray sky, but the light brightened the land enough that I could see vendors stirring in the market. My breath puffed out in clouds as I pulled my hood farther over my face. The sooner I could get this over with, the better.

The stones crunched beneath our feet as we walked down the center of the market. The guards stayed annoyingly close to me but never attempted conversation. More footsteps sounded from a path beside us. I glanced over to see Sadie Bloughtry, bouncing happily in a beautiful green dress. Why did she only have one guard? Behind her, a couple walked closely together, the woman's arm linked with the man's. They smiled and chatted as they strode toward the market. Once they came closer, I recognized them from their picture in the newspaper. The man, Mr. Harold Carpenter, had recently become engaged to Miss Olivia Shanseid. Mr. Carpenter had said he was willing to trade his heart for anything Miss Shanseid desired at the upcoming Heart Reign.

The twinge of feelings I had experienced with Silas bloomed inside me again, and instead of the two people walking together, I pictured Silas and myself. Heat spread through my cheeks as I turned away. No, Silas had never had any interest in me. I was a burden to anyone who entered my life.

My own guards halted abruptly, crossing their long, pointed rods in front of me to cease my steps as well. The image of Silas and me together fled from my mind as I stopped, squeezing my fingers twice before I looked up at the large iron gates. A shudder went through my body as I remembered every detail of the last time I had been here. The tall table with the book of Traders' names, the guard with the green quill, it was all the same. I tried to take a step back, but the guard behind me didn't waver from his position, blocking my retreat with his armored chest.

The Reliance, the group of previous Traders who believed in the fairytales of the Mender and Ophidian, were beginning to gather around the gates. Because of their infiltration of past Heart Reigns and violent fights they caused with Traders, Governor Willow had banned them from the festival altogether.

I studied them closely as they grouped together on the other side of the gate. There was something about them that raised the hair on the back of my neck, giving me an eerie feeling. Their eyes were hollow with darkened circles beneath them. Their lips were frozen in straight lines. Their clothes were tattered and torn, yet layered to an extreme extent. Even if the fairytales were true, they didn't look any better off than those who didn't believe in the Mender. In fact, they looked worse.

I looked back toward the gates, squeezing my fingers and trying to avoid making eye contact. Unfortunately, I caught the eye of an elderly member with a knitted cap, and he started walking toward me. I tried to take a step away from him, but the guard to my left wouldn't budge. I looked at the soldier with disbelief and confusion as to why he wasn't doing anything about this man, but he continued to stare steadily at the gate.

"There is another way, miss. You don't have to trade your heart for nothing," the member of the Reliance said, his voice low.

I tried to ignore the lack of competency in Governor Willow's enforcement. I didn't respond but turned toward the man, leaning slightly closer than I should have.

A satisfied look crossed his face, knowing the bait had

worked. "There is a man who can fix all hearts. Little, gray, broken, bruised—nothing is impossible for him. He is called the Mender."

My eyes narrowed as my lips formed a reply. If the Mender could mend hearts, why didn't he prevent the trading of hearts? Why had he never come to save Nana? Or my parents? Or Lyle? It was all lies, and these people believed it. Why chase something that didn't exist?

"He doesn't exist," I said flatly, my eyes darting to the gate, praying it would open soon. A line began to form behind me. All the excited whispers, commenting on what their trades would be, swirled through the air. I pulled my hood down farther over my head and turned away from the man.

"You're so sure?" he replied with a huff. "Well, we'll see now, won't we?"

The man turned and continued his way back toward the Reliance outside the gate. I breathed a sigh of relief, knowing I had gotten off easy. *The Barracks Conversation* had documented full-blown fights between those ready for Extraction and the followers of the Mender, resulting in more injuries for Doctor Magnum to fix and more banishments for Governor Willow to enforce.

Swallowing, I looked to the tall table. A different guard than the one from Lyle's Heart Reign sat behind it with the same green quill and look of boredom.

"Adelaide Tye?" he questioned.

The whispers from behind me immediately ceased as all eyes bore into the back of my head.

"Did he just say Adelaide Tye?" someone whispered.

"It can't be," another added. "I heard she went crazy and killed herself."

I winced at that remark, knowing there was some truth to it.

"Did you see she has *three* guards? It's probably because she'll try to ruin Heart Reign for the rest of us. Just like she did for her brother."

I clenched my fingers tightly, breathing steadily under their words.

"I bet her heart isn't even worth one trade." Snickers erupted from the last comment, and I blinked back tears. This would all be over soon. I just had to keep going.

"Adelaide Tye?" the bored guard repeated, this time peering down at the crowd.

"Yes," I said, more confidently than I felt. A small part of me was satisfied when the snickers died down at the sound of my voice.

"You are hereby granted entrance to Heart Reign and are free to trade your heart for anything you desire, so long as it is extracted immediately," he droned on, motioning to the guards.

The large gates opened, and the guard behind me nudged me forward, hurrying me through so the next Trader could proceed.

I quickened my steps, breathing heavily as I analyzed

all the vendors busily setting up their displays of bright colors and enticing items.

Each vendor I passed eyed me like their next meal, almost as if they could see whether or not my heart was ripe and were eager to rip it from my chest. Uneasiness filled my stomach, and I quickened my pace, averting my eyes.

The clocktower still stood tall in the center of the market, barring the same banners of the lands of Decim as it had seven years ago, but that was the only similarity. After the clocktower had rang out and announced Schism's arrival, it had stopped ringing althogether. There had been several advertisements in the newspaper, seeking clockmakers or tinkerers to repair it, but none prevailed. So there it stood for seven years, its face marking the exact time when Schism had brought ruin upon Barracks.

Settled at the end of the lane was a small stone hut with a thatched roof. That was where my pain would end, and my plan would begin: The office of Doctor Montgomery Magnum.

The Barracks Conversation had once published an interview with Doctor Magnum. Apparently, he had traded his own heart for a long, youthful life, which showed in the picture they included with the article. Doctor Magnum looked the epitome of health. His muscles had been long and lean, and his skin was beautifully bronzed, bright and clear of any blemishes or wrinkles. I remembered from the article that the doctor had explained the only fault to his overall youthful appearance was the long white hair that grew from his scalp. Though it was rumored that his hair had always been white, Doctor Magnum explained he would always pull it back into a single braid so it wouldn't get in his way.

From my limited knowledge about him, Doctor Magnum had always been kindhearted, greeting the patients coming in for extractions with a smile.

Still, my breaths came out short, and my palms turned moist as I drew closer to the hut, thinking about Nana's journal and the emptiness and pain the Extraction left behind. I paused until I felt the hand of the guard to my right pushing me back on course. Irritated with their lack of actual guarding, I shrugged my shoulder away from him and walked on.

Silas's story came back to my mind as well. For Doctor Magnum to knock him out without telling him why didn't make sense. And giving him someone else's heart? How did Doctor Magnum even get his hands on an extra one? I shook my head, trying to rid it of thoughts of Silas. I needed to focus on what was ahead.

As I continued moving, my mind became so consumed with trying not to think about Silas that I didn't hear the second pair of footsteps crunching quietly beside my entourage. Before I could react, a hand whipped through my trio and wrapped around my waist, pulling me hard against a sturdy chest.

"Adelaide," a sultry voice whispered in my ear. "I hear you received my invitation."

I pulled away violently, turning to see the enchantingly smug smile of Lord Farmount. I sent a pleading look to my guards, who had stayed in their triangular formation, staring straight ahead. What was the matter with them? One offense was dismissible, but two?

Letting out a huff, I squeezed my hands together and stared back at the lord. He was handsome in all the ways Barracks' women thought a man should be. Because of his dark brown waves and his bright green eyes, women swooned over him wherever he went. If that didn't work, one of his dazzling smiles would do the trick.

"Yes," I replied curtly, remembering Silas's enraged reaction to the golden invitation.

"And?" He quirked an eyebrow.

My eyes scanned the market for a possible escape. All the other vendors were setting up their booths for Heart Reign, not paying any mind to me or the sleek vulture that stood before me, blocking me from their view. Stiffening, I focused on Lord Farmount, who watched me in a way that chilled my skin more than the cool air. "And what?"

He wrenched my hand that was holding the other and held it tightly. "And are you going to accept?" He leaned closer, his eyes serious as he whispered. "Once you accept, I can protect you from all this."

I blinked, confused. Protect me from what? I looked into his eyes and was surprised to see genuine anticipation, like I wasn't just another woman, but someone special.

The women of Lord Farmount would say how it was a delight to trade to the handsome lord. After a solitary year of companionship, they were given their own plot of land with a residence. My mind dwelled on that for a second before I let it pass.

I was leaving this wretched place and had no need for land or a home.

Retracting my hand, I backed away from him, stepping back in line with my emotionless guards. The sincere look in Lord Farmount's eyes vanished, replaced with something hard and unfeeling.

"Very well," he said coldly as he clenched his gloved fingers into a fist. He opened his mouth to continue, but a wave of giggling caused both of us to turn toward the vendors. Fluttering happily up the road was Lord Farmount's harem, linking arms with one another as they smiled and chatted like everything was right in the world.

When the clucking hens saw him, they squealed and ran toward us. Lord Farmount sighed before looking back at me with a saddened expression.

"I'm disappointed with your decision, Adelaide. Know that it will haunt me forever." Before being consumed by the frills and frocks of his women, the lord grabbed my hand once more and kissed it softly before turning away.

As I watched Lord Farmount saunter toward the

market, I wondered if he had recognized the unhappiness his trade brought him, just like Nana had.

A harsh breeze and the resuming steps of my guards snapped me back to my senses. I focused on Doctor Magnum's office, forgetting the arrogant lord.

Walking up to the wooden door, I hesitated. Fortunately, the guard to my left decided to do his duty and knocked for me.

The light of the mid-morning sun descended on the land, indicating that the official start of Heart Reign was approaching. It was almost midday. *He* would be here soon.

I drummed my fingers against my thighs as I waited anxiously for the door to open. After a few moments, a creak came from the door.

"Adelaide?" a voice whispered. "You're quite early. Nurse Rawlings isn't here yet."

As the door opened wider, Doctor Magnum came into view, looking exactly as the picture had depicted him several years ago. His body was still lean. His skin was still clear. His hair was still white. His face was still young. But his eyes were sunken, like he hadn't slept in weeks.

"She has been selected by Governor Willow to have her heart extracted first," the guard behind me boomed. I jerked slightly at his loud voice.

Doctor Magnum gave a quick nod but didn't allow either of us inside the office.

There was something deeply troubling the man. Swallowing, I found some courage and asked, "Doctor Magnum, are you all right?"

As if realizing the state he was in, Doctor Magnum quickly straightened, running his hands across his clothes as he flashed a winning smile at me, his perfectly straight teeth gleaming from his flawless chestnut skin. "Yes, of course. Where are my manners? Please, come in, come in."

As I walked into the hut, Doctor Magnum quickly shut the door behind me, locking my guards outside.

I stared at the closed door, my body tensing as my senses went on alert. The thumping of my heart pounded between my ears as I swallowed the knot rising in my throat. I drew in a few breaths, a sterile scent consuming my lungs as I clasped my hands, studying the room before me. Perfectly placed chairs lined the perimeter of the light gray walls. A small table in the corner was piled with children's books and toys, while a stack of twenty-year-old *Conversations* sat atop another table. I assumed this was all to keep patients occupied while they waited. Curious about the old newspapers, I was about to pick one up when Doctor Magnum spoke up.

"So, Adelaide." He rubbed his hands together with another striking grin. "Today's the day. How are you feeling?"

I stared at him, not knowing what to say. There were so many emotions ricocheting off one another that I didn't know how I felt.

I gave a nonchalant shrug and waited, trying to avert my eyes from the doctor's scrutinizing stare.

Doctor Magnum gave me a quizzical look, as if that wasn't the response he had been expecting. He then sat down in one of the waiting chairs with a sigh.

"I know I'm not supposed to say this, but I'm deeply sorry about what happened to Lyle." He paused. "And the others."

I looked at him, my mouth ajar. No one in Barracks ever mentioned what happened to Lyle. And people definitely didn't talk about the disappearances of the others. The citizens of Barracks didn't like to remember the obvious evil in the past. When Heart Reign occurred, they only cared about themselves and making a good trade. After that, their emotions disintegrated, so their feelings toward others didn't matter. But the evil wasn't just in the past, but in the present and future. For Doctor Magnum, of all people, to mention it was beyond my understanding.

Coughing, he quickly transformed back to his cheerful self, slapping his hands on his knees before standing. "Let's have a look at your heart, shall we?"

I nodded, grateful. I wanted to get this over with.

Doctor Magnum quickly led me to the back room, casting a wary glance at the front door on the way.

Four blindingly white walls greeted me. The matching white cabinets on the far wall accentuated the black, marble table that stood perfectly in the middle of the sterile space. Next to it was a silver table scattered with various shining instruments I didn't want to know about.

I squeezed my hands, taking in the room and thinking about all the people who had laid on that table, willingly giving up their hearts. And I was about to do the same.

CHAPTER 8

"*P*lease." He motioned to the shining ebony table.

I swallowed, trying desperately to calm the ferocity of my heartbeats. When I pulled the hood of my cloak back, my long ponytail spiraled down my left shoulder. I had tied it back this morning with a red ribbon Silas had given me a few years ago.

I sat on the hard surface before laying completely flat. The chill of the black marble seeped through my wool cloak, causing cold bumps to cover the entirety of my flesh. I took a deep breath and clasped my hands over my stomach as I stared at the crisp white ceiling. Everyone had to extract their heart. Everyone *wanted* to extract their heart. So why did I feel nothing but dread?

Shuffling and clanging sounds came from my right. I twisted my neck and watched as Doctor Magnum arranged a variety of instruments on the small table with his back to me.

"So," he mumbled, picking up a very sharp object as long as my arm. "How's your friend doing?"

"Um," I stammered, unable to take my eyes off the instrument in his hand. "I'm sorry, what friend?"

"You know" —Doctor Magnum turned slightly, revealing a rather casual smirk—"the one who's always visiting you. What's his name? Stephen? Stifle?"

"Silas," I whispered. I absentmindedly reached for the ribbon in my hair, trying to think of him right now. I knew Doctor Magnum had done this hundreds of times before, but handling my Extraction like a normal appointment felt wrong. Bringing up Silas felt even worse.

"Ah, yes, Silas. Is he well?" he asked above a piercing clink of metal.

It took all my strength not to vomit as he picked up an even larger object, this one with several blades sticking out. "Yes."

"That's good, that's good." Doctor Magnum turned around with his polite smile and motley collection of torture devices. "Now, forgive my memory. A long, youthful life doesn't mean a long, youthful brain!" He chuckled at himself. I stared at him until he cleared his throat and turned back around. "But I seem to have forgotten what he traded his heart for."

I squeezed my fingers tightly, nausea filling my stomach. If what Silas had said was true—that he never had a heart of his own and was given someone else's—wouldn't Doctor Magnum already know since he was the one who had performed the Extraction? And for me to reveal that Silas was still holding onto that heart without trading it would bring serious consequences.

I gave the doctor a weak smile, trying to fabricate the best lie I could. "Silas wasn't really into Heart Reign."

"Wasn't?" Doctor Magnum stiffened. It was odd how he could emote so easily. It had been decades since he traded his heart. "What happened to him?"

Panic rose in my throat, and I squeezed my fingers. "I'm not sure."

Doctor Magnum turned his full attention on me. "Is he not attending Heart Reign?"

"I don't know," I mumbled, hating that my heart felt like it would burst.

"That's very . . . interesting." Doctor Magnum paused for a few moments, his silence like a needle injecting anxiety into my veins. The clinking of metal tools echoed throughout the room until the doctor cleared his throat. "Well, I'm sure he'll be fine." He whipped back around.

A churning sound came from in front of him, and I shut my eyes for a second. I wanted this to be over.

Answering my silent plea, Doctor Magnum turned around. My heart froze once I saw what was in his hands: a long metal cylinder equipped with several sharp gadgets protruding from it. The different blades were at least two inches in length, shining like fangs. All the blood drained from my face. Doctor Magnum laughed heartily. How could he laugh?

"Oh, Adelaide, don't worry. This isn't the setting we use for Extractions."

He pressed a button, and the sharp objects retracted into the cylinder. At one end, a smooth, rounded tube slid out. Sharp minuscule teeth jutted from its metallic circumference that was just wide enough to cover the area of skin above my heart.

"That doesn't look much better," I muttered.

Doctor Magnum laughed again. "I always enjoy Extraction conversations. Most people are too eager to extract their heart and never question my methods."

"That's reassuring," I squeaked.

Doctor Magnum walked to one of the cabinets and pulled out a simple white dress with two giant pockets in the front. "Before we begin, you must put this on."

I stared at him, hoping he wasn't serious. His stern look didn't waver. Swallowing, I sat up and grabbed the dress. As I began to untie my cloak, I shot a glare over my shoulder.

"You can't stay in here."

He snorted. "Of course not. I'll be waiting outside. Just knock when you're ready."

After he closed the door, I studied the dress. There wasn't much to it. The neck scooped lower than I would have liked, but I could surmise that it was designed with the purpose of an Extraction in mind.

With some regret, I pulled off Lyle's light blue sweater and my pants, changing into the white gown. The fabric tumbled to the ground, touching the tops of my boots. The cool winter air sent chills up my exposed arms and chest, causing the bumps to return. The last time I had worn clothing without sleeves was at Lyle's Heart Reign, when the weather was still warm and welcoming.

I knocked on the door and within moments, Doctor Magnum returned. He stopped briefly and stared at me as if in a trance.

"You look just like her," he said, barely above a whisper, his face paling. I stared at him in confusion. Shaking his head, Doctor Magnum smiled politely, forcing his casual demeanor to return. "Shall we get started?"

Laying back down on the table, I felt like an animal being led to slaughter.

Doctor Magnum stood next to the table, looking down at me. A piece of his white hair slipped from his braid, framing his youthful face. With a stern look of concentration, he placed the cool metal tube on my chest, causing my whole body to tense.

Sensing my fear, he smiled and said, "Don't worry, this won't hurt a bit."

In one motion, he turned the cylinder, causing a churning sound as pressure hit my chest. I let out a gasp when the cool metal pierced my flesh. As the tiny metal teeth cut deeper and deeper into my skin, I shrieked, but Doctor Magnum continued placing pressure on the cylinder. The crisp metal descended on my heart, and my body pulled in two different directions. When the cylinder made contact, my heart let out a cry, trembling as it fought the ascending pressure. I gripped my fingers tightly, feeling tears well in my eyes before they streamed down my cheeks. They were probably my last. I was being stretched to the point of breaking.

Then I heard it. A snap reverberated inside my ears, and my eyes shot open. It was as if I had lost the entire essence of my being. Everything that had made me who I was vanished.

Gasping, I sat up, placing my hand where the device had just been. My skin was cold, drained of all life, leaving a void behind. A thin white line traced where the circular device had extracted my heart. Everything felt empty.

I looked over to see Doctor Magnum still holding the Extraction device, staring at something in his hand with a look of awe.

"Doctor Magnum, where is my heart?" Although it was no longer within me, I still felt it brimming with fear.

"It's been years since I've seen anything like this." He looked up, his eyes wide with terror. "Adelaide," he whispered. "You must leave Barracks."

"What?" I exclaimed. What was going on? What was wrong with my heart?

"You must leave now!" he yelled suddenly, pulling me from the table and pushing me toward the door.

"But, why?" I spun around, evading his grasp to face him.

"I—I never thought it was possible or that I would see it again. I've only read about such things before, but never thought . . . people will find out. *He* will find out." A look of horror passed over Doctor Magnum's face. "He'll come back." He pushed his fingers through his hair, moving the strand that had fallen from his braid.

"Doctor Magnum, what are you talking about?"

Grasping my wrist, Doctor Magnum pressed something into my hand. Something warm, vibrant, and teeming with life. He leaned over and said harshly, "Run, Adelaide, you must run!"

I looked down, unable to believe what was in my hand. My heart wasn't small. My heart wasn't gray.

It was big.

Red.

And alive.

CHAPTER 9

"*R*un!" Doctor Magnum screamed again.

I pulled my gaze away from my heart, my brain unable to comprehend what was going on. My heart wasn't supposed to be red and pure. What did this mean? What was going to happen to me?

Looking around in panic, I quickly grabbed Lyle's sweater and wrapped my heart in it before sprinting out of Doctor Magnum's office. The frigid air encased my limbs, but I couldn't stop. A line of Traders waiting for their Extractions stood in front of his door, bending around the hut. All those of age chattered with excitement until they saw me, clutching Lyle's sweater to my chest. I didn't give them time to question me as a sprinted past them, running straight into Governor Willow, just as I had seven years ago.

"Adelaide." The governor puffed a cloud of purple

smoke from his pipe. He locked his thumb into the small pocket on his vest before he twitched his mustache. The fabric strained over his rotund stomach with each inhale he took. "It's been some time since we've seen you at Heart Reign." His gray eyes darted from my face to the bundle in my hands. A hungry look appeared on his face, causing me to take a step back and clutch the warm ball tighter. "Have you had your heart extracted yet?"

Just then, a local vendor rushed up to Governor Willow, complaining about how the place for his display had been taken by another traveling vendor.

Taking advantage of the distraction, I quickly turned and ran in the opposite direction, farther into the market.

It was absolute chaos. People were everywhere, shuffling about each display, lost in the revelry of Heart Reign. I pushed past them as they laughed at charismatic performers and ate delicious foods, completely unaware of what was happening around them. The winter air bit at my exposed skin, and I held my arms tighter to my chest. This wasn't part of my plan.

"Hey, watch it," a thick-bearded vendor with beady eyes sneered as the crowd pushed me into his display. Recognition swept over his face, and his upper lip curled. "I don't take just anyone's heart. Especially a fool's."

My newly extracted heart pulsed against my arms through Lyle's sweater, and I held it close, ignoring the vendor's words.

"Isn't that her?" a local gossip whispered as I pushed past.

"It should be a good show if the Leper of Barracks is back again," a previous Reigner commented with a cruel smirk.

But I kept running through the crowd, ignoring odd looks, crude insults, and vocal acknowledgments of my identity.

The last report of a fully red heart was before Schism descended upon Barracks. After he came, they had vanished.

I paused for a moment, swinging between two displays to catch my breath. The glow seeping out from between the fibers of Lyle's sweater was barely containable. Though my heart was light, I felt a strong power emitting from it. How could someone like me have such an extravagant heart?

Even though it was no longer within me, I could feel it palpitating with excitement and fear as I nestled it close. My heart had been extracted, but I could still feel.

A large crowd of people rushed past the alley, some of them stumbling into it as they pushed and shoved one another. I felt as if I had been transported back in time, seeing the same scene play out in front of me from seven years ago.

I clutched the pulsing ball of fabric, walking closer to see the crowd. The people looked like a horde of animals that had been starved for months. They tore at each other to get to where Schism had first appeared, all to trade their hearts for an unknown choice—something we had been void of for many years. But a choice of what? Happiness? Life? They didn't even know what kind of choice they were making. But I did.

I pushed my way into the crowd, ending up a few rows back from where Governor Willow stood. His thick white mustache curled at the ends. He took the pipe from his mouth and grimaced.

"Traders and previous Reigners, welcome to Heart Reign," he said with mild enthusiasm. But the crowd, still possessing wisps of their emotions, cheered wildly. Governor Willow's men stood on the inner rim of the crowd, attempting to block any Traders from breaking through.

"As is tradition, we are going to begin the first trade with our most popular vendor," the governor said.

The crowd cheered again as a black plume of smoke erupted behind Governor Willow. The warmth of my pure heart dulled at the flashy entrance of Schism Breaker. I laced my fingers around it, feeling the fear consuming me once more.

The blood-red doors appeared on either side of the monster with the sparkling smile. The crowd roared with applause as people lifted their hearts in the air. A few people in the front swooned at the sight of his beautifully pale skin and long hair and had to be pulled out from under the feet of the demanding, pressing crowd.

Governor Willow returned his pipe to his mouth and grimaced as he clapped at Schism's arrival.

"My good people of Barracks," Schism said, his head bowed, hushing the crowd with his soothing voice. Slowly lifting his head, he flung out his muscular arms. "Welcome to Heart Reign!"

Once more, the crowd exploded, shoving one another to get to the front. I attempted to hold my ground, but it was as if an invisible force directed the crowd, pushing me right into the face of the man who had ruined my life.

An unnerving grin bore down on me. "Are you brave enough, little Addie?"

I stared Schism straight in the eye, unwilling to let him see the fear I still felt. I took a step forward, and the crowd gasped before going silent. The grin widened across Schism's flawless face.

"Let's get a round of applause for this very special" — he took my hand, caressing my pure heart in the process, and kissed my knuckles— "and very beautiful young lady."

My heart recoiled as I ripped my hand away from his frigid grasp, causing him to chuckle as the crowd's applause grew louder. The people cheered all around me, encouraging me to do the same thing. The same thing Lyle had done. But I wasn't here to trade my heart for an unknown choice. I was here to get my brother back.

It was excruciatingly loud. The chants and cheers of the crowd bounded off the cobblestones and wooden buildings, polluting the air with adoration for a monster.

The noise overwhelmed every one of my senses. I shut my eyes against the cheers, trying to block them out. All sounds floated away until I was left with only one: the solitary beating of my pure heart.

A surge of strength filled me with determination as I opened my eyes to find Schism staring at me with a grin more wicked than the last. We both knew what was about to happen.

"Now, you all know the rules." Schism turned to the crowd that cheered at his will. He turned back to me with an evil glint, palm opened. "A payment is needed."

Narrowing my eyes, I stood still, waiting for the opportune moment. Schism circled me like a predator, then leaned in close. "Are you brave enough, little Addie? Brave enough to choose like your dear brother did all those years ago?"

In a flash, he was between his blood-red doors, pushing on the doorframes of each. They swung open simultaneously, and the crowd roared. Each door revealed nothing but the white birch Wintertide trees behind them.

Schism walked back to me, his grin transforming into a scowl. For a moment, the whites of his eyes darkened to black. Like pits of tar, they stared into me, seeming to suck out any life nearby. After a moment, they shifted back to normal, but I had already seen enough.

The image of the crumpled piece of paper Lyle had dropped came to my mind. The script was distinct and sharp. I had only known one person to write in that way, and that was my father. The hope that Lyle had discovered something about our parents was enough to give me the strength to find him at any cost.

A new wave of courage I had never felt before poured into my veins as I glared up at Schism, holding my head high. "Are you brave enough to let me?"

The muscles in Schism's neck tensed as his feet moved mechanically away from the doors, allowing me an opening to rush toward the door on the right, the same door Lyle had chosen. A mixture of sounds filled the air, but each passed through me as one singular sound. The crowd was still roaring with applause mixed with gasps, thoroughly enjoying the dramatic display. My heart pounded with each step.

As I approached the threshold of the door, a string of voices wound together, entering my mind.

Do you think you're clever? they asked.

As I ran toward the door, I searched the crowd around me, trying to find the source. But I realized the voices spoke only in my thoughts.

We know who you are, Adelaide Tye. You can't hide your pure heart from us.

I gasped but kept running. Darkness surrounded me as cold air ripped at my skin, but I didn't stop.

The voices spewed threats and curses. But they were cut off by a new voice, one I'd never heard before.

"Run, Addie. Run!" The tone was gentle, unlike Doctor Magnum's harsh command earlier.

I pumped my legs hard and looked at the crowd once more. It felt as if time had stopped. The crowd held a mixture of faces. Some rippled confusion, some contempt. Schism glared at me, his lips curling back into a growl as his fingers flexed at his sides, but he never moved to stop me. The veins in his neck bulged, almost as if he was being restrained. A flash of gold hair caught my eye but vanished before I could recognize it. Turning back toward the doorway, I took the final step, the door slammed shut behind me, and I was greeted by a black abyss.

CHAPTER 10

*A*ir whipped all around me as my body fell into darkness. I clutched my heart close to my chest, not knowing what was coming next. The rapid fall vibrated through my body before I slammed into the hard ground. Grunting, I ran my hands over my limbs, making sure everything was in the right place before sitting up, wincing from the pain.

The abyss was dismal, the air thick with fog. And it was cold, much colder than Barracks. I looked all around, not recognizing anything. Where was I?

I rubbed my exposed arms, and panic choked my throat as I searched for my heart until my eyes caught a pink hue glowing in the dark. Breathing a sigh of relief, I gathered the bundle in my arms. The air seemed to drop a few degrees, and I shivered. Maybe I needed a little more protection than my bare skin.

Looking down at the bundle, I decided to use Lyle's sweater for an extra layer of warmth. I slowly unwrapped my heart, allowing the bright red light to shine. I couldn't help but let out a gasp, fascinated at the sight. The warm strength of it seeped into my hand as I held it. And it was feather-light, so light that if it wasn't for the power throbbing from it, I wouldn't have realized it was there.

An eerie feeling suddenly arose from the surrounding darkness. I quickly placed my pure heart in one of the pockets of the dress, feeling its warmth against my thigh, before I fully unwrapped the sweater.

Lyle's sweater fit perfectly over the white gown, covering everything that the dress didn't. I stood and adjusted the sweater before looking around once more.

A black void greeted me in every direction. I laced my fingers together, knowing I would get nowhere by standing still. A musky scent filled the air as I sucked in a deep breath and took a step. The ground surrounding my foot immediately ignited with a gray light. The light was dim, only showing a few feet of ground, which was covered in a thick layer of fog. Looking around once more, I saw no other option but to take another step. As I did, the light extended, illuminating more of the gray ground.

The obsidian abyss wrapped itself around me as I continued down the path, squeezing my fingers with each step. I needed to keep my mind and heart focused and not allow them to drift back to everything that had just happened. And everything I had left behind.

After I traveled some distance, I slowed my pace and squinted in the dim light. There was something ahead. The beating of my heart quickened against my thigh. My heart. Did its bright light awaken something within these dark depths? I squeezed my fingers tighter, feeling the fear that had already planted itself within my heart rise to a new height.

The fog whipped to my right, a rush of scratching following it. Panic gripped my heart as I turned in the direction of the sound. I had no protection or defense. I was alone.

The fog whipped again behind me, and I spun back around, suppressing a shriek. My heart raced as it swung with my movements.

Scratching came from where I had been facing, echoing into the emptiness as chills rippled up my spine. I breathed in deeply, squeezing my fingers numb. I wanted to close my eyes and pretend this was all a nightmare. But I knew it wasn't. And I knew I couldn't.

A long claw with skin like worn gray leather pierced the dull light. I took a step back, my heart trembling as the claw moved forward, revealing a sickly being attached to it. Its arms and legs were like a human's, but deformed, as if they had been stretched too far. The claws on the ends of its fingers were as black as the void surrounding us and created a high-pitched, spine-tingling sound as they dragged along the ground.

The creature crawled into the light, and I gasped in horror as its face came into view. Sewn shut with black cord, its mouth only allowed an awful moaning sound to escape from its thin lips. Its eyes were black, staring unblinkingly at me. My heart might as well be dead, for I knew I would be soon.

The creature moaned again, scratching the long, black claws that extended from its elongated fingertips against the hard ground. The sound penetrated the darkness, and I hunched over to cover my ears at the loud vibrations. The creature moaned and scratched again before falling silent. I stayed huddled, breathing deeply, not knowing whether to flee or cry as the monster stared.

The entire void rumbled at once. The sound of numerous claws scratching against the ground suddenly began, perfectly in sync with one another, as if performing a ritual. With each moment I wasted, the scratches came closer.

The first creature moaned, and a multitude of other moans answered, coming closer by the second. Fleeing was my only option, and I ran in the direction I had just come.

Extending its long, black claws, the monster swiped at me as I attempted to escape. Though my heart was still intact, the tips of the claws tore straight through the white gown to my thigh, slashing through the flesh. I let out a cry but found the strength to wrench away and continue running.

My heart beat in terror as I sprinted away from the creature. I could still only see the few feet ahead of me that the gray light gifted me, leaving no clues as to where I was headed. My body screamed in pain, my lungs gasped for air, but still I ran.

The moans followed me, the claws sounding as if they were inches from my skin. My legs were exhausted and covered in blood. Wasn't there anyone else here? Anyone to help?

I tried to keep going, but my injured leg crumpled beneath me. Letting out another cry, I tumbled to the ground.

All my running meant nothing, for the creatures were no more than a few strides away. I tried to move once more, but an immense pain shot up my leg. I cried out again, digging my fingertips into the hardened ground, breaking the tips of my nails as I tried to pull myself away. I thought I would last longer than this once I went through Schism's door. I thought I would have found Lyle before I died.

Shadows shrouded the corners of my vision, blurring what little light highlighted my fallen body.

The scratches and moans were practically on top of me, but there was nothing I could do. I reached my hand toward my pocket, hoping my pure heart would take away the pain of being punctured by claws, when a yellow light sparked in the distance. My body tensed as I narrowed my eyes enough to see a person running toward me, holding what looked like a lantern and a giant black rod. The light from the lantern revealed thousands of creatures like the first, lurking in the shadows. Panic seized my heart as the light exposed the evil in the dark.

The person ran hard and fast. I shifted my body, trying to move out of the way, biting back the pain in my leg. Grasping my leg with my hands, I moved it a few inches, choking back wails. Sweat ran down my temples as I shuffled across the ground, leaving a bloodied trail behind me. I looked back to see where the figure was when a dark mass jumped over my body. I shielded my face, thinking it was the end.

A crack sounded through the air, and I turned to see the figure simultaneously swinging the lantern and rod at the creatures that were surrounding me. The figure moved gracefully, shielding and striking like an experienced warrior, battling one creature after the next.

The rod collided with a creature's face, causing it to moan loudly. The surrounding scratching and moaning stopped.

Shoulders heaving, the figure stood, hands gripping the rod. He or she would not back down until the creature began to slither back into the shadows, accepting defeat.

Relief filled my heart until my savior turned, walked toward me, and shoved the lantern in my face.

"This is new," a voice huffed, sounding distinctly

female. I tried to speak, but only a pathetic squeak came out.

"Don't talk," the figure hissed, placing her hand with a soiled, fingerless glove over my mouth. "They'll come back."

The figure pulled back her rod, a crack echoed within the abyss, and I was greeted by darkness once more.

CHAPTER 11

$\mathcal{W}$armth hugged my skin as the clanging of pots sounded in my ears. Was I back home? Silas had to be downstairs in the kitchen. I listened to the clanking of cookware for a minute longer, my head exploding with pain. My hand went to my pounding head, feeling a giant bump on the side.

Was it all only a dream? Hope rose in my heart before I realized my heart wasn't where it was meant to be. The harsh reality weighed on me as my eyes flew open, darting around to figure out where I was. When I moved, a sharp sting pierced through my thigh. Gasping in pain, I sat up, knocking over a bowl that had been next to my leg. A green liquid flowed out of the bowl as it shattered on the ground.

A sigh came from behind me. "That was my favorite bowl."

The fear billowed over, and I panicked. Flailing to the side, I attempted to escape from my captor, only to find that my injured leg was completely numb. Falling forward, I landed on the hard floor with a grunt.

"Calm down, girl," the voice commanded as my captor approached and helped me back into bed. "Reacting like that will get you nowhere in here. Especially when you have no idea what you're doing."

Heat filled my cheeks as I reluctantly laid back down. I clasped my hands in front of me, squeezing tightly as I breathed. Cloves and cinnamon swirled through my nose as a woman a few years older from me, stood before me. A tousled bun of curled white hair protruded from her scalp with a midnight streak standing out in front. Several strands hung around her face, barely concealing the mix of scars and fresh scratches on her copper skin. Yet as the firelight danced across her face, I could just see a smattering of freckles across her short, thin nose.

Layered with a brown vest and matching pants, the woman wore a man's shirt that was probably once white, but was now yellowed with age. Her hazel eyes beamed with curiosity as they studied me, but her mouth was set in a devious smirk.

"Not what you were expecting? Well, you definitely weren't what *I* was expecting, either." Her eyes traveled to my injured leg.

I followed her gaze to my white dress, torn to the thigh and stained with red blood. Dirt and grime covered the remaining areas that weren't red. My injured leg was covered in dirt, blood, and the green liquid that had spilled from the bowl. Curious, I unwove my fingers and placed my hand on the wound. A tingling sensation fluttered beneath my fingertips.

"What were those things?" I asked the woman, fearful of eye contact. But a sliver of hope seeped into my heart, seeing how this odd woman had helped me instead of feeding me to the monsters.

The woman crouched down and began gathering her broken bowl. "Siti."

"What?" I had never heard of such a creature.

She stood up and discarded the broken pieces in the back room. The fire was small, making it hard to see beyond the few feet the two of us were in. The clash of the broken pieces being set down echoed across the room before footsteps approached again. Pulling out a cracked wooden chair, the woman sat down next to me.

"Siti, or Life Parchers. They feed on all life that enters this realm. They were once humans, but now . . ."

A shudder ran up my spine and down my arms as I imagined those monsters as humans. How could they have traded their hearts to become such horrid creatures? Another shiver danced on my nerves when alarm rang through me. I couldn't feel the beat of my own heart. Frantic, I reached toward my pocket. The feeling of the familiar thumping brought instant relief.

The woman watched me suspiciously before her eyes

widened in understanding. "So that's why they were after you."

My shoulders tensed as my hand grasped my heart protectively. What was she talking about? I slid my eyes back to her, not moving my hand from my pocket.

She frowned, and a slight wrinkle formed between her white brows. "No one ever gets past that wretch at the gates with their heart. I could practically feel the life coming out of you when I carried you here."

My body relaxed a bit. So that was how I got here. "Thank you."

"Don't mention it," the woman said, clasping her gloved hands behind her head as she leaned back. "I'm surprised and impressed you got past Fracious with your heart."

"Fracious?"

"Yeah, you know." She sat up, motioning. "Long dark hair, beady eyes. Arrogant."

I knew someone who fit that description, but his name wasn't Fracious. "You mean Schism Breaker?"

"Is that his name in your realm?" She barked out a laugh. "How pathetic."

I bit my lip, hesitating as I tasted a salty mixture of sweat and grime. I feared the answer to my next question but asked anyway. "What realm are we in?"

The woman's face immediately hardened. "Don't be stupid, girl. How could you jump through the gates and not know what you were getting yourself into?"

"Schism never said where the doors led."

She huffed. "No, he wouldn't, would he?"

"Wait," I said, trying to understand. "Where are we?"

A hardened look passed over her face. "Ophidian's Realm."

"What?" I gasped before I could stop myself. I knew Schism's doors led to somewhere bad, but I never thought it would be somewhere fictional. Ophidian wasn't real . . . right?

I looked back at the woman. By the scowl on her face, I was sure she wasn't lying. I turned toward the shadowed wall before me, trying to remember the small bit of knowledge I had on Ophidian. He was practically evil incarnate and held the power to create nothing but hate and violence within a heart, turning it black.

Black hearts. Just like my dream.

But if Ophidian was real, was he the one behind everything happening in Barracks?

"Don't be stupid, girl," the woman chided, interrupting my thoughts. "You should've known you were damned the moment you walked through those doors." The woman's face relaxed slightly, the wrinkle between her brows disappearing. "So, where's this home of yours that allows victims still with their hearts to enter into the realm of evil?"

I looked down at Lyle's sweater, unwilling to let the woman see the fear I felt in realizing I was in Ophidian's

Realm. My fingers fiddled with the light blue fibers as I swallowed the saliva building in my mouth. "Barracks."

The relaxation instantly fled from the woman's face, the wrinkle between her brows returning, deeper than before as she clenched her jaw. Her muscles tensed so tightly, I thought she had turned to stone.

"Are you all right?" I asked.

I began to lean forward to offer comfort when she recoiled, shaking her head as if trying to rid it of a bad memory. After a deep breath, she looked back at me. The muscles in her jaw slackened, but the intensity in her eyes stayed.

"Yes. Sorry, I just haven't heard about that place in a long time."

Hope lightened my heart. "You know about Barracks?"

The woman turned her back to me and strode toward the fire near the back room. Her steps were sure and confident as she took her black rod and poked some of the sticks, causing the flames to brighten. The space we were in was barely big enough for the two of us. If it wasn't for the domed ceiling, we would have had to crawl around to get anywhere.

Although the room was small, it was well kept. A series of colorful bowls and spoons lay on a wooden table next to the fire, each one stacked inside the other. A mat, woven with birch bark, sat close enough to the bed to reveal the intricacy of its work. In fact, everything besides the bowls and the black rod seemed to be made of wood.

After the woman finished poking the fire, she returned to my side with a bright red bowl, similar to the ribbon surprisingly still holding back my hair. She sat back in her chair and began to layer more of the green salve on my wound. The mixture stung my skin on contact, and I sucked in a sharp breath. But as it seeped in, the cool tingling erased the pain, allowing the numbness to enter once more.

As she rubbed the green liquid into my wound, she said in a hard tone, "Barracks used to be my home."

I watched as the liquid hardened, turning from green to white, creating a plaster cast around my thigh. I lifted my hand to feel the hard surface, noticing I hadn't been grasping my fingers in fear since this conversation had begun. "It's not anymore?"

The woman took the bowl in her hands and walked back to the table beside the fire. She slammed the bowl down, causing me to jump. Her shoulders were tense as she gripped both sides of the table. "That cursed place will never be my home again."

The hatred in her voice silenced me from asking any further questions. Luckily, I didn't need to. Years of fury and pain had apparently given the woman a need to vent her frustration.

"My mother always loved to learn." She stared intensely into the fire. "She had stacks of books all over our house, each one with a different piece of paper marking the page where she had left off." My father would always laugh at her when she piled several open books, one on top of the other, trying to read them all at once. You could say knowledge was her addiction; she couldn't get enough of it. She wanted to know everything about everything.

"Heart Reign was a day away, and the discussion of what I wanted to trade my heart for came up at dinner that night. I said I hadn't decided yet but was thinking about trading it for beauty." She absentmindedly ran her hand over her white hair. "But my mother forbade it, saying beauty wasn't worth the price of my heart. What I should trade it for was knowledge."

She had my full attention. I had never heard of anyone trading their heart for knowledge, nor had I seen or known of any vendors who offered it. It was an unattainable gift. After all, who would know everything about everything and be willing to trade it for a dying heart?

"I didn't know then, but her actions would lead to my destruction," the woman said as she released her hair and grabbed her rod. She jabbed it fiercely into the fire once more, her movement strong and direct. Shadows danced violently across the walls in response.

"She claimed I could trade my heart for all the knowledge in the world and then rushed out of the room. She came back with an old book. It was written in an ancient language that's no longer used, but my mother deciphered enough of it to learn about Aeternam Scientia, the trade for Eternal Knowledge."

"Eternal Knowledge?" Is that why Lyle had traded his heart to Schism? He, too, enjoyed learning about everything. Was there some knowledge about our parents that he wanted?

"Yes," the woman snapped, causing me to, once again, lace my fingers and squeeze. She eyed the reaction but said nothing. "Aeternam Scientia, or Eternal Knowledge, is an ancient magic that was thought to have disappeared. It's a strong-willed power that is deadly to those who are too weak to contain it. Those who possess Eternal Knowledge are able to influence and control the will of anyone who crosses their path."

I swallowed the knot building in my throat as the hair on my neck stood on end. I prayed it wasn't true, but I feared that was exactly what Lyle had traded his heart for.

"A man who was tall and handsome to the average eye stood on the page she had shown me. He was facing another man who was kneeling before him, offering his heart toward the Heavens. I remember my mother pointing excitedly at the page, saying how I could learn all the secrets about our realm and the realms around us." Pulling the rod out of the fire, she tightened her grip on it. "I almost agreed with her until I turned to the next page."

The woman drifted away from the fire toward the bowls, her shoulders sagging slightly as she let out a heavy sigh. She rummaged through them until she found a bright lavender one, a beautiful color I hadn't seen in years.

Taking a rusted kettle from an adjacent table, she poured a brown liquid into the lavender bowl before squaring her shoulders and striding back to the broken chair. "Remember how I said the siti were once human?" she asked before sitting.

I nodded.

"Well," she murmured, her eyes distant. "Once you give up your heart for Eternal Knowledge, you become a monster worse than the siti. Your mind is unable to handle the knowledge around you, and you continuously thirst for any source of life to give you more knowledge. You go mad. You don't eat. You don't sleep You're unable to live in any world except the one of the monster who gave you the knowledge. And that's only because your heart is just like his: black."

A chill of horror ran through my heart as I remembered the nightmare that had haunted me for the past seven years, confirming my earlier suspicions that it was true.

The woman sipped from her bowl again, examining the liquid after she swallowed. "My father grabbed the book out of my mother's hands and cast it into the fire, yelling she was insane. He tried to reconcile with her, but it was too late." She sipped more of the brown liquid. "Her eyes began to blacken, and her voice sounded as if many people were speaking through her."

"What did they say?" I asked, wrapping my arms

around my waist as I leaned forward, engrossed and terrified at the woman's tale.

"'A trade has been made. We will have the heart, or you will perish.'"

Another chill shot through me, and I unwrapped my arms, squeezing my fingers together, which drew a frown from the woman as she looked back into her bowl, swirling the contents once more.

"I thank the Heavens for my father in that moment, because I was frozen where I stood. He grabbed his favorite walking rod from the wall and battered my mother, whatever she was, out of the way without hesitation. Grabbing my hand, we ran out of our home toward the market.

"When we got to his office, he began taking off his clothes, telling me to change into them. I never questioned him." She looked up from her bowl and stared at the curved, stone wall to my side, clutching one of the buttons on her vest. "He then performed my Extraction in a matter of moments." She placed her hand on her chest where her heart should have been. "I'll never forget how it felt to be ripped in two."

Opening my mouth, the beginning of a question was on the tip of my tongue, but I stopped, watching the woman stare at the far wall, lost in the past.

"He told me to run far away, and he would follow as soon as he could." She paused before looking back at me, a slight glimmer of tears in her eyes. "I was so scared. I turned to leave but was thrust back by a . . . force. When I sat back up, the man from the book stood in front of me." She shuddered. "I'll never forget the first time I saw those yellow snake eyes."

She looked down at the liquid again, rotating the bowl in silence.

I placed my hand on my beating heart in my pocket. Heat flowed through my palm. "What happened?"

Sighing, she shrugged off her earlier emotions. "My dad ran away, the Beast took me captive, and here we are."

I stared, wide-eyed in disbelief. Was she really unmoved or just acting like it? It was obvious she could still feel, despite having an Extraction, but that story was horrendous.

I watched the woman continue to sip from her bowl before she poked at the plaster around my leg.

"Sorry about the long ramble. I haven't talked to anyone in a while."

I looked away briefly, fidgeting with Lyle's sweater. "What happened to your heart?"

"Don't know." She shook her head and shrugged again. "But I know it's still out there."

"How?" My fingers clutched the fabric as I looked at her.

She shot me a wide grin. "Because I haven't given up. Though these years have been torture, I know I won't stay in this cursed realm forever. The Beast can try to take my heart, but he'll never take my hope." All too soon, the grin faded. "If I don't hold onto that, what else do I have to live for?"

My heart reached out to the woman, knowing the same feeling.

"You see," the woman said, looking at me, her smirk returning. "You and I are the same. We're both damned because of the choice of someone else."

I stared at her, trying to hide my surprise. "How do you know I'm here for someone else?"

The woman shook her head, letting out a soft chuckle. "Don't be stupid, girl. No one with a pure heart would plunge into Ophidian's Realm for themself." She stood up, leaning her weight on her black rod. "I'm here because my possessed mother tried to trade my heart to the Beast. The question is, who are you here for?"

I swallowed the lump building in my throat. Though I hadn't wanted to be a worthless burden in Barracks, I knew I wouldn't survive here alone. But I didn't know anything about this woman. Could I trust her not to attack me like the siti had? And what if this was all a trick to lure me to Ophidian?

I looked down at my leg. The plaster had begun to dissolve, revealing the smooth contours of my skin, perfectly healed as if nothing had happened. This woman had healed me. She had saved my life without knowing who I was. The least I could do was trust her.

Taking a readied breath, I attempted to bend my knee

and stretch my leg. The rush of warm blood gushed through my veins as the feeling returned. When I looked back to the woman, she gave a confident smile, as if knowing and understanding why I had doubted her.

"I'm here for my brother," I said, swinging my legs over the side of the bed. "He chose to trade his heart and walk through one of Schism's doors seven years ago. I haven't seen him since."

The woman nodded, her face hard. "What's his name?"

"Lyle."

Her eyes bulged as her shoulders tensed, straightening her body as stiff as the rod she held.

Fear struck my heart as I watched the transformation. The beating in my pocket rapidly thumped against my leg.

"Do you know him?" I asked anxiously.

The woman nodded slowly, her face changing once more from horror to grief. "I know all who walk through the doors. It's my job to see them through the Seven Choices."

"The what?"

Before she could answer, a loud moaning came from a short distance away. My blood turned cold as I recognized the call of the siti.

The woman looked at me, her eyes hard. "No time to explain." She ran to the back room. In seconds, she was back with a bundle in her hands.

"Here," she said, shoving a shirt and pair of black pants at me. "You're like a signal calling them with your heart so exposed and wearing that awful dress." She crinkled her nose. "Change quickly if you want to survive."

I stripped off Lyle's sweater and the dress and changed into the black pants and shirt, pulling Lyle's sweater over it. Reaching into the pocket of the dress, I removed my heart, noticing it wasn't as bright and red as before.

"Whoa," the woman exclaimed, staring at my heart.

"Do you have something I can carry it in?" I asked, trying to hide it from her gawking eyes.

The woman nodded and sprinted to the back room. When she returned, she held a leather satchel and opened the front flap. Carefully, I wrapped my heart in the tatters of the dress and placed it in the satchel before taking it from the woman and slinging the strap across my body.

"Excellent." She smiled widely, placing the strap of another bag over her shoulder. "So, your brother. You want to find him?"

I nodded, though I was unsure of what finding Lyle entailed.

"Very good." The woman smiled again, then placed her hand on her chest where her heart should be. "Well, strange girl, I swear on the empty cavity in my chest that I will help you find your brother at any cost."

I blinked a few times at the strange promise. "Thank you."

With a satisfied look, she turned and began to walk toward the front door.

"Wait! I don't even know your name."

Pausing, the woman looked over her shoulder. "Claire Magnum."

CHAPTER 12

*A*s we raced through the void, Claire yelled, "There are Seven Choices within Ophidian's Realm that every person who trades must go through." The scratching and moaning had faded into the distance, but not far enough for my liking. "At the end, if you survive, Ophidian will give you what you seek. If you're not stupid, you just might be able to have Lyle returned to you and escape this place alive."

Claire shoved the lantern at me to hold as she gripped her rod. As we ran, the fog began to clear, revealing a door with the same rounded arch as Schism's doors. My muscles tensed, straining my heartbeats. Another door? Wasn't the first one enough?

Yet, instead of it being painted blood-red, the door was blue like the sky in Barracks used to be. Panting hard, we stopped in front of the door.

"What do you mean by 'Choices?'" I asked, placing my hand on the satchel to make sure my heart was still there. The steady thrumming eased my anxiety as I looked up to see Claire holding a set of keys, each one worn and rusted.

Claire let out an irritated sigh as she flipped through them, her creased brow resembling Doctor Magnum's, until she found the one she was looking for. She held it out to me. The light reflected off what little metal could be seen beneath the rust as I shined the lantern over her gloved palm. Studying the key quickly, I could barely make out the head of a goat molded into the top. Before I could ask what it meant, Claire spoke again. This time, though, her voice was not her own.

A silky voice came from Claire's mouth, dancing with pompous undertones. "Welcome to my realm, Adelaide. I knew you would find your way here one day."

I gripped the strap on the satchel with both hands, squeezing it as terror flooded through my heart. Claire's eyes hadn't turned black like the siti, but a thick, white fog clouded her gaze. Though the voice was speaking through Claire's mouth, I had a good idea who and what I was talking to.

"Where's my brother?" I demanded, attempting to sound brave.

Claire laughed a deep chuckle, making the hairs on my neck stand on edge as I squeezed the satchel strap harder.

"Quick to the point," the voice muttered. "I always liked that about you, Adelaide. Your brother has been keeping me company for quite some time now. I must say, he's quite the ambitious young man."

I unclasped my hands from the strap, balling them into fists. "What have you done with him?"

"Nothing he didn't choose." A wicked smile contorted Claire's face. "The only way you will reach him is if you choose the same as he did."

Claire wrapped her fingers around the goat key and walked toward the light blue door. She began to put the key in the lock when her arm paused, shaking.

"No," Claire's normal voice pled, straining against the other voice. "This isn't right. She didn't trade . . ." She began to pull her arm away. It stopped mid-air as she tried to fight the being controlling her.

She wrestled with the invisible force. One hand gripped the other, fighting to keep the key away from the lock, pulling and straining. I wanted to help, but I had no idea what to do.

Claire's arm wavered. In that small moment, her hand shot forward, shoving the key into the lock. While she sunk to the ground, her eyes shifted from white to hazel for just a moment. "I'm sorry," she whispered before her eyes glazed over once more.

Quickly standing, she twisted the key in the lock, causing the door to fly open. A rush of warm air blew through the doorway, wrapping around me. I crossed my arms in front of my face, shielding it from whatever may appear. But it wasn't what was coming out that was the problem. The air reversed and, as quickly as it had rushed out, it rushed back in, sucking me—and only me—into its depths.

I grappled for anything to hold onto. "Claire!" I screamed over the rushing wind. "Claire!"

But Claire stood quietly, watching with her fogged eyes as I slipped further away.

The door immediately shut, fading from sight, leaving the lantern as my only light. Cautiously, I took a step, praying to the Heavens that this wasn't a lair filled with siti. As my foot hit the ground, nothing happened. No gray path appeared. No light to show the way. I was once again alone.

Thankful for the lantern, I gripped the handle, listening to the darkness. The only sound that filled the void was the soft thumping of my frightened heart.

Clutching the strap of the satchel, I took a few hesitant steps as I held the lantern in front of me to light the way. Each step I took led me farther into the darkness, with no known exit ahead.

As I traveled deeper into the void, a green haze began to flow toward me, surrounding the ground around my ankles. Gasping, I took a few steps back, only to be met by something hard. I turned, expecting to see the light blue door again, but was greeted by a stone wall. I placed my hand on the cold stone. The wall wasn't there a moment ago. I pushed my hands against it, thinking it would move. It didn't. I was trapped.

The green fog swirled up around my knees. The air thickened with heat and humidity. Beads of sweat formed on my neck as I frantically held up the satchel, trying to keep my heart as far away from the haze as I could. My knees trembled with fear. I wasn't sure what the haze was, but nothing in Ophidian's Realm could be good.

The haze moved faster, rising to my chest. The spirals thickened, spinning faster as they circled me. It seemed alive and eager for a fresh meal.

I stood on my tiptoes, trying to hold my heart as high as I could above my head. The haze reached my chin, its earthy scent trying to tickle its way up my nose, tempting me to breathe it in. Knowing there was only one way this could end, I took a deep breath before the haze reached my mouth, ready to hold it for as long as I could.

The fog felt thicker, spinning around me like a violent hurricane. The haze smothered the lantern, extinguishing the last source of light I had left. My heart cried out with fear as darkness surrounded it. My lungs weakened, begging for air, but I knew if I took a breath, it would be my last.

The haze enclosed me, bathing my body in its intoxicating scent. I tried to hold on, but I couldn't much longer.

The deep green fog had engulfed me, squeezing and constricting my body. Tears ran from my eyes as I held in my breath, but I couldn't hold it any longer. I gasped for air, allowing the green haze to plunge down my throat.

CHAPTER 13

he haze continued to pour into my mouth, filling my throat with an awful burnt taste. Straining, I tried to close my lips, but couldn't. More and more haze filled my lungs. I coughed, trying to rid it from my throat, but only more haze entered until—

It didn't taste so bad.

The haze felt smooth, like a soothing syrup sliding down my throat.

All at once, my arms slumped to my sides, allowing the satchel to hit against my leg. I looked down. Why did I have this satchel again? I drew in another deep breath and sighed with delight. Whatever was in the air was delicious. I tried to take a step and stumbled to the ground, barking out a loud laugh.

"Hey, there, honey," an enticing voice said from the hazy shadows.

Struggling to stand, I smiled at the stranger. The green haze around him illuminated his high cheekbones and lush pink lips. His sun-kissed skin sparkled as the haze swirled through his wavy, brown locks. I let out a small gasp. He was the most handsome man I had ever seen.

"Hey, there." I waved, wriggling my fingers childishly. I looked down and saw a bag hanging from my arm. The haze cleared from my mind. There was a reason why I had come here.

I took in a deep breath, and my muscles relaxed once more.

The man wobbled forward and slinked a lanky arm around me, placing his full weight on my shoulders. "Come on, honey."

Who was this guy? He didn't feel familiar. He didn't feel like . . . I took in a breath. What was I thinking about? I breathed in again and looked over at him. We were going somewhere. I wrapped my arm around his thin waist as we helped each other walk to our destination.

I took a few steps before tumbling over, giggling frantically on the ground as the man leaned over me and laughed wildly, clutching his sides. Once our amusement faded, he reached down and helped me back up.

I stumbled against him, trying to find my footing. He placed his hands on my shoulders to try to steady me. I smiled, then felt a sharp pain, leading me to look down at the satchel. Something felt wrong. A harsher pain struck, and I cried out, bending over with my head in my hands.

"Just breathe, honey," the man said, rubbing my back in soothing circles.

I drew in a deep breath through my nose and immediately relaxed. My mind began to clear, and I took another breath for good measure. What was I thinking again?

I gave the man an amused smile, which he returned. We wrapped our arms around each other once more and continued walking. After several strides, we arrived at a small wooden house surrounded by the green haze.

Something about the house seemed strange. I wasn't sure if I should go in. I breathed in deeply. There was nothing to worry about. I would be fine.

The man swayed to the door and opened it. "Come on in, honey."

I gleefully wobbled through the doorway after him. The man immediately closed the door behind me and locked it. Alarm jolted through me, clearing my head for a moment. Where was I?

Something pressed against my leg. What was it? I looked down. A bag? When did I start carrying a bag? What was inside? Why was . . . I breathed again.

The man turned and gave me a droopy grin before taking my hand. He began pulling me down a wooden stairwell. I took another breath and followed him with a smile.

The stairs gave painful creaks with each step we took. It was a miracle we made it to the basement without crashing through the staircase.

The green haze was a thick sheet encasing the lower level of the house, prohibiting me from seeing anything.

"Hey!" a voice from the fog yelled groggily. "Where have you been?"

"Out," the man answered, slumping down onto something soft on the floor. Our fingers were still interlocked, so I landed on top of him, laughing wildly.

He laughed, too. "You're funny, honey."

"Funny honey!" another voice exclaimed through the fog.

An eruption of chaotic laughter sounded from the fog, sending my senses on alert once more as I whipped my head toward the voices. My mind cleared long enough for me to let go of the man's hand. He quickly grabbed it back again.

"Just breathe, honey."

Obeying, I took in another breath. Of course there were other people here; why wouldn't there be? This place was great.

Smiling at the man, I slid down next to him, breathing in the earthy scent of his clothes. With each breath, my muscles melted into the soft cushion, and I became more relaxed. I let out a yawn. I hadn't felt this at ease in a long time.

"That's it, honey," the man murmured, wrapping his arm tightly around my shoulders. "Just breathe."

I breathed in and out again, allowing my eyes to close.

"Isn't this great?" a voice from the fog said, causing my eyelids to open ever so slightly.

"I love it," another voice responded. "I love just lying around. And" —the voice paused for a deep breath— "doing nothing."

"Nobody telling you what to do," a voice added from another part of the fog. "Nobody expecting you to do anything."

"Or be anything," another voice said sleepily.

Exhaustion hit me, and my eyelids shut entirely. I'd been running for so long, and I was tired. Why couldn't they all be quiet so I could rest? I sucked in a deep breath. The air tickled my nose, causing me to giggle.

"Shh," the man said, running his fingers in circles on my shoulder. "You need rest."

"I do. I do need rest," I replied, peeking an eye open as I playfully poked him with my index finger.

"And sleep," he added.

"Sleep," I whispered, cuddling closer to him.

"You don't need anything or anyone."

Why would I need anything? Everything I needed was right here. And why would I need anyone? I needed nothing. I needed no one. I breathed in deeply, beginning to close my eyes once more.

"There's no one you need to take care of."

He was right. No one I needed to take care of.

But . . . it felt as if there was someone who took care of

me. Someone kind. Someone who was my friend. Someone who was more than a friend?

I breathed in. It didn't matter. There was no one I needed to take care of. Closing my eyes, I settled into the man's side, breathing heavily.

"There's nowhere you need to run."

There's nowhere I needed to . . . run.

Run.

Running.

I was running.

I was running away.

Away from where? Where was I running?

Run . . . run . . . run . . .

I breathed in deeply. Who wanted to run when you could sleep?

"Run, Addie, run!" a voice screamed in my ear.

I sat up with a gasp, my heart racing. My eyes shot open to see people—hundreds of them—lying all over the place. Some were in seats, others on makeshift beds made from pillows and blankets. But most of them were heaped one atop another, breathing in the addictive green haze.

I began to pull Lyle's sweater over my mouth when a hand yanked my arm down.

"You're supposed to be sleeping, honey."

I looked up, expecting to see the attractive man I had seen before. Only he was anything but. He was hideous. His dark hair was matted with layers of grease. His skin was pale and splotchy, as if he hadn't bathed in years. But his eyes sent needles down my spine. Those eyes, which were once big and green, were replaced with the cold, dark eyes of the siti.

"It's time to sleep," he said, forcefully pulling me down.

Reacting on instinct, I kneed him in the stomach and stood up. Pulling Lyle's sweater over my nose, I ran toward the stairs.

"It's time to sleep," more voices said as the wood creaked beneath my feet. Grabbing the strap of the satchel, I sprinted up the stairs and ran toward the front door.

Once outside, I looked around in hope of finding a way out of this realm. Dragging footsteps echoed around me. I stepped back as hundreds of people from the basement poured out of the house, their black eyes fixed on one point: me.

"Sleep," they moaned, sounding like the call of the siti.

I clutched the strap of my bag tightly, trying not to breathe as I took a few more steps back. Claire had said the siti were once human, right? Was this what she meant?

I started to take another step back when my foot hit something hard, and I stumbled backwards. Terror seized my heart until I saw the light of the lantern shining right beside the house. Relieved, I grabbed it and ran.

The moans died down as I pumped my legs. The void extended around me as the lantern swung from my fingertips, its light illuminating the dense, hazy air a few paces ahead. My lungs were dying for fresh air, but I couldn't breathe. Hot tears of frustration streamed down my cheeks as I ran faster and faster. My chest heaved in pain. I felt so weak.

"Run, Addie, run," the voice whispered to me softly. It was the same voice that had yelled earlier.

"I am!" I growled between huffs. I held Lyle's sweater tighter over my nose as I kept running.

But the void continued. The green haze thickened the farther I ran. I was so tired. It would be so much easier if I gave up. Who was I kidding? I couldn't save Lyle. I was always the one who needed help, not him.

Just as I was about to slow my pace, a light blue door glimmered in the distance. A layer of hope clung to my heart as I sprinted toward escape.

I pumped my legs as hard as I could, the door growing closer, and a figure with white hair that beamed brightly against the green haze appeared next to it.

"Claire!" I shouted through Lyle's sweater.

But Claire didn't respond.

CHAPTER 14

*W*hen I finally reached Claire, I realized why she hadn't responded. Her eyes were still glazed over. Ophidian was still here.

"I'm impressed, Adelaide," the Beast said through Claire's lips. "Most fail at the First Choice. A life of laziness and sleep is such a temptation for most. No accountability or responsibility."

I clenched my teeth, anger replacing my fear as I gripped Lyle's sweater around my nose. "I passed your test. Now tell me where Lyle is and let Claire go."

Claire let out a deep laugh that pricked my skin. "Oh no, this was only the First Choice. You have six left before you can see your brother. Choose wisely."

Claire's body swayed back and forth before it slumped forward. Rushing to her, I caught her wrist before she landed on the ground.

Moaning closed in behind me, turning my blood cold. Darting my head around, I spotted the sleepwalkers. While I was talking to Ophidian, they had caught up to me. My heart beat in a frenzy before I remembered Claire's set of keys.

Frantically, I patted her pockets as she stood with furrowed brows and a frown on her lips, still recovering from Ophidian's full-body takeover. When my fingers brushed the rusted metal, I yanked the keys out of her vest pocket and searched for the one branded with a goat.

The moaning grew louder.

I flipped past a lion and a snake, not wanting to know what doors those unlocked, until I found the goat key. The cool texture of the metal was refreshing compared to the humid haze infecting the air. I held the key in my free hand and rushed to the door. When I didn't hear footsteps following my own, I looked backed to see Claire still standing in the same spot as before.

"Claire, come on," I said through Lyle's sweater.

She didn't move.

I turned and walked back toward her. As I got closer, I saw that Claire's eyes were closed. Reaching out, I grabbed her hand. Her skin felt like ice. I wasn't sure what Ophidian had done to her, but we had to get out of here.

Looking back over my shoulder, I clearly saw the outline of the sleepwalkers against the green haze. Grasping Claire's arms, I hoisted her onto my back, then took a deep breath before the protection of Lyle's sweater fell from my face. It would be impossible for me to unlock the door, hold the lantern and rod, carry Claire, and cover my own mouth all at the same time.

The green haze wrapped around my nose, prodding me to let it in once more. I bent over slightly to balance Claire on my back, then strung the lantern through the rod as I clutched the keys. My fingertips buzzed with energy as they wrapped around the cool metal rod, but I disregarded it, thinking it was an effect of the haze.

My lungs squeezed in my chest as I jammed the key into the lock. With a small click, the door flew open. The rushing air returned just as it had before, sucking both Claire and me through the doorway and leaving the sleep-walkers behind.

Dirt filled my mouth as we slammed into the ground. I groaned when Claire's entire body weight crumpled on top of me. Heaving her off, I coughed and gasped, praying the haze had disappeared. Bile rose in my throat, possessing the same burnt flavor as the haze. The delicious taste I had once loved was now gone. Leaning over, I gagged until my sides ached, hoping to rid my body of Ophidian's addictive poison.

Finally able to stand, I wiped my mouth with the back of my hand before inhaling. The air was fresh and crisp, chilling my lungs in a pleasant way. It almost felt as if I was back in Barracks, breathing in its cool winter air. But I knew I wasn't. I drew in another breath, not able to get over how clean and pure the air tasted.

After I had filled my lungs, I walked over to where the lantern and rod had landed. Removing the rod from the lantern ring, I felt the hum of the cylinder again before dropping it to the ground. It was an odd staff, that was for sure. I held out the lantern, hoping to figure out where we were now. Though its light didn't shine far, the lantern reflected off branches and large, dark leaves.

Images of my nightmare flooded into my mind, and my palms began to sweat. I tried to block them out, praying that this forest was a different one. Holding the lantern farther out, the light exposed straight, tall trunks instead of the arched ones I had come to dread. I breathed a sigh of relief, my heartbeat slowing to normal.

Loosening my death grip on the lantern, I took a step to investigate when a groan came near my feet. I clutched the lantern, ready to use it as a weapon against any siti or sleepwalkers.

"Wh—"

I let out a sigh of relief, thankful to hear Claire's own voice again. I lowered the lantern to see her face covered in dirt from our rough landing. Crouching, I held the lantern closer to her. Although she sounded like herself, I wasn't about to take any chances.

"Get that stupid light away from my face," she spat, pushing the lantern away as she covered her eyes with one hand.

"Sorry." I smirked, trying to suppress a chuckle. "I'm just trying to make sure you're not possessed anymore."

Claire let out an irritated groan before wiping the dirt off her face, revealing her freckles once more. "I hate it when he does that."

I placed the lantern between us before slumping to the ground next to her and lacing my fingers together. My mind ran over everything I had learned: Claire was Doctor Magnum's daughter, and I was stuck in Ophidian's Realm with Seven Choices to go through. I squeezed my fingers tightly, biting my lower lip as the lantern's warm light illuminated the branches above. The darkness seemed dismal against the flickering light.

The forest was eerily quiet compared to what I had seen of Ophidian's Realm so far. No moaning pierced my ears. No scratching claws appeared in my periphery. For once, my heart beat at a steady pace. I hadn't looked at it since I was in Claire's hut, which now seemed like ages ago.

As Claire continued to mutter curses toward Ophidian, I unclasped my fingers and reached into the satchel to pull out the white bundle. I carefully peeled back the shreds of the white dress and looked at my life force. It was still red. It was still big. But the brightness of it had dimmed. Maybe I was still feeling the effects of the green haze. Confused, I studied the warm, glowing heart as I turned it around in my hands.

"I figured that would happen," Claire said, making me jump. I looked back to see her peering over my shoulder.

"What would happen?"

She pointed to my heart. "Your heart. It's not as bright anymore."

I looked back at my heart with a frown.

"Don't feel bad," Claire continued, picking at a leaf on the ground. "No one has ever made it through Ophidian's Realm with their whole heart. One did come close, though."

"What do you mean?"

Claire leaned back, pressing into her hands and stretching her feet out in front of her. She looked up at the trees, her white hair reflecting the lantern light. "It's a story I heard long ago, before I was traded here. Unfortunately, my psychotic mother told it to me."

I crossed my legs, cradling my heart in my hands as I waited for her to continue.

Claire looked back at me and sighed. "Fine. " She laid back down, placing her hands under her head before she began. "There was once a young man who was very kind. He always cared for others, but no one ever cared for him. When he was a boy, his father didn't want him, so his mother traded him for a spool of silk. In mere moments, he became an orphan, traded to a horrible man who made him work long hours as a blacksmith.

"The man was a young boy then and didn't know anything about the rules of blacksmithery. Day after day, he lifted the metal, pounding it into submission. Day after day, the horrible man beat him, never satisfied.

"By the time the boy was old enough to run away, he

chose not to. He tried to be kind and love the horrible man. After all, the man had provided him with a place to live, food to eat, and had taught him a trade. So, the boy continued to work for the horrible man until he became one of the most acclaimed blacksmiths in all the land. Everyone wanted to trade their hearts for his custom-made swords and daggers. People would come from the far ends of Julal just to get a glimpse of his work.

"The young blacksmith usually shied away from the attention, never liking to be in the spotlight. He only took the requests the horrible man gave him and never asked any questions. Until one day, he received a most peculiar request."

I quirked a brow, trying not to interrupt Claire's explanation as I rewrapped my heart and placed it in the satchel. With a sigh, I stretched out my legs against the soft soil that covered the ground, enjoying a moment of rest while she continued.

"A stranger walked into the workshop. Usually, the young blacksmith only saw the horrible man; outsiders were never allowed inside the forge. But this man didn't seem to know that rule. Or didn't seem to care.

"Though he walked into the hut with authority and grace, he was dressed as a layman. He walked over to the young man, who was pounding away at a new sword. The young blacksmith looked up, astonished to see a different man than the one who had ruled over him for so long."

Claire's voice deepened. "'If you could trade your heart for anything, what would it be?' the man asked.

"The young blacksmith looked at the stranger, surprised. No one had ever cared enough to ask him what he would trade his heart for. No one had ever seen him as anything more than a slave. The blacksmith cleared his throat and said he wouldn't trade his heart.

"The stranger smiled and asked, 'What would you do with it?'

"The young blacksmith looked down at the tools he had been working with for almost his entire life. He created things that people wanted all the time. He couldn't understand how they were so willing to trade their hearts away for something so insignificant. He could never trade his heart away for something meaningless. So, he replied that he would give it away to someone he loved."

My own heart melted a bit at the sentiment. What a nice thought. But then, that's what happened to Nana. Love was a fickle choice for a heart, leading only to destruction.

Claire continued the story, acting out each part. "The stranger smiled kindly before he walked toward the young blacksmith, picking up the sword the blacksmith had been working on.

"'Love is a gift, isn't it?' the stranger said. 'Something that can't be traded or pawned away. It is never earned, only given and received.' The stranger then gripped the sword, and the blade glowed pure white. The young blacksmith backed away in fear. The stranger loosened his grasp on the sword, then handed it to the blacksmith.

"'Your heart is purer than any heart known, and for that, you will be blessed,' the stranger said. 'But you will also be condemned. People will hate you, ridicule you, and turn against you for your kindness. But, worst of all, your pure heart will be hunted, for a pure heart contains much power. There are those who won't hesitate to destroy you to get their hands on it.'"

I frowned. This was new information. Grabbing the satchel, I peered inside once more. The red hue around the white strips of cloth pulsated softly. Did it really contain power? If it did, why had I never felt it before?

"The young blacksmith's fear grew stronger," Claire continued a bit louder. "The stranger clasped the young blacksmith's fingers around the sword and said, 'When they come, and they will, use this to protect yourself.' And with that, the stranger disappeared."

CHAPTER 15

I sat up, holding the satchel in my lap. This blacksmith, if he was real, hadn't done anything wrong. Why was he so mistreated? I looked over at Claire, who had stood during her retelling to better act out each part. The white bun on her head had become loose and was filled with pieces of dark soil from when she had previously lain on the ground. Enjoying her theatrics, I waited for further explanation.

But instead of continuing, Claire laid back down with her hands under her head as she stretched out her legs. "Yeah, that was one of my favorite stories growing up."

I gave her a pointed look. "You didn't finish it."

"Hmm?"

"I'm assuming the young blacksmith got to Ophidian's Realm?"

Claire nodded.

"Well," I said, motioning to her. "How did that happen?"

Claire gave me a questioning look. "You don't mind me talking?"

I shook my head.

She studied me once more before sitting back up. "Well, okay." She brought her fist to her mouth and coughed a few times, exaggerating the clearing of her throat. When I laughed, she grinned before straightening her posture to continue the story. "The young blacksmith was amazed at the magical man but terrified of what he had said. Not long after the man had vanished, a mob of angry townspeople burst through the door, demanding to get their hands on the young blacksmith's heart. He immediately held up the sword, sending a shining light through the crowd, blinding them all. While they stumbled in their new darkness, the man fled from the town, never looking back."

The Traders' loving cheers for the beautiful Vendor and their hateful jeers at me never fully left my thoughts. It was too easy for them to choose a stranger instead of one of their own. Just like the townspeople who had turned against the young blacksmith in the blink of an eye.

Claire paused to brush the soil from her hair before readjusting the bun to sit atop her head once more.

"What happened next?"

"Well," she said, securing a few stubborn hairs. "He went in search of the man who had given him the enchanted sword. But everywhere he asked, no one had heard of him. If he stayed in a town more than a month or two, the people would find him and demand he give them his heart."

"That's awful," I whispered, looking down at my glowing heart once more. A pure heart had caused the blacksmith tremendous pain. With that, he and I could relate.

"That's not even the worst part." Claire looked back at me. "One night, while the blacksmith was camping in a forest, he was approached by a man dressed all in black, who offered him a choice: he could trade his heart to the man and be free of its burden forever or continue to be hunted wherever he went."

My fingers froze around the satchel. A choice. Why did it always come down to a choice? To split fate into one decision. One path is chosen, one destiny accepted. Another path is chosen, a different destiny accepted. Why was that? Why did the young blacksmith have to choose? Why did Lyle have to choose? Why did I have to choose?

"What did he do?" I asked, shaking my head in frustration.

"At that moment, the stranger who had given him the sword appeared and said, 'There is always another way. Give me your heart, and I will protect it until it is time.'"

I opened my mouth to ask more questions, but Claire shot me a death glare, causing me to promptly close it.

"The young blacksmith looked between the two men,"

she continued with a satisfied look. "To the average eye, they appeared to be two regular men. But, because of the purity of his heart, the blacksmith could see the difference between them: one outlined in light, the other in darkness. The blacksmith gripped his sword in one hand and pulled out a dagger with the other. With the dagger, he cut a circle in his chest, allowing his pure heart to fall into his hands. He was so astonished by the brightness of it that he never saw the man outlined in darkness running toward him. The blacksmith cried out in pain as his heart was slashed in two, the man in darkness stealing half of it before disappearing into thin air."

I wrapped my arms around the satchel, hugging it to my chest. The young blacksmith's heart was cut in two, and he survived? I glanced at Claire, about to ask another question, but she continued acting out the next part of the story.

"The man outlined in light picked up the other half of the blacksmith's heart. 'I can mend this,' he said.

"'But what about the other half?' the young blacksmith asked."

"'You must retrieve it on your own,' the stranger replied. He picked up the sword and handed it to the young blacksmith. 'I will be with you when you are in need.' The stranger ripped open the air around him, revealing a dark, shadowy void."

"Ophidian's Realm," I whispered, connecting the significance of the story.

Claire nodded, then pointed across the air. "'Go!' the stranger said, 'Retrieve your heart, for you are more powerful than you believe.' So the young blacksmith went. He made it through all Seven Choices with the help of the man in light and was about to gain the other half of his heart when Ophidian offered him another choice."

I scowled, increasingly hating Ophidian with his stupid realm and stupid choices.

Claire gave me a look of agreement, then spoke in a tone that was so similar to Ophidian's I almost thought he had possessed her again. "'Young man,' Ophidian said, 'I will offer you a choice for the other half of your heart.'" Her voice returned to normal, allowing me to breathe easier.

"'No more choices,' the young man said with his sword high above his head. 'I've made enough choices.'

"'Life is all about choices,' Ophidian sneered. 'Our choices define our lives and who we are. If we do not choose, we do not live.' Ophidian then took the young man's heart in his hand. 'If you leave this half of your heart with me, I will spare the one whom you would give it to.'"

I let out a small gasp, lacing my fingers together around the satchel, pulling it closer. "The love he was going to give his heart to?"

Claire nodded with a somber look. "Before the young man agreed, Ophidian showed him what she looked like. Though the man had never met her, he humbly conceded, leaving his heart to the Beast and never returning."

"What did she look like?" I asked anxiously.

Claire shook her head. "The story doesn't say."

I pursed my lips, irritated. "Why wouldn't it say what she looked like?"

Claire huffed. "All we know is that she has the mark of the Mender."

I frowned. "The what?"

"You know," Claire said, shrugging. "When the Mender mends a heart, he leaves his mark on the heart so Ophidian can no longer claim it. Those who bear the mark of the Mender can defend themselves against Ophidian's forces. For centuries, Ophidian has been trying to rid the realms of them."

"Is this true?"

Claire glared at me. "Of course it's true. Why wouldn't it be?"

I looked away, unconvinced.

Claire swatted the air in my direction. "Believe what you want. But the only thought that has helped me through years of hell is that the Mender will somehow find my heart and save me."

I immediately regretted my suspicions. I had no idea what life had been like for Claire. She was taken against her will and forced to be Ophidian's puppet.

"Not everyone has a choice, Addie," she said, using my name for the first time. I was surprised she even knew it. "My heart is gone, lost. I have no choice but to obey Ophidian. You have no idea what it's been like." She gave me another pointed glare and placed her hands on her hips, waiting for my reply.

"Claire." I reached out and touched her arm. "I'm so sorry." When she didn't respond, I let out a sigh. "Look, once we get through the Seven Choices, we'll find your heart."

Her eyes remained skeptical, but her wrinkled brow smoothed in surprise. "You would do that? How would you even find it?"

I shrugged. "I don't know. But if you know your heart's still out there, we'll find it."

"I guess you really do have a pure heart," Claire muttered.

I let the comment pass. "So," I said, deciding now was as good a time as any to ask something I'd been wondering for a while. "How do you know Lyle?"

Claire sighed. "Like I said before, I helped guide him through the Seven Choices. I helped him as much as I could while Ophidian was preoccupied. Which was hard, considering Lyle was an arrogant know-it-all."

A smile came to my lips. That definitely sounded like my brother. I'm sure he and Claire bickered all the way through the Seven Choices.

Claire met my smile with a solemn face. "Whenever he would get in a tight spot in one of the Choices and thought he wouldn't make it, he would always say, 'Tell Addie I'm sorry.'"

My smile vanished, my heart searing with pain. After

all these years of worry and regret, Lyle had never forgotten me.

"It wasn't until Ophidian said your name through me that I understood. I was too preoccupied before with saving your life from the siti to connect everything." Claire gave a grin. "You've definitely grown up a lot."

I gave a small smirk. "Thanks for that, by the way."

"Don't mention it," Claire said before her grin turned grim. "Addie, there's something else you should know."

My fingers gently cradled the outside of the satchel. By the pained expression of Claire's face, I knew whatever she said next wouldn't be good.

"The Seven Choices. Each one will challenge you in a different way. Ophidian knows the weaknesses of humans, so he makes sure those weaknesses are amplified as you enter each Choice. He wants you to stay in one of the doors, so he makes each one more appealing than the last. Every time you walk through a new door, you must choose whether to stay or leave. Either decision has a consequence of its own."

A chill rippled up my spine, tensing my muscles. That must be why I couldn't resist the haze in the First Choice. Ophidian had stacked the odds against me before I even entered. I looked in the satchel, glancing once more at my heart before closing the bag. Regardless of Ophidian's tricks, I had to try to make it through to Lyle. "That's why the humans turn into siti, isn't it? They never exit the door of the Choice they were in."

Claire nodded before standing up and brushing the dirt from her pants. "Yep. So unless you want to become a life-parching monster, I suggest we better get moving." She grabbed the lantern and rod and began walking through the forest.

Taking in a deep breath, I tried to calm my racing thoughts. I had no idea what to make of everything I had learned. My only hope was that I could figure it out before it was too late.

CHAPTER 16

*L*ike the void when I first entered Ophidian's Realm, the forest seemed to go on forever. The lantern swayed in Claire's hand, shining only a few feet ahead to show us the next section of thick tree trunks that were identical to the last. We had been walking long enough for me to realize we were going nowhere. The path never twisted, never turned—a straight path to nothing. When were we going to reach the next of the Seven Choices? I just wanted to get them over with.

While crossing my arms over my chest, my footsteps became more pronounced as I stomped through the soil. Claire glanced over her shoulder but said nothing. I stomped a little louder, trying to get her attention so I could complain. I was ready to get to the next door. I wanted her to hurry up and get me there.

Just then, a bright yellow door appeared in front of Claire, causing her to stumble back a few steps.

"Finally!" she said, throwing her hands up before placing the lantern on the ground. "I was wondering when you would figure it out."

Making a face at her exaggeration, I asked, "What are you talking about?"

Claire shook her head as she rested her rod next to the lantern. She pulled out her set of keys and began to flip through them. I took a step back, hoping she wouldn't be possessed by Ophidian again.

"Don't worry," Claire said, taking note of my retreat. "He's preoccupied with something else right now. He can't be everywhere at once."

I nodded, not completely reassured. "So, the door?"

"Yeah, yeah." Claire waved a key with the head of a frog pressed into it. "In order to reach the second of the Seven Choices, you have to want it with all your heart."

"What do you mean?"

The wrinkle between her brows returned, but this time, her eyes filled with concern. "You'll find out soon enough."

Without saying another word, Claire placed the key into the lock and turned it. I braced myself, expecting the door to fly open like the other door had, but it didn't. Instead, the yellow door eerily creaked on its hinges, causing the hair on my neck to stand on end as my heart trembled within the satchel. Claire motioned me toward the open door.

Steadying my thumping heart, I couldn't but drag. As soon as I crossed over the threshold, I would be more susceptible to whatever trap lay ahead. But still, I walked toward the door, also knowing I was one step closer to Lyle. Before I crossed the threshold, Claire placed her hand on my shoulder.

"I'll see you on the other side."

With a wary nod, I clutched my hands and walked through.

The world inside the yellow door was much different than that of the light blue door. It looked exactly like the market in Barracks: a long, stone path separated endless rows of stands, and I expected to hear the yells and shouts of vendors, but there were none. Only empty displays lined each side of the path.

As I breathed in the crisp air, I almost believed I was home. The structures, the colors, the smells—they were all the same. But a loud clock ringing in the distance reminded me that I was far from home. The clocktower in Barracks had stopped chiming as soon as Schism arrived. Startled by the sound, I ran to the nearest display and crouched behind it, squeezing my hands together.

When the clock rang for the sixth time, people poured into the streets of the market. I peeked over the top of the display to see. These people were, by far, the strangest I had ever seen, and Barracks had some very odd people.

Some were clothed in layers of fine silks and ruffled fabrics. Others looked content in displaying their different body types without any fabric on them at all. Although there were a variety of shapes and sizes among them, the townspeople all carried on throughout the market, chatting with one another as if it were an ordinary day. A desire to investigate this strange place pumped through my veins. Keeping my fingers laced, I gathered my courage and stepped into the busy street.

As soon as my feet landed on the stone path, vendors appeared on either side of me. They peddled their wares to the clothed and naked people with vigor, drawing crowds to each of their displays. I tried to walk by unnoticed, but the glittering items popping up all around me were too much to resist. My eyes wandered to the closest display, which held a mound of sparkling gems. The suggestion of walking closer flitted through my mind, and my feet obeyed.

"Gold and jewels beyond reason!" a vendor wearing a hat with an elaborate spread of shining feathers yelled. "I have all you want! But how bad do you want?"

"I'll give this silk gown!" a woman wearing a pink silk gown said as she began to strip in the middle of the crowd.

My jaw dropped at the woman's rash reaction. I wasn't sure whether to look away or cover her up. No one else seemed to bat an eye. This place was definitely odd.

"I'll give this gold watch!" a half-dressed man wearing

black slacks and two red ties around his neck yelled as he ran frantically through the crowd, ferociously shoving others out of the way.

The vendor immediately shifted his attention from the almost-naked woman to the half-dressed man. I kept my eyes on the vendor as the whole crowd turned toward the half-dressed man. The vendor appeared to be drooling at the sight of the gold watch, his eyes growing abnormally wide, starving for it. But before I could take a closer look, something jabbed in my ribs, and I let out a yelp, turning to see a short, round man barreling his way through the crowd. Once he had passed, I looked back to the vendor, noting that his face was as it had been before.

As soon as the gold watch touched the vendor's hand, he and his booth disappeared, showering the half-dressed man in an abundance of golden coins and brilliant jewels. As the coins clinked along the stone path, the crowd shifted their attention from the vendor to the man being showered in riches. My hands clenched the satchel strap, a chill running through my body as the marketplace became eerily quiet.

The entire crowd, whether naked, overly dressed, or half-dressed, surged upon the man, grasping for the coins and jewels. They turned ravenous, like wild animals that hadn't eaten in months. Their teeth chomped at the air, growls escaping from their lips as their hands clawed at the man. He did his best to evade them, swatting at them while never releasing his handfuls of gold, but there were too many. The cries of the half-dressed man were soon silenced by the feet trampling over his body.

I looked on with horror as the crowd retreated with their prizes, revealing the mangled body of the half-dressed man. What would possess these people to act in such a way? Valuing wealth over a life? Even the people of Barracks had never acted in a manner such as this. I started to back away when I heard another vendor shouting.

"Happiness! Love! Joy! I have all you want! But how bad do you want it?"

Though it sounded like the trap Claire had warned me about, I released the tight grip I had on the satchel and was drawn into the crowd. A vendor selling happiness? Was that even possible?

People crowded uncomfortably close around me, filling the air with a salty stench as the vendor set out his jars. My focus shifted from the foul smell to the colorful, glowing bottles. My breath caught as my lips parted into a smile. Each bottle sparkled like a rare jewel. I couldn't remember the last time I had felt happy. There had been brief moments, mere glimpses, but never full happiness since Lyle disappeared.

I looked at the gleaming little bottles. Was it really that easy? With one small bottle, could all my troubles be dealt with? The idea rolled through my mind, convincing my heart to proceed. All I needed was happiness, and I would be fine. I nodded. Yes, that sounded right. If I had happiness, I wouldn't need anything else. I wouldn't want anything else. But I knew what I wanted. Happiness meant Lyle never left Barracks. Happiness meant our parents had never died. Happiness meant my grandfather never disappeared, and Nana was healthy. Happiness meant Silas would smile and laugh with me. Happiness meant I was no longer alone.

My eyes narrowed at the sparkling yellow bottle, blocking out everything around me.

I wanted it.

I needed it.

I wanted it.

It would be mine.

CHAPTER 17

I pushed through the crowd of people, desperately trying to close in on the happiness. *My* happiness. These people had no idea what I'd been through. Why should they receive happiness when I deserved it? They had probably never had an ounce of sorrow in their lives, whereas I had lost everything. Every*one*.

The vendor, wearing a gold jacket adorned with shining stones edging the cuffs, asked again, "How bad do you want?"

A balding, naked man held up one of his shoes, waving it with vivacity. "I have real leather shoes!"

A growl escaped my lips. A pair of shoes for happiness? Happiness was worth more than that. That man didn't want it as much as I did. He shouldn't get it. Happiness was for me and me alone. Happiness was worth more. It was worth . . . I ran my fingers along my long, pulled-back hair, twirling the strands between each finger. Happiness was worth the price of beauty. My hair had meant something to me, but that didn't matter now. I wanted to be happy, and I would do anything to get it.

"I have genuine human hair! Never been tampered with!" I yelled loudly, silencing the other cries of payment.

The entire crowd turned, forming a circle around me as they focused on the long curls cascading down my back. The short, round man from before caught my eye, his eyes widening as the vendor's had: abnormal, large, and ravenous. The faces of those around him mimicked his actions, but I didn't care. That bottle of happiness would be mine. I couldn't wait to see Lyle again, or to hug the mother I never knew. To meet my father and learn all sorts of things from my grandfather. No one was taking my happiness from me. It was mine.

Drool spilled from the vendor's mouth as he jumped from his booth and met me in the crowd. He licked his lips like he was about to devour a savory meal.

"Human hair is hard to find these days," he said, wiping his mouth with one of his glittering cuffs, revealing a wry smile. Grabbing the bottle from the table, he held it out to me.

My skin tingled as every cell in my body became aware of the glowing bottle before me. It was as if it was a part of me, and I wouldn't be whole without it. I needed it. I wanted it. Just one little bottle. That was all. One little bottle, and everything would be taken care of. It was all I needed. It was all I wanted.

The tingling sensation grew more intense, persuading me to reach my hand out toward my happiness. Warmth cloaked my body as I grew closer to my prize. But when the vendor pulled the bottle away, the feeling vanished, leaving me as cold and empty as I had been before. No, colder. I growled at him, and he barred his teeth, handing me a knife instead.

"The hair, girl," he demanded, his voice turning dark.

I growled again but took the knife. I needed Lyle to be safe and back with me.

I bundled my hair in one hand and raised the knife high, using the red ribbon Silas had given me as my mark. The entire crowd's eyes were glued to me. I focused on the little bottle. I needed Silas to smile and enjoy spending time with me. Drool tumbled over my lips and rolled down my chin. I needed Nana to be young and healthy. I needed my parents to be alive.

I brought the knife down fast as a voice entered my mind: *Run, Addie, run.*

I stopped the blade before it cut through the first hairs. What was I doing? I raised my wrist to my chin, feeling the cool saliva on my skin, reminding me of those nights I stayed up too late reading and slept well into the after-noon of the next day. Silas would wake me up, and I was always so embarrassed of the dried spit on my cheek. Wiping it away, I looked at the knife in my hand. The memory of Silas was real, but this desire for me to sacrifice the memory of my mother for false happiness wasn't. How could I have fallen so easily into Ophidian's trap?

My grip tightened around the knife, and I took a step back as I watched the vendor's eyes turn black and his skin change to dark gray. A deep growl escaped his lips.

Terror seized my heart as I looked into the crowd and saw the woman who had been undressing earlier transform as well. Her once creamy complexion was now dismal as her bright amber eyes dulled to charcoal. I gripped the knife in my hand, not knowing what to do. The vendor and the crowd continued to morph, waiting for my next move. The soft thumping of my frightened heart echoed in my mind.

Run, Addie, the soft voice rasped once more, and that was all I needed to hear.

Immediately, I turned and sprinted through the crowd, not looking back at the sounds of their growling, not even when I heard their footsteps gaining on me.

I had almost reached the clock tower when the echo of shattering glass reached my ears.

Horrorstruck, I looked back. The bottle of happiness had fallen to the ground, the glass broken into tiny shards as the yellow glow faded into the darkness.

Breath escaped my lungs. My heart stopped.

The image of Lyle walking out of Schism's door, unharmed, with a smile on his face vanished. My mother, whose beautiful hair was long and thick, just like mine, faded. Silas's beautiful, crooked smile disappeared as if it had never existed. Nana's youthful appearance was sucked from her body, rendering her frail and broken once more. Tears gathered at my eyes. My happiness was gone.

I blinked hard, noticing the crowd around me. My happiness was gone because of these people. My shoulders tensed and my eyes narrowed. My skin flamed as I grasped the knife in my hand. They had taken happiness away from me.

And it was mine.

All mine, and I wanted it. I needed it.

Harsh palpitations pounded between my ears as I let out a loud roar and held up the knife, ready to strike. Let them come. I would do anything to get my happiness back.

The possessed stared at me, their black eyes showing their readiness to devour. But I didn't care. I wanted happiness, and they took it from me. The crowd growled. I growled back.

I lifted the knife, ready to charge, when a soft beating thumped against my leg. I stopped, feeling the beating again. It was delicate, but powerful.

Run, Addie, run, the voice whispered, coaxing the pounding of my heart to a steady drum. A cool wind wrapped itself around my flesh, extinguishing my burning anger. Once more, I had been broken out of my trance.

Shaking off the thoughts of my greed, I spun around,

doing my best to ignore the intensified growls behind me. I ran hard and fast.

Just as I whipped into an alleyway, a hand grabbed my hair and yanked my body backwards. It felt like a thousand needles piercing my scalp. I cried out as the possessed tried to rip my hair from my head. The harder I tried to yank away, the harder they pulled.

In one swift motion, I swiped the blade behind me, causing the possessed to jerk away long enough for me to free what was left of my long strands. Their deformed arms rushed toward me again, claws cutting through my skin in a desperate attempt to snatch their prize. Bundling my hair in my fist, I brought the blade down and sliced where Silas's red ribbon bound it, trying not to remember my mother's beautiful locks or the gift that held mine. I cringed as the knife made its mark on my curls, condemning them to death.

The possessed were locked onto my every move, drooling pools of saliva onto the stones. I threw my hair into the crowd. They bit and clawed one another, trying to get a single strand.

I took off running, hoping I was near the end of this horrid Choice. If there was anything I wanted most, it was to get out of here, and fast.

CHAPTER 18

*A*s soon as the thought passed through my mind, a yellow door appeared in the distance with a figure standing in front of it. I shook my head. Of course, I would have to want to leave in order to find the exit.

I ran until I reached the door, thankful the possessed in the market didn't follow me. Leaning over my knees, I caught my breathe. Claire lifted an eyebrow at me, hands on her hips. "Nice haircut."

I glared up at her. "Gee, thanks, I did it myself. Added the blood for extra color. Can we get out of here?"

She held up the frog key in surrender. "Okay, okay, calm down. We're going."

Claire turned toward the door, then looked back at me over her shoulder with a smug smile. "Are you sure that's what you really want?"

If my glare could kill, Claire would be dead. She let out a laugh before placing the key in the lock.

The yellow door creaked inward, revealing tall trees. Relief came over me as Claire picked up the lantern and rod that she had left outside the door. I was ready to be done with the Second Choice. But before she proceeded through the doorway, she held the lantern up to my head and let out a low whistle.

"They really did a number on you."

I lifted my hand to feel how much hair I had cut off. As I reached past my shoulders, my stomach dropped. My hair ended at my chin. Though I intended to cut it for trading, I loved knowing I looked like my mother because of my hair. It was the only resemblance I had to her, and I was willing to give it away. And for what? A bottle of happiness? I shook the remainder of my curls while we stepped over the threshold. Happiness couldn't be bottled.

"All right, let's get you cleaned up before the next Choice," Claire said, pulling out a small bottle and a piece of fabric from her vest pocket.

I winced as she applied the same green salve to my head as she had used on my leg. It stung at first before numbing the pain.

"So," she said after a while. "How did it go?"

"How do you think it went?" I responded curtly.

Claire chuckled before her lips thinned into a stern line, and her brow furrowed. "Hey, considering what I've seen, you look pretty good."

I studied the depth of the wrinkle between her brows, realizing it indicated how Ophidian's Realm had tried to oppress Claire and failed. "What have you seen?"

She put the cork back in the bottle and sighed. "Things I will never forget." Placing the bottle back in her pocket, she picked up her rod and the lantern before continuing her strong strides forward. I followed.

"When I was first taken by Ophidian, I couldn't go through the Choices because I didn't have a heart to trade," she said matter-of-factly. "Since Ophidian didn't know what to do with me, I was given the job of opening the doors for the Traders and *only* open the doors." She jangled the keys dramatically.

"It was difficult at first." A grim look overcame her face. "The siti were so ravenous for any form of life that as soon as someone walked through the first door, they would attack." She paused and whispered, "So many people were lost because of me, and I didn't even know who they were."

I thought about offering words of comfort, but I had no idea what to say.

"Anyway, I was searching for siti when another person walked through the red door. I knew the siti were close and hungry, so I ran toward the stranger, hoping I would save him in time. When I got there, they had surrounded him, breathing in the last drops of life he had from the blood spilling out of his chest."

"What did you do?" I asked.

A smirk flickered across her face. "I saved him, just like I saved you. I took him back to my place and cleaned him up. I knew I was disobeying Ophidian's orders, but I couldn't stand to hear the horrible cries of another victim of the siti." She shuddered. "It's a terrible sound when they finish off their prey."

I cringed, knowing that if Claire hadn't saved me, I would've been lost to the siti, never having a chance to attempt to find Lyle.

"Once I cleaned and bandaged him, I recognized him." She stopped again to turn and look at me. "Your brother was the first person I saved."

"You knew Lyle before you got here?" I asked with only mild surprise. After Lyle disappeared and Silas came into my life, I began to wonder if my brother had an entirely separate life from the one I knew.

Claire nodded, and it may have been the flicker of the lantern, but I could've sworn I saw a tint of pink come into her cheeks.

"He used to come to my father's office on his way to work at the market and would always explain some new fact he had learned, or how it would be better if we organized the equipment a new way." Claire rolled her eyes with a small smile. "He was extremely smart, even if it was annoying."

I let out a small laugh. Before his Heart Reign was even a thought, Lyle was always ready to learn. Whenever he discovered something new, he would be engrossed in it until he knew absolutely everything about it. That's why his trade to Schism was so odd. Lyle had never been spontaneous about anything.

"And I would willingly join him in combat," Claire said sadly as she began walking again. "We would debate about everything: why people traded their hearts, why the chairs were lined up against the wall, why I was wearing a purple sweater. Life was so much simpler then."

I nodded, wondering if Claire's feelings for my brother were a lot deeper than what she was confessing.

"I saved him from the siti, but I probably sent him to his death." She gave me an apologetic look. "I had to send him through the Seven Choices." She shook her head. "That stupid idiot traded his heart for a choice, and I'm bound to take anyone through who made that first choice."

We were silent for a while, the sound of our footsteps padding through the soil of the shadowed forest. The lantern squeaked with each step as it swung from Claire's fingertips, never failing to light our path.

I inhaled the cool, damp air before she spoke again. "Why did he do it, Addie?" she whispered. "Why would he ever trade his heart for this?"

"I don't know." But I wished I knew. I had ideas of why Lyle traded with Schism, but I was never absolutely sure. Not knowing had haunted me for the last seven years. If it hadn't been for Silas, I would have gone mad.

The image of Silas's crooked smile flashed through my

mind, causing a heaviness to weigh on my heart. I missed Silas. He always made sure I was well fed and protected. He had always been there for me, fixing my home and keeping me company. I never thought I'd see a day when he wasn't around.

I wished he was here with Claire and me, trying to figure out this puzzle that had no clear answer. Though he wasn't as analytical as Lyle, Silas always did the honorable thing, no matter what.

When I was younger, Silas came to my house with a bag full of exotic fruits from Piet. As we rolled them out on the table, he picked one up and placed it back in the bag before leaving without an explanation. After an hour or so, he returned with the bag empty. I asked him if something was wrong, and he replied, "I didn't pay for eight. I paid for seven." At that moment, I realized he had walked all the way back to the market to return the extra piece of fruit. Since then, I always relied on his guidance to steer me back on the right path.

Claire stopped walking and set the lantern down in the dirt.

"Well, you're following the same path as Lyle, that's for sure," she said as she plopped to the ground.

"What do you mean?" I asked, sitting next to her.

"You both have this undying perseverance to make it through to the end. Even when things got tough, Lyle made it through to the next door." She rummaged through her pockets, looking for something. "But to be fair, you're going through the Choices a lot faster than he did."

I hugged my knees to my chest. "How do you know?"

"Time flows differently here. It took Lyle what seemed like years to make it through one door. Trust me, I remember the arguments we had during those long times." She rolled her eyes. "Whereas, for you, it's only taken a few moments." She shrugged. "I don't know. It may have to do with your big heart."

"You were with him the whole time?"

"I tried to be," Claire responded quickly. "I knew I wasn't supposed to, but I couldn't stand on the sidelines as he came out of each door beaten up." She peered at me. "Seems to be a family trait."

I frowned at her, then reached up to touch my hair, now sticky with sweat and dried blood. I nodded in agreement. If Claire hadn't fixed my leg and now my head, I didn't know where I'd be.

"So, I fixed him up as best I could," she continued. "But as he got further into the Choices, he began to forget things."

My heart trembled against my leg. "Like what?"

Claire took out a small, yellow bag and started eating some kind of nut. "It was little things at first, like why it was dark and why his chest hurt. I thought he was just exhausted from being here, so I wasn't worried. But when he began to change, I knew something was really wrong."

My stomach twisted into a knot. "Change?"

Claire stopped, her hand midway in the bag, as if her mind was searching back to the past. "He couldn't remember who he was. Each time he finished another Choice, he would lose more and more of himself. First it was only forgetting his identity, but then he couldn't remember me." She turned, refusing to look me in the eyes. "What was worse was that he began hitting himself where his heart had been extracted until his chest was black from bruising."

I swallowed the lump in my throat as I clasped my hands. I couldn't imagine Lyle trying to hurt himself. What had this place done to him? My heart felt cold at the next thought. What would this place do to me?

"Before he entered the final Choice was the last time I saw him briefly return to his full self."

Claire took a deep breath. "He said, 'Tell Addie I'm so sorry.' Like he had before, but this time he added, 'Tell her I would have chosen differently, if given the chance.'"

The pain returned to my throat. I tried to restrain it, but I couldn't. Tears welled in my eyes, rolling down my cheeks with each blink. After everything, Lyle still thought of me. He wanted to change his choice. How I wished I could go back in time and convince him to choose another way.

I buried my head in my knees, squeezing my arms around my legs. I could tell Claire was unsure of how to react. Thankfully, she sat still and let me cry.

I wanted to see Silas. With Lyle gone, he was all I had.

Whenever my nightmare threatened my dreams, Silas was there. Whenever I was hungry, Silas made sure I ate. He had comforted me and helped me all those years when no one cared. My heart ached as I choked out more tears until I had nothing left. I'd lost Lyle. I'd lost Nana. I'd lost Silas. I'd lost everything.

If our parents hadn't died, Lyle wouldn't have had to care for me on his own. The thought wove a strand of realization through my mind before adding another. If he hadn't had to care for me, he wouldn't have felt desperate to leave. My blood heated as I continued connecting the series of events. If Lyle never felt desperate to leave, he never would've met Schism. If he had never met Schism, he would never have walked through that red door. If it wasn't for that red door, Lyle would've never traded his heart for this choice. And if he had never traded his heart for a choice, he would still be with me.

The final realization clicked into place, and my heart pulsed with fury. Who was the one who taunted everyone at Heart Reign to make a choice? Who was the one who stood directly in front of Lyle at Heart Reign, coaxing him to trade his heart for the unknown? Who was the one who had haunted me for years in my sleep?

Schism.

I unraveled myself from the ground, standing with a new flame to fuel. Clenching my fists at my sides, I gritted my teeth.

A few feet away, a blood-red door appeared out of thin air. Claire looked up; her lips parted as her brows shot up.

"Whoa," she said, putting away her snack. "That was faster than I thought."

I was too angry to answer her. I stared at the door, remembering the first time I had seen that shade of red—at Lyle's Heart Reign. Because of that door, Lyle was gone.

Rage burned through every part of me, unleashing something I never knew was inside. My blood boiled beneath my skin, and my heart thumped wildly. My pulse pounded between my ears as a different emotion took over. I clenched my teeth as I thought of every moment of fear I had experienced, every second I was without Lyle. The heat in my chest increased as I glowered at the blood-red door before me. A small warning whispered through my thoughts, saying I should lock down this feeling and control it. But unlocking my wrath felt fantastic, and I was tired of being sad.

I wasn't sad, not anymore.

CHAPTER 19

"**A**ddie," Claire said, cautiously stretching her hand toward me. "Calm down."

I jerked away from her, ignoring her words. Stalking toward the door, I was ready to avenge my brother for all the pain and torment he had experienced because of one person's prompting. There was only one thing on my mind: Schism. His name tasted like bitter fruit poisoning my lips. Everything bad that had happened in my life was his fault. If it wasn't for him, I would have Lyle. If it wasn't for him, I wouldn't be in this hell. He had to pay, and I would make him.

A red tint, like a shade, dimmed my vision, coating everything crimson.

"Addie," Claire repeated in a worried tone. "You need to keep your head."

The scarlet tint grew more vibrant across my eyes as I

remembered every sleepless night, every empty morning without Lyle.

"Open the door, Claire," I growled.

With a sigh, Claire pulled out her keys, flipping through them until she held the one bearing the head of a bear. She placed the key in the lock. Before she turned it, she looked at me hard. "Don't be stupid, Addie."

I narrowed my eyes at her. I wouldn't be stupid. I didn't know what I wanted in going through the previous doors, but this time I did. I didn't want happiness; I wanted revenge.

Claire shot a glare back at me and turned the key. The door swung open with such intensity, it sounded as if it hit an invisible wall, causing a loud crack to reverberate through the forest.

Without another word, I stomped through the doorway, ready to destroy anything that stood in my path.

The door slammed shut behind me as I readied my stance for battle. I stood seething, but nothing attacked me. In fact, there seemed to be nothing around at all. I shifted my eyes, searching the dark abyss. Nothing.

It wasn't until I took a step that a bright light from above shined down, revealing a dirt floor with a large white circle traced into it.

I was suddenly hot, beads of sweat forming at my brow, as I stared at the white circle, unsure of what to do. My heart pulsated into overdrive as it thumped loudly in the satchel. The red thickened over my eyes. I needed revenge and didn't care how I got it. Heaving in rage, I stormed over to the circle.

"Didn't I say your time would come, little Addie?" The mocking voice of Schism Breaker rang through my ears, bringing me back to the day I first met him.

I growled as the red tint outlined Schism's taut chest and muscular arms in a bloody shade. The dark hair on his scalp gleamed as I directed my glare toward him.

"What do you want?" I spat at the demon.

"I believe I should be asking you that," Schism said, cocking his head to one side with an arrogant grin. "You're the one who summoned me here." He took one step into the circle. "I must say, I never thought *you* would invite me into Ira's Vindicae." Giving me an innocent smile, he asked, "What have I done to upset you?"

Baring my teeth, I snarled and began to charge into the circle when Schism held up his hand.

"Proceed with caution, little Addie. Once you enter Ira's circle, you cannot leave until you win."

All rational thought fled from my mind, the veins in my neck pulsing along with the revenge pounding in my heart. Sweat rolled down my temples as I continued toward the circle.

Yet, before I crossed over the white barrier, the gentle voice echoed in my thoughts.

Run, Addie, it whispered. *Run.*

But I didn't run. I wouldn't run. Not this time. I had suffered too much because of Schism. I could never erase the years of torment I had endured from the people of Barracks, but I could make him pay for starting it all. Pushing the voice away, I crossed the white line, not caring about the consequences.

A too-wide grin spread across Schism's face, causing my fury to turn cold.

"Oh, you silly, stupid, little girl," he said, his voice beginning to intertwine with others. "You're so naïve, just like your brother."

At the mention of Lyle, my rage turned full-force, and I charged at Schism, wanting him to choke on his words. Seconds before I reached him, he was gone.

"Did you really think you could seek your revenge on *me*?"

I whipped around, ready to charge again, when I stopped dead in my tracks.

Schism's pale, smooth skin transformed into a color deeper than the abyss surrounding us. His eyes shifted from black to a bloody shade of red as his body stretched higher and higher until he was at least nine feet tall.

My heart froze, my limbs paralyzed as I took in the transformation. Swallowing hard, I tried to take a step back, but my foot stopped just before it hit the white line, as if it had created a barrier.

"I told you," Schism said as he leaned toward me. "Once you step in, you can't leave until you win."

I placed my hands behind me on the invisible cage, realizing there was no escape. I clenched my fingers in front of me, the terror overwhelming my heart as I breathed deeply. What had I done?

Schism rushed toward me, extending his arm to reveal a set of long, black claws. Piercing pain shot up my arm as his claws dug deep into my flesh. I cried out, paralyzed in terror and leaning against the invisible shield.

"Scream, little Addie," he murmured with satisfaction. "Scream. No one can hear you."

As he retracted his claws, I clutched my arm against my chest. The opening between his long legs yelled escape, and I dashed between them.

But as soon as my frantic retreat led me far enough away, I slammed into the barrier of the circle. I didn't have time to blink before Schism was there. It took all my strength not to cry out again as he sunk his sharp claws into my leg. Bile and bitter blood coated my tongue as my teeth dug into my lower lip. Tears rolled down my face, but I stayed silent, unwilling to give Schism any more satisfaction.

When he retracted his claws once more, I let out a gasp and crumpled to the floor, whimpering in fear. There was no way I was going to make it through this Choice alive.

I was stupid for not listening to Claire. I couldn't look past my rage to see that she was trying to protect me from this. Now, I didn't know if I would ever see her again.

The pounding of Schism's footsteps vibrated against the invisible cage around us. Acting on instinct, I rolled away, narrowly avoiding another encounter with his claws. I knew there was more to Schism than his beautiful appearance. My heart had felt it long ago when I was a child.

While he had monstrous abilities to slay his opponents, though, I had nothing. No weapon, no defense. Only my wrath, and even that was gone now. But there had to be something I could use to protect myself.

I rolled again to avoid his claws. The pain in my arm competed with the pain in my leg, and I gritted my teeth, trying to hold back my cry.

Clutching my injured arm, I made an attempt to stand when the iron scent of blood hit me hard. Puddles of red mixed with the dirt on the ground, creating a revolting sight. I looked down at my thigh, my vision blurring as I stared at the canyon-like gash Schism's claws had left behind. I wasn't going to win. I should have listened to the voice and run while I still had the chance.

As if the Heavens heard my thoughts, a light began to form at the base of my feet. Like new-fallen snow, a beautifully crafted sword materialized atop the blood-stained dirt. Wincing, I carefully reached down and grasped it with my hand. It was sturdy and strong, but light enough that I could wield it easily. The only people I knew who had held weapons were Governor Willow's men, and those blades were only used for intimidation.

My fingers brushed against the emblem before they wrapped around the golden hilt. It was a circle with a line running through it, almost as if it had been slashed in half.

Before I could ponder it, a loud roar cried out from the far side of the circle. I whipped my head toward the noise, realizing too late what my self-doubt had cost me.

Like leather sails, a pair of gray, decrepit wings loomed over Schism's shoulders. The gust from their beating slapped against my face. Not having any other option, I gulped down my fear and lifted the sword over my head, hoping the instincts that had saved me before would save me again.

Schism let out a horrible laugh. "I see you've received some help. Something your *brother* never got. How I enjoyed his screams every time I sliced open his pathetic human skin."

Fury rose in me once more, but this time it was different. My vision didn't turn red, and my thoughts weren't cloudy and filled with ideas of murder and revenge. Everything was crisp and clear.

I looked at the sword grasped in my hands. Its luminous tint blazed through the dark void. Fear trickled into my heart as I felt the power flowing through the metal into my hands. The power was so ferocious, I almost dropped the blade. But it didn't feel evil, as if it was trying to devoid me of life like the siti. It was the opposite, like it was purifying my rage and using it to strengthen me.

I looked down at my injured leg, surprised to find my thoughts about the sword were correct. While the gash was still there, the bleeding had slowed, each cell of my body slowly working to clot the wound. Gripping the hilt with both hands, I raised the sword high above my head, knowing someone or something had given me more time.

I straightened my shoulders and held my chin up. Although the monster, with his long claws and sail-like wings, was terrifying, a peace overtook my mind as images of all those who had been swayed by Schism's lies flickered through my mind. The baker's daughter, who had traded her heart the year after Lyle, had meant to marry the year following her Heart Reign. And Headmaster Clive's son, who we all thought was going to trade his heart for wealth, had also traded for an unknown choice. My jaw clenched as I recalled the stories of their trades. They were the real victims, cheated out of their most valuable possession by a creature who cared nothing for them.

Pure white light erupted from the satchel, merging with the blade. The hilt cooled beneath my grasp as the weapon glowed.

"I will defeat you, Schism Breaker," I said in a voice much more valiant than I actually felt. "But not for my own revenge."

For years, I had wanted to destroy the beast who had taken my brother, but I had been too fearful to face him. Now, I knew that the monster in front of me was only a pawn, a distraction from the real monster behind the destruction in my life.

"If not for your own revenge, then who's?" Schism

snarled, extending his long claws as he flew high above me, ready to dive.

Taking a deep breath, I stared straight up at Schism, righteous rage beating furiously in my heart. "Everyone else's!"

Schism let out a bloodcurdling roar before tucking his wings against his body and diving straight toward me.

I held my stance, not breaking eye contact with the black mass. Could I die? Yes. But would I die? Something told me that I wouldn't. Not yet.

I knew there was an extremely high possibility that I would lose the battle of Ira's Vindicae. If I failed, I would be stuck within this door and become a siti forever. I would never find out if Lyle was still alive. I would never see Claire again and help her find her heart. I would never see Nana again and tell her how happy she made me. I would never see Silas again and tell him how much he meant to me. Everything they had done wouldn't matter anymore. But there was still one thing I would be able to do to help them all. I would do everything in my power to destroy Schism, once and for all.

As my fingers gripped the sword tighter, the emblem lit up, glowing brightly to match the brilliant blade. Once the monster was close enough, I swung with all the strength I had. Every muscle in my arms burned as the blade made contact with Schism's iron body. A loud roar erupted from his black lips, amplifying as it rebounded against the walls of Ira's Vindicae. My breath quickened as I dropped to the ground and covered my ears.

As I crouched, one of Schism's clawed hands landed in front of me, black blood oozing from the freshly severed wrist. I stared at it, wide-eyed, before I looked at the sword. Did *I* just strike Schism Breaker? An energizing warmth radiated through my body, filling me with a power I never knew I had. Relaxing my muscles, I readied my stance to strike Schism once more.

But he was too quick. With his other clawed hand, Schism swiped it across my chest, cutting the strap of my satchel. The bag fell to the ground, the white bundle rolling out into perfect view of the monster.

CHAPTER 20

$\mathcal{I}$ rushed toward the bundle, only to be blocked by Schism's monstrous body.

"I know it's in there," he growled, standing over the white bundle, mesmerized by it. His chest heaved as he spoke. "I can feel its power."

The rhythmic beating of my heart pulsed through my thoughts. What did Schism want with my heart? And why hadn't he taken it already?

Schism stood still, his red eyes gawking at the bundle below him. He began to bend down, but then reared back, growling.

Why was he acting like that?

Not wanting to waste another moment, I carefully raised the sword again, using the distraction my heart had given. But as I lowered the sword, Schism broke his gaze from the bundle and flew high into the air, my blade missing him by inches.

I grunted at my slow reflexes and lifted the sword again, ready to finish him off once and for all. But Schism didn't dive this time. He grasped his handless arm and stared down at me as if I was the most repulsive creature he had ever laid eyes on. He looked like he wanted to finish me off but couldn't.

"This isn't over, little Addie. The next time we meet, I *will* be able to hold your heart." Flapping his wings, Schism roared once more and disappeared from the white circle.

Confusion wove through my mind as I watched him disappear. Why couldn't he touch my heart?

As soon as he vanished, the barrier around the circle evaporated, allowing me to cross over the white line. I breathed a sigh of relief before dropping the sword and rushing to my heart. The white fabric surrounding it was more shredded and soiled than before, but my heart was still intact and undisturbed. I didn't want to think about what could have happened if Schism had been able to take it.

Crouching down, I winced at the pain in my leg. Though the bleeding had stopped, the ache burned. I gathered my heart back into the satchel and tied the severed ends together as best I could.

As I stood to leave, the twinkling of the sword gleamed in

my peripheral vision. I had expected it to disappear with Schism, but it was still lying in the mess of black and red blood. Limping over to where I had dropped it, I stared down at the weapon, I stared down at the weapon, studying the metal in the light beaming down from above. The overall design of the sword was simple, but there was beauty in that simplicity. The iron of the blade extended past my arm and seemed to weigh several pounds. Hesitantly, I reached down and grasped the hilt, whipping the sword around like a true swordswoman. The blade moved swiftly, feeling lighter than air. Like my arms or legs, it felt like an extension of my body, moving and gliding with my thoughts.

Ceasing my movements, I looked down at the golden hilt. There were no markings except the circle with the line slashed through it. I ran my thumb over the emblem. Whoever made this weapon had definitely put a lot of time and care into making it perfect.

I gripped the sword in my hand and left the white circle. A sword this spectacular shouldn't be left in the shadows.

Once my foot stepped outside the circle, the blood-red door reappeared, sending waves of relief through my aching muscles. Though I hadn't defeated Schism, I was excited to tell Claire about his severed hand.

Standing to the side of the red door, Claire stood with her hands on her hips and a scowl on her face, waiting.

I kept my fingers around the hilt of the sword, feeling

less confident. This fight could be worse than the one I had just endured.

As I walked closer, I gave her a small smile. "Hey, I'm, um, alive."

Claire narrowed her eyes at me. "I can see that."

"Sorry about earlier," I said sheepishly.

Sighing, Claire picked up the lantern and rod and took out her keys while shaking her head. "Yeah, yeah. I'm just surprised and glad you're still alive." She flicked her hand before placing the bear key into the lock. As she opened the door, she glanced back over her shoulder with an exasperated sigh. "That was my favorite bag."

Giving her an apologetic smile, I tried to cover where Schism had sliced through the strap of her satchel. Sighing once more, she shook her head and walked across the threshold.

I followed Claire through the doorway, expecting to find myself back in the forest once more. But as I walked through, I let out a gasp. We weren't in a forest. In fact, there wasn't a tree in sight.

As I took another step forward to investigate, a searing pain shot through my leg. Letting out a cry, I grasped the spot on my thigh where Schism had sliced through my skin. When I pulled my hand away, my fingers came away bloody, and sharp pain flared from the wound on my arm. I attempted to take another step, only to fall. My face planted straight into the warm, black sand covering the ground around us. Footsteps soon rushed toward me, spraying sand with each step.

"I have to admit, I was impressed when you first came out and could still walk," Claire said. She dug through her pockets, probably for more of that green liquid. With a huff, she flipped me over and popped the cork out of the bottle. Soon, the familiar sting of the salve ignited against my nerves. I sucked in a sharp breath but relaxed as my wounds began to numb.

"Most people come out with hundreds of cuts or missing limbs. But here you are, summoning Ophidian's right-hand monster from the Shadow Realm with only two gashes."

I sunk into the contours of the sand, allowing its warmth to seep through my body.

"It may seem like nothing," I said, glancing over to see that Claire had settled herself on the sand next to me, examining the salve on my leg closely. "But it wasn't going very well in the beginning."

"Oh, I was sure he was going to slice you like bread," Claire said a little too confidently.

I frowned. "Thanks."

"Well, I told you not to be stupid, but what did you do? You ignored me and were stupid." She recorked the bottle and sat back on the black sand, crossing her arms over her chest.

I couldn't help but let out a laugh. Even though Claire

continuously called me stupid, she faithfully patched me up, saving my life again and again.

"I'll try to listen next time. I promise."

Claire stared at me with a quirked eyebrow. "Speaking of slicing . . ." Her eyes locked onto something beside me. I moved my arm, following Claire's line of sight straight to the sword. Reaching my hand out, I grasped the hilt and drew the sword toward us.

"Addie," Claire said, her eyes not wavering from the sword. "Where did you get that?"

I studied the sword as I had before. There was such a magnificence about it, I wondered if it was owned by a king or some kind of royalty.

"I don't know," I replied, looking up at her. "It just came to me."

"While you were in Ira's Vindicae?"

"You know about Ira's Vindicae?"

She scoffed. "Just because I can't experience the Choices myself doesn't mean I don't know what lurks within them."

"Does that mean you can tell me what's in the next one?"

Claire shook her head. "I've tried that. If I tell you what lies ahead, Ophidian possesses my body, sealing my own thoughts shut. Now, don't change the subject. You got that sword in Ira's Vindicae?"

I nodded. "Hasn't that happened to everyone?"

Claire shook her head again, still staring at the sword.

"No one has ever come out of the Third Choice with a weapon. I told you before, most of them have lost their limbs. Very rarely does anyone come out with all four still intact." She eyed me, trying to piece my story together.

"Claire, I don't know," I replied, suddenly defensive of the sword. "I was bleeding to death, and then the sword came and helped me get through the fight in one piece." I looked down at the sword and smiled, thinking of the confidence it had given me to overcome my fear of Schism. I had a strong feeling that it was the same enchanted sword Claire had told me about earlier, but why would a magical weapon come to me?

"That's how I remember you," Claire said, pulling my attention back to her.

"What?"

"Your smile," she said as she pulled out a small green sack. "Whenever I saw you and Lyle at the market, you were always smiling. It must have been hard to be alone all this time."

I swallowed, remembering the trips Lyle and I made to the market and how I always looked forward to them. Lyle would promise me one small item if I behaved. But now I only had the memories. A thickness coated my throat as tears welled in my eyes. Shuddering, I placed the sword on the ground between us before lacing my fingers together to try to prevent the tears from falling.

"Does that help?" She motioned to my hands.

I gave a slight nod, squeezing them together.

"Hmmm." She opened the small sack, pulling out yellow berries and popping them into her mouth as she stared off into the black desert.

I watched her closely, willing my heart to ignore the years of torment. "Where do you get all that?" It was a question I had been wondering for a while. Now, since I was being healed again and we weren't going anywhere, was as good a time as any to ask it.

Claire had been living in Ophidian's Realm for who knew how many years, but never seemed to grow hungry or thirsty, *and* she had her own home. Where did it all come from?

"All what?" she asked mid-chew, glancing over at me.

"All that. Your things." I unclasped my hands and pointed to her bag, then to the bottle of green liquid in the black sand next to her.

"Oh." Claire swallowed. "That."

I stared at her intently, waiting for an answer. By the look on her face, Claire wasn't in a divulging mood. She fiddled with the bag of berries, making me more curious of their origin. Letting out a sigh, she placed the bag back in her vest pocket.

"When I was first brought here, Ophidian was set on never letting me leave. Apparently, my mother's trade with him included all of eternity." She waved her hand in the air, rolling her eyes. "Ophidian wanted to stick with that."

She tried to sound nonchalant, but I could see the pain on her face.

It was still difficult for me to wrap my mind around the fact that Claire was Doctor Magnum's daughter. Never once had he mentioned her. No one had. To think he had held onto the pain and torment of losing his only daughter all these years. I couldn't imagine it. At least I had Silas to confide in after Lyle disappeared. Doctor Magnum had lost both his wife and daughter to Ophidian.

"But," Claire said, pulling me away from my thoughts. "I coaxed him into a trade." She rolled her eyes again at my surprised expression. "It's not like I was extremely cunning or anything. You'll learn Ophidian loves to trade. Especially when there's a heart involved. So that's what I traded."

I frowned. "How would that work? You don't know where your heart is."

She shrugged. "Easy. I told Ophidian I would trade him my heart, the one promised to him by my mother that he never got, if he allowed me to leave his realm and look for it."

I blinked a few times, not understanding what Claire just said. *She* was willing to trade her heart to Ophidian, too? Confident, strong Claire was willing to give her heart to the Beast?

"But why?" I stammered. "Why would you give your heart to that monster?"

Claire's eyes turned cold, her voice sharp as she

replied, "Unlike Lyle, no one is coming to save me. I have to look out for myself."

I bit my lip and looked away, not knowing how to respond. I felt the burn of Claire's glare on my cheek before she continued.

"Ophidian accepted the trade right away. But there was a catch."

"Of course there was," I muttered, glancing at her. There was always an underlying aspect to every trade.

"I would be able to leave to look for my heart, but only when I brought someone successfully through all Seven Choices." Her voice lightened from its icy tone, sounding defeated as she looked past my head into the abyss of the black sand. "A terrible thing, isn't it? I get rewarded by bringing someone else to their death."

"How many people have you led through the Seven Choices?" I tried to bite back the question after it left my lips. The look on Claire's face was enough to shame me for asking.

"I can't remember," she mumbled. "I remember Lyle." Her face was stern, her mind focused, spinning as she tried to find the answer. "But I can't seem to remember the others. I know there have been many. So, so many. I remember their cries and their screams. It used to keep me up when I tried to sleep. But after Lyle, it's all a blur."

How could Claire know she had taken people through the Seven Choices, but not remember doing it?

Warmth flowed through my muscles, alerting me that

the salve had healed me once again. I stretched out my legs before bringing them to my chest. Rocking slightly, I hesitantly asked, "How many times have you been allowed out of Ophidian's Realm?"

"Only a few. That's how I have all my things. I looked for my heart, but along the way, I gathered supplies to bring back here to survive." She stared down at her empty hands. "Sometimes I would visit my dad, just to see how he was doing. I would watch him work in his office, helping patients. But he never saw me."

"What do you mean?" If Claire had been lurking around Barracks, someone would have seen her.

She let out a long, tired sigh before looking back at me. "Ophidian owns me. I belong to him in his realm. In our realm, I'm nothing but a shadow—a ghost drifting between two worlds, never belonging anywhere."

My heart beat slowly inside the satchel, weighted by the burden Claire had to bear.

She noticed my pained expression and quickly added, "But it's been a while since I've left."

I nodded, acknowledging she didn't want to talk about Doctor Magnum. But there was something else that did need to be discussed. Something that didn't seem to fit.

"You said there was a catch," I began, stretching my legs into the sand. "And I think there is." Claire nodded in agreement, waiting for me to continue. I reached out and grasped a handful of the midnight granules, allowing them to pass through my fingertips. "I think Ophidian wants you to believe you're making the choice on your own. But, really, he decides when you leave."

Claire let out a sigh. "Unfortunately, that makes sense."

I nodded. But there was still something about the agreement that didn't seem right. Why would Ophidian want Claire to save people until the end of the Seven Choices? Wouldn't he want them to be picked off in the earlier Choices, only the strongest surviving the end Choice?

The image of the black heart of my nightmare flashed in my mind. Ophidian was the only one who could create a black heart. There had to be a connection between Claire saving Traders and the black heart.

But every heart needed an owner, including a black heart. The horrid reality struck me to the core.

I swallowed. "Remember how you said you lost the people when you first came here—that they were attacked by the siti?" She nodded. "Then you began to save them, patching them back together and helping them heal."

She nodded again before the wrinkle returned between her brows. "Do you mean Ophidian *wants* me to keep saving Traders so that they can make it through the Seven Choices?"

I gave a wary nod. I didn't know what was at the end of the Seven Choices, but I knew Ophidian was too conniving to allow Claire so much freedom. He had to have another plan. While I still didn't know the meaning behind my nightmare, the mere fact that Ophidian existed gave me the feeling that my hunch was correct. Ophidian wanted to turn the Traders' hearts black.

"But that means . . ." A look of terror crossed her face as she clamped her hand over her mouth. "I—I've been helping him all this time! I thought I was being clever in trying to go back into my realm and find my heart, but he's the one who came out on top." Claire dropped her head and clenched her fists. "That dirty snake. I swear, I'll make him pay."

As Claire muttered threats to Ophidian, I brushed the sand from my hands and legs before standing. A twinkle caught my eye, and I looked over to see the emblem on the sword. It gave off a quick flash of light before returning to its normal color. I paused, staring at it.

"Addie, what's wrong?"

"It's this symbol," I said, reaching out to the sword. "I've never seen it before."

Claire followed my gaze to the emblem, her face quickly shifting from anger to a knowing smile. "Well, now I know why you were fine coming out of Ira's Vindicae."

I pursed my lips, not agreeing with the word "fine," but too curious to know what she knew. "Why?"

A smug smirk appeared on her face. "Because" —she pointed to the emblem on the sword— "that's the mark of the Mender."

CHAPTER 21

*M*y expression was not kind.

"The mark of the Mender," Claire repeated, giving me an equally unfriendly look. "Don't be stupid, I know you remember the story I told you."

I remembered the story all right, of the young blacksmith and his pure heart. How he had lost half of it to the Beast to try to save his love. But I didn't know what the Mender had to do with the enchanted sword. He hadn't been seen for hundreds of years. Why would a sword with his mark suddenly show up to help me? I didn't even believe he existed. He had never helped me before; why would he now?

"Don't tell me you still doubt," Claire replied with narrowed eyes.

I plunged the sword into the black sand, using it to

heave myself to my feet. Once I regained my balance, I pulled it back out.

"It's not that I doubt," I clarified, sliding the sword through the ring that held the satchel's strap. "It's that I can't believe."

"Isn't that the same thing?" Claire questioned sarcastically before standing. She picked up the lantern and rod before tossing a smug look over her shoulder. "If I can't make you believe, I'm sure going to laugh in your face when you're wrong."

I smirked then let it fade away. I genuinely hoped I was wrong and that the Mender would save us from this nightmare. But so far, he hadn't. Why would he now?

We began the trek across the black desert toward the next Choice in silence. Claire walked ahead of me, barreling through the sand as I followed behind, squeezing my hands. I hadn't meant to upset her.

But as we continued forward, the sand began to shift beneath our feet. Like spirals of snow on the icy ground, the sand pulled us to and fro as a harsh wind blew gusts at us. In a matter of moments, we had sunk knee-deep into the thick grains.

"What's going on?" I yelled to Claire over the howling wind.

"It's Ophidian!" she yelled back, her face turning pale as the dunes shifted her away. "I don't know why, but he doesn't want you to succeed!"

I dodged to the left, narrowly avoiding a wave of black sand as it crashed next to me.

None of this made sense. Ophidian had wanted all the other Traders to make it through the Seven Choices. Why not me? Unless there was something at the end of the doors he didn't want revealed.

"Addie!" Claire yelled, her voice whisked away by the wind. "Watch out!"

I turned in the direction of her voice only to be met by a towering wall of sand. I pushed my thighs against the granules, attempting to move myself out of range. Instead, I sunk to my waist.

I slugged through the black sand, grasping at it in handfuls as I pulled myself through, hoping to outrun the giant wave. But as I attempted to flee, it continued to follow me.

I looked over my shoulder and gasped. I no longer saw the wave behind me, but, instead, a towering, thin man made of black grains. His chin was perfectly chiseled with a strong jaw bone that could slice through wood. The granules surrounding his eyes shifted and swirled in the shape of two serpents slithering from his temples and down his neck. His cropped hair flowed with the wind, black particles at its edges flying into the abyss. A wide, sharp grin extended across his face. The only parts of him that weren't sand were his eyes. A pair of yellow eyes, narrow as a snake's, stared down at me as I tried to keep my head and chest above the sand that was insistent on pulling me down.

"Well done, Adelaide," he said. "I hear from my ward that you put up quite a fight."

I scowled as soon as I heard the voice, recognizing it from his earlier possession of Claire. Ophidian. Of course he would come here to finish me off after I had sliced Schism's hand off.

"I don't plan on dying here," I replied, making sure I stared straight into the Beast's snake eyes. The sand around me continued tugging at my body.

Ophidian cocked his head to the side, his lips peeling back over sharp teeth. A thin snake on his face twisted and curled around one of his eyes. "You don't? Well, that's good to hear. I can't have you dying when there's someone who's been trying to live long enough to see you again."

I let out a gasp, my heart bursting with excitement and dread as the sand opened beneath Ophidian. Rising as if suspended on invisible strings, a lifeless body with dark curls and spectacles, covered in black sand, appeared.

"Lyle!" I yelled, fighting against the sand to get to him. He was motionless. My throat tightened, and my stomach squeezed as I feared the worst.

As soon as I reached my brother, the sand closed around him, burying him once more.

"Lyle!" I dug my hands through the whipping sand. The hammering of my heart quickened as I threw handfuls of granules out of the way.

"Don't fret, Adelaide. Your brother is safe with me. However, I have come here to offer you a choice." His voice was calm and comforting, as if consoling a child. But there was something beneath it, tugging at my heart to surrender.

I gritted my teeth against the hard grains in my mouth, straining to keep my thoughts straight. Another trade, another choice. You choose one, you lose the other. Another choice that would affect what happened to me from this point on. It was amazing how such a simple concept controlled the entirety of my eternity.

"What kind of choice?" I growled.

Ophidian's toothy grin remained plastered to his face, almost gleaming against the black sand. "I will give you back your brother, heart and all, on one condition."

The whirring of the sand around me vanished, the rhythmic pounding of my heart the only sound I could hear. After all these years, could I really have Lyle back? Could he really get his heart back and have a chance to relive the past seven years? My own heart began to beat with a flicker of hope.

I opened my mouth to accept when a memory entered my mind's eye. A memory that wasn't mine.

I was standing before Ophidian, just as I did now. Except he looked older and frail. But that couldn't be right. Was this a vision of what was to come?

"No more choices," I replied, my voice sounding strangely like Silas's. "I've made enough choices."

"*Life is all about choices,*" Ophidian wheezed. "*Our choices define our lives and who we are. If we do not choose, we do not live.*"

I blinked, realizing what the memory was. This was what happened between the young blacksmith and Ophidian.

"*If you leave this half of your heart with me, I will spare the one whom you would give it to,*" Ophidian said.

My mind reached back to the story Claire had told me. Ophidian showed the young blacksmith who his love was. Maybe if I could see who she was, I could figure out what had happened to the blacksmith. Maybe it had all worked out, and they were together. I let that childish thought dissolve. Nothing ever worked out, especially when dealing with the Beast.

The memory began to fade from my mind, and I struggled to keep focused, wanting more than anything to know who this mystery woman was, the woman who bore the mark of the Mender.

As the light dimmed around the memory, old Ophidian revealed who the love of the blacksmith was.

Long dark curls.

Bright blue eyes.

A curious smirk on her lips.

The woman who bore the mark of the Mender wasn't a stranger.

The woman who bore the mark of the Mender was me.

CHAPTER 22

I gasped as the memory fled, my mind returning to the swirling black desert. Ophidian still loomed over me. Black sand pulled away from his body as the wind whipped around him. Did he know what I had just seen?

"If you give me half of your heart, I will give you your brother," Ophidian continued, apparently unaware of my vision.

Why did he only need half? But then I realized what he was bargaining for. He still only had half of a pure heart from the young blacksmith. I didn't know what would happen if Ophidian gained the power of a wholly pure heart, but I knew it couldn't be good.

My heart ached as I remembered the image of Lyle's lifeless body ascending from the sand. I loved Lyle with all my heart and wished more than ever that I could be with him now, but I couldn't allow Ophidian to become stronger.

I readied myself for the Beast's abuse when I felt the same cool power from the Third Choice coming from beside me. It was strong, radiating toward my heart. Reaching through the coarse sand, I pulled out the sword, its refreshing energy flowing into my veins. It glowed brightly, a halo of pure light beaming from the blade.

The particles that made up Ophidian's body immediately scampered away from the glowing light. The Beast's once-grinning face transformed into a horrible scowl. He let out a roar as I held the sword high, the power of it surging through me.

"No more choices!" I yelled, the emblem radiating brighter as I spoke. "No more trades!"

Ophidian snarled at the light and slithered away, looking more snake-like than before.

"You will die, Adelaide Tye," he growled. "I'll make sure of it. Once I have a pure heart, I will live for eternity and will watch you die a thousand deaths."

"You will never have my heart!" Acting on instinct, I gripped the sword with both hands and plunged it into the black sand in front of Ophidian, causing the black particles to freeze in midair.

The light from the blade washed over the entire desert of black sand, transforming it from darkness to light.

Ophidian roared again, his body turning to pure white granules before crumbling to pieces and colliding with the brilliant ground. A final gust of wind blew the last grains away, erasing any mark the Beast had left. And all was silent.

Panting, I pushed on the hilt and hoisted myself out of the white sand. Exhausted, I lay still on my back, feeling the strength of the sword leave my body as it retreated back into the metal. The chill of the frosted granules relaxed my racing heart as I ran over Ophidian's words: *Once I have a pure heart, I will live for eternity.* That was why he needed a pure heart: to become immortal.

"That was incredible!" Claire yelled from a distance.

I turned my head to see her racing down the calm white dunes.

"I can't believe you did that," she said, gasping for air with a grin on her face, eyes sparkling with joy.

"I didn't really," I replied, pushing myself into a sitting position before studying the sword again. "It was all the sword."

She placed her hands on her hips and leaned to one side, the lantern she held squeaking with the motion. "You're saying the sword just stabbed itself into the sand and got rid of Ophidian?"

I frowned. "Well, no, I did that."

"Don't be stupid, Addie. That sword came to you for a reason! I mean, look!" She motioned to the clean, white sand with another giant grin. I followed her arms, taking in the crisp dunes stretching beyond sight. The pearly grains sparkled as Claire moved the lantern, reminding me of the nightly snowfalls in Barracks. It was amazing, knowing that the area had been a void of darkness but had transformed into a beacon of light. "Things like that don't just happen."

I stood and brushed remnants of white sand from Lyle's sweater. "I know." I didn't want to think about why this sword came to me and what I had to do with it. I just needed to focus on a way to save Lyle and keep my heart away from Ophidian.

What pressed my mind even more was the image from the memory. Ophidian had known all this time who I was. Had he lured Lyle here to get me here, too? I ran my thumb against the emblem on the hilt, thinking about the rest of the memory. *I* had the mark of the Mender. I wasn't sure how that could be true, because I didn't have a visible mark. There was also the fact that a young black-smith was out there, missing half a heart, all for me. Why would anyone do such a thing? He didn't even know who I was, yet he was willing to sacrifice half of himself to the darkness so I could be safe.

A nagging thought pulled at the back of my mind, one I was surprised to acknowledge. While I saw the young blacksmith's memory, the familiarity of his voice had struck me. I almost thought it could have been Silas talk-ing. My heart fluttered at the thought, and I frowned. That couldn't be right. The young blacksmith's memory was full of life, emotion, and passion—all things Steady Silas didn't possess.

I shook the thought away as I looked down at the satchel. The darkness invading its edges had faded, replaced with a pure white. A crisp, invigorating chill spiraled through my arm as I placed my hand over my heart. It was transforming into something else. Something powerful. Swallowing, I made a promise to myself. When I got out of here, and when Lyle was safe, I would find the young blacksmith, whoever he was, and I would help him get his heart back, no matter what.

My own heart beat in excitement. There was still another adventure that waited for us after this one finished. And I was ready for this one to end.

CHAPTER 23

$\mathcal{I}$ opened my mouth to ask Claire whether we should keep moving when a royal blue door appeared amidst the white sand. I groaned, tilting my head back in frustration. I had forgotten there were still four doors left.

Claire let out a laugh. "Well, that's the first time I've ever heard that response." She pulled out her keys, pinching the one with the head of a snake on it.

Dread filled my heart as I focused on the rusted key. I didn't like snakes. Especially after Ophidian. I had hoped I wouldn't have to deal with that key so soon.

As she placed the key in the lock, she turned around and faced me. "Now, please take note when I say *don't be stupid.*"

I gave her a wary smile. "I'll try not to be."

Shaking her head, Claire patted me on mine. "Good girl. This one's going to be tough."

Before I could ask what she meant, Claire opened the door. Swirls of shadows spiraled out, contaminating the pure sand. My breath caught as thick, warm strands snaked around my body, enticing me to fight another Choice. I went without a struggle, reminding myself I was one step closer to finding Lyle.

After they had pulled me through, the door closed softly, and the shadows released me from their grasp. Surprisingly, my heart pulsed calmly, no longer fearful of the night.

Raising the sword, I took a step, and a long hallway etched with golden markings appeared before me. My muscles tensed at the quick change.

The teal carpet muffled my footsteps as I strode cautiously, anticipation rising in my heart. My shoulders scraped along the gilded walls, barely clearing the narrow width.

Suddenly, the hallway opened into a red-tinted room filled with smoky haze. Holding my breath, I strained my eyes, hoping the haze wasn't like the First Choice. A variety of different shapes moved within the smoke. The longer I looked, the more I recognized the shapes as people dancing. I exhaled and inhaled, allowing the scent of jasmine to tickle my nose. I couldn't remember the last time I had smelled something so fragrant. A soft melody wove throughout the room, beckoning me to loosen my tight grip on the sword as I watched the couples sway rhythmically to the tune, holding each other close.

It seemed harmless enough, like the dance halls that used to be in Barracks. Only then, there wasn't nearly as much smoke. Or hugging, for that matter.

As I took my first step toward the marble dance floor, a tingling sensation slipped from the top of my shoulders down to my ankles. No longer was I wearing Claire's shirt and pants beneath Lyle's sweater. Instead, a shimmering evening gown draped my frame, blue as the color of the door. The material was cool on my skin, slinking against my curves.

I gasped as I looked down at the dress. I could see straight down my chest, almost to my stomach, the neckline plunged so deep. And it stretched so wide, it left me almost fully exposed.

My elbow bumped against a chilled gold chain that twisted around one side of my chest. It then crossed my body around to my back, creating goosebumps as it brushed against my bare skin.

I reached my hand to my back to discover there was no back to the dress at all. The fabric covered so little, I might as well have been wearing nothing at all.

The chain snaked back up my shoulder and repeated its pattern on the other side of my body, clasped between my almost-exposed breasts. When I looked down again, a small snake of gold stared up at me with two yellow eyes.

I felt like vomiting. If this disgusting display of my body was Ophidian's idea of a sick joke, I wasn't laughing.

A small, golden purse dangled from my right shoulder, and as I shifted, it fluttered against my side. I breathed a sigh of relief. I still had my heart, and my sword now hung from my left hip in an ornate sheath. I had a feeling I would need it. The sword felt warm against my side, strengthening me as I covered myself with my arms.

I would never wear something like this. In Barracks, I would have frozen to death, but it also just wasn't me. There were many people here who had traded their hearts for a different body or hair. But I had never considered it.

I watched the surrounding couples dancing to the beat when a glow of golden hair framing a familiar face caught my eye. My heart jumped, a jolt of electricity searing through my veins, making my knees weak. It couldn't be. I moved to another area of the room to get a better look. My stomach fluttered as my heart hammered in my chest. It was him.

In the center of the dance floor was Silas, dancing with a beautiful woman with flowing, blonde hair. A red silk dress hugged her voluptuous body as Silas crushed her against him. A silver necklace with a yellow stone melded into it glittered as she swayed with the soothing music.

I swallowed the knot in my throat as I laced my hands together. The room grew hot, closing in around me as I squeezed my fingers tightly, allowing the fear to creep back in. How could I have ever thought Silas would want someone like me?

Unweaving my hands, I gripped the hilt of the sword for stability while turning to flee from the wretched Choice when a soft clacking of shoes echoed across the marble floor.

My knuckles turned white, tightly wrapping around the hilt as I kept my back turned. I refused to watch as the figure approached. Two strong hands reached out to me, cupping my shoulders and spinning me around. I let out a small gasp before looking up into a familiar set of brown eyes. Eyes I had yearned for since I entered Ophidian's Realm.

"Addie," Silas murmured, drawing closer to me. "You look amazing."

My heart pounded with an intensity I'd never experienced before. There was no way my Steady Silas would ever say that. I looked at the creamy complexion and tousled locks, then back into the chestnut eyes gleaming down at me. I wasn't sure I minded the desire I saw within them. But I was still in Ophidian's Realm. This couldn't be real. I took a step away, but Silas reached out, grabbing my wrist.

Before I could break his hold, a cool surface rose up behind me, and I froze. Looking over my shoulder, I saw another wall had blocked my escape. My hair stood on end as my limbs refused to move. But the light touch of

Silas's fingers on my wrist was enough to bring relaxation to my tense body.

Silas took a step closer and ran his fingers up my bare arms, sending pleasant chills up my spine. Standing so close to him, I could smell the cold air of Barracks on him. This had to be him. But how did he get into Ophidian's Realm?

"Don't cover up," he whispered, his hot breath tickling my ear. "You're so beautiful." His hands slid from my arms to my bare back, his fingers beginning to twirl the gold chain, sending my heart into a frenzy.

"Silas . . ." I barely whispered, my breath escaping my lungs.

"Too long you've kept me waiting, Addie," he said. "You're all I've ever wanted, for so long." He took a step back, holding his hand out to me.

Entranced, I laced my fingers through his, allowing him to lead me to the dance floor, where the other couples still swayed. I felt oddly light as we glided across the polished floorboards.

He pulled me close to his firm chest and whispered, "Dance with me."

My heart almost stopped, it was beating so fast. I sucked in a breath and nodded quickly before my rational side could catch up with me again. Silas grinned, and I paused. Silas never smiled. He couldn't.

But before I could think, his calloused hand hugged the small of my back, making my skin tremble beneath his touch and flushing away my suspicions. I took a small step closer.

My heart pulsed harshly, banging against my leg in warning. But for it to feel this good, I didn't know what to think. Could something this wonderful really be that bad?

"Addie," Silas whispered again. "I'm not going to hurt you."

Holding my breath, I took another step. He drew me closer until my body was pressed against his. The smooth fabric of his soft shirt tickled my chest as we swayed back and forth.

The music continued to hum in the background as I tried to keep my mind alert to all that was happening around me. But the melody was so soothing and, with Silas holding me, my thoughts of danger slipped away.

There had been a small part of me that wished for Silas to see me as more than the little girl he looked after. I thought it was too late when he didn't show up for my Heart Reign, but I was wrong. Silas had come back. He had changed, and I liked it.

The tempo of the music picked up slightly, causing the dancers to sway faster. I could feel Silas's hand press harder into my back, pushing me closer into him. The touch of his rough skin against my bare back ignited the nerves beneath. A pleasant shiver coiled down my spine as I allowed him to bring me close.

Suddenly, my left hip felt lighter. Glancing down, I saw that the sword had disappeared. I shrugged it off, and I leaned into Silas. If the sword was gone, it had to know that I was safe now. I didn't need it anymore.

Soon our bodies were swaying against one another in perfect time to the music. I knew I shouldn't be enjoying this. My heart knew it wasn't real. But I let my body react otherwise.

The music started to play faster, adding a harsher tone to its tune. Silas let go of my hand, placing both of his hands on my back. I immediately wrapped my arms around his neck and pulled myself closer to him.

As my body swayed harder and faster, I pulled myself closer, my breaths quickening with each movement of his body against mine. My fingers ran up and down his neck, feeling the smooth strands of his silky hair. He was an intoxicating poison I couldn't wait to drink.

His breath heated my neck, making my heart forget everything my head was thinking. And when his lips caressed my neck, a burning sensation followed, but I ignored it.

He kissed me again and again. Each time, the pain shot through my skin, but I suffered through it. His hands ran up and down my back, but instead of bringing pleasure, the touch began to sting.

Somewhere between desire and pain, I continued to dance. I was able to ignore the discomfort as my heart beat with passion. Silas let out a small groan as I pressed my body fully against his. His hands began to move their way up my back, pressing me harder into him as he burrowed his face into my neck.

The delight of his lips was unlike anything I had felt before. Until a hard nip pierced my flesh.

A bright light flashed through my mind, alerting my nerves of danger. I let out a yelp and pulled away, my limbs tightening at the sudden movement. Placing my hand on my neck, I felt a warm liquid coating my finger-tips. There was only one guess as to what it was.

I stared at Silas, who was wiping the blood from his mouth with the back of his hand.

"I'm sorry, Addie," he said, walking closer with a different gleam in his eyes. "I got a little carried away."

"Just a little," I snapped, wiping more of the blood off my neck. What was the matter with him?

He began to wrap his arms around me again, but I took a step back, extending my arm between us. "I don't know about this, Silas."

He then smiled a beautiful, crooked grin that I had never seen before, making my knees weak. "Addie, it's me, remember? I would never hurt you."

Reaching out, Silas cupped my face, his rough fingers caressing my cheek. A shudder spiraled throughout my body, and I shut my eyes, savoring the sweetness of his delicate touch. I wanted to push him aside and rid myself of whatever was happening, but my body drew closer as I allowed myself to succumb to his embrace again. His strong arms moved from my neck to my waist, wrapping tightly around me. The icy scent surrounding him relaxed my muscles, and I held onto him as if nothing else mattered. It wasn't long before I was completely lost in him once more. Our bodies moved perfectly in time with one another as the music thumped faster and faster.

"I just want to eat you up, to drink you in, to feel you," he whispered in my ear, kissing my neck and shoulders.

I let out a gasp as he pushed me back against the wall. A whimper escaped my throat as my spine collided with the stone.

"Shh," Silas said softly, running his hand up my thigh.

I held my breath as he leaned closer, his face only inches from mine.

Run, Addie, the soft voice said.

I knew I shouldn't ignore it. The last time I did, I had almost died.

But as I began to unwrap myself from him, Silas cupped my cheek and crushed his cold, thin lips against my mouth. It was like fire and ice, heating me up and cooling me down all at the same time. So pleasant and yet so—

The smell of burning flesh washed over the room, and I pushed Silas away, feeling my neck and shoulders. The skin where he had kissed me was raw, red, and decaying.

The dim light of the room revealed terrible burns that covered almost everywhere Silas had kissed me. How had I missed it?

Silas stood before me, studying every part of my body.

The same gleam in his eyes had returned. Leaning down, his lips reached for mine once more. My heart raced, pounding as if it would explode. Terrified, I tried to back away, but the wall trapped me.

"Silas, st-stop . . ."

"Oh, Addie." Silas's voice began to change, becoming entwined with other voices. "It doesn't matter if it's right or wrong. I will get what I want."

Blood drained from my face. I tried to run away from him, but his hands reached out and clenched my wrists.

His hands felt like fire. Every follicle, every nerve, seared beneath his touch. I gagged as I smelled my own flesh burning.

I screamed. But no one heard me. No one would save me.

I desperately tried to dodge the lecherous kisses from Silas as he pressed his weight against me. Wriggling with all my strength, I jerked my arms forward, attempting to break the hold he had on me.

"I don't think so," he growled with a grin that was no longer Silas's.

I tried to wrench my arms free once more, but he only grasped them tighter. The harder I struggled, the more painful it became. My body ached. New burns were forming, branding my skin.

I shouted in surprise when a flash of light descended into the room, causing the sword to materialize at my side. Thankfully, Silas was too consumed with holding me to notice.

Knowing this was my only chance, I braced myself as a perfectly thought-out plan entered my mind. Taking a breath, I relaxed my trembling limbs, causing Silas to loosen his grip ever so slightly.

In that moment, I quickly reached to my side and grabbed the hilt of the sword. The power within the sword immediately flew through me, feeding my hope once more. Like a cornered animal, I reared back before shoving Silas in the chest.

He moved back enough for me to scramble out of his grasp. I clutched the sword with both hands, heaving. Silas leaned his head back and laughed with a voice that had become the Beast's. "Do you think you can defeat me with your little sword? Oh, Adelaide, you know nothing."

The beautiful brown eyes that were once Silas's darkened into the life-parching depths of the siti. The body that had fooled me for Silas leapt at me, a horrible moan escaping its lips. Ignoring the brands of painful lust on my skin, I held the sword high and charged at the monster. I didn't care if I was desirable. I didn't care if being with him felt good.

My hands gripped the hilt tightly as Silas's hands grabbed for my body. Fiery lips bit down on my mouth, sending shock waves of piercing pain into my flesh. Struggling, I lifted the sword and plunged the blade straight through his chest.

CHAPTER 24

*S*ilas choked, his black eyes widening in shock. A haggard breath escaped his lips as he staggered backward. I couldn't stop the tears from filling my eyes. I knew the monster before me wasn't Silas, but a sharp pain pierced my heart. Nausea boiled in my stomach as black blood poured from his chest.

I quickly untangled myself from him, jerking the sword with me. Siti Silas groaned, falling to the ground before his body began to transform. His eyes were still black, but his skin faded from Silas's normal, smooth complexion to a grayish, leathery one. The fingernails on his hands grew into long claws, scraping the stone floor.

I gripped the sword tightly as I watched a single cord of black rope thread itself through his lips, preventing him from ever speaking again.

The creature's body moved, its limbs stretching until

they were horribly thin. I whipped my head around, frantically looking for an exit. I spotted one on the opposite end of the room. Not giving the siti another look, I raced away with all the strength I had left.

A horrible moaning from the siti trailed after me. I ran faster, wishing I hadn't been so easily lured in. I should have listened to the voice—and my heart—the first time they warned me.

The hollow feeling from my Extraction returned to my chest as I ran, the cold emptiness of my heart magnified by a moment of pleasure that didn't amount to any ounce of love.

Suddenly, the sword glowed in my hand, shooting warmth up my arm. Glancing down, I watched, amazed, as several pieces of yarn appeared in midair, looping back and forth, stitching together as they traveled up my arms and legs. Soon, my body was clothed once more in the familiar comfort of Lyle's sweater and Claire's clothing, my heart hidden in the old satchel.

The scratching of claws behind me pushed my thoughts back to escape as I pumped my legs faster. I soon stumbled onto another dance floor, where the dancers were undressing themselves and openly groping one another while their bodies shifted into monsters. I looked away, horrified. Was that what I was about to do? Become so completely lost in physical lust that I didn't care about who was around?

I shook my head and kept running. The only sounds I

heard were my own footsteps pounding in time with my beating heart.

After a while, realizing no one was closely pursuing me, I slowed to a jog, exhausted from all the Choices. Either the siti had gotten tired of me, or it had become lost in another lecherous act. I shifted my pace into a slow walk until the royal blue door appeared ahead of me, accompanied by the lantern light illuminating Claire's figure leaning against it.

I hung my head and allowed the sword to fall until it dragged behind me. The burn marks on my skin hadn't faded away. With every step, the sharp memory broke through my mind, reminding me of my sensual desires. I kept my focus on the pattern of the teal carpet as I drifted toward the door, unwilling to see the disappointment on Claire's face.

My mind kept showing Silas's bleeding body over and over again, branding the image into my memory. My head knew it wasn't him, but my heart ached, seeing Silas transform into a monster. Tears rolled down my face before I reached the door to exit this horrid Choice.

Claire's footsteps sounded just beyond the threshold. I didn't care if she called me stupid. I just wanted to get out of here.

Before I could tell what was happening, two arms wrapped around my shoulders, pulling me into a tight hug. That was enough for my waterworks to fully release.

I cried into Claire's dirty vest while her gloved hand stroked my short curls.

I cried for Nana. I cried for Lyle. I cried for Silas. I cried for Claire. But mostly, I cried for myself. My stupid, stupid self.

A loud crack resonated through my ears. My muscles quivered beneath my skin before a rush of boiling heat flooded into my chest. A guttural scream erupted from my throat as pain encased my nerves. I touched the circle on my chest, only to remember my heart was no longer there. Pulling away from Claire, I frantically searched through the satchel until my fingers latched onto the white fabric. Carefully peeling back the pieces, I saw the pulsating heart still alive and beating. But it had changed so much since this journey had begun. While the center was still pure red, the outer edges of my heart had changed from red to pure white to a dark gray.

I wiped the tears off my face before I spotted a small crack in the middle of the top of my heart. It wasn't very large, but it was enough to paralyze my body. I took a deep breath before rewrapping the cloth. I didn't know what was happening, but I knew I needed to get through these doors, and quickly.

Wiping my face with my hands once more, I ran my fingertips along my cheeks to make sure all the tears were gone before I looked up. Claire gave me a sympathetic glance, then turned the snake key in the lock.

"I told you this one was going to be tough," she said

softly. "You can break all the bones in your body, but nothing can compare to the pain of a broken heart."

Swallowing the knot in my throat, I tried to hold back more tears. The pain from that tiny crack was worse than anything I had felt so far. I didn't want to know what would happen if it cracked more.

"Okay," Claire said, clutching her rod and the lantern. "Let's get out of here."

With an aloof nod, I followed her through the doorway. The bright sand shocked my eyes as we returned to it. I cupped my hand above them to lessen the impact of the blazing force. I hadn't seen anything so brilliant since the sun shone in Barracks, which was years ago.

As I squinted, my eyes slowly adjusted to the light among the darkness. The bright white sand against the midnight black sky reminded me of the first time I had seen snow. It was a hot summer in Barracks, and Lyle had traded one of his springs for a ball of freshly packed snow from the Shalley Mountains. I loved how it sparkled and shined in the sunlight. A soft warmth filled my chest as I replayed the memory while looking out over the clear, white sand. It was incredible to see anything this pure in a place so dark.

A light breeze caused the short hair around my face to tickle my cheek, reminding me of the doors I had gone through and that the memories I had of Lyle were in the past. I brushed a curl away as I continued to follow Claire through the desert, the tip of the sword forming a rut in the sand as it dragged behind me.

Twice, the sword had saved me from my stupid decisions. Twice, when I had pushed the warning voice away, it was still there. I didn't know why either one had chosen to come to me, but I was thankful they had.

"So," Claire said over her shoulder as we walked through the sand. She used her rod as a staff in one hand and clutched the lantern with the other. "Do you want to talk about it?"

The sword continued to drag as my feet dragged along with it. That last door had completely broken me; I didn't know how much more I could handle. Stopping in the sand, I collapsed, crossing my legs on the sandy ground.

Claire turned around with an irritated look. "Is that a yes?"

I stared blankly at her until she let out a huff and slumped down on the ground as well.

"After Lyle left, I thought I'd be alone forever," I murmured, immediately catching her attention. "But this boy—this man," I corrected myself, "came into my life right when I thought I had no one. He was a miracle. He took care of me when I was sick, fed me when I was hungry, and listened when no one else would." The large knot in my throat resurfaced. "And I just *stabbed* him through the chest and watched him transform into a monster." My voice wobbled as I tried to control the tears from running down my cheeks again.

"Addie, you know that wasn't really him. That was Ophidian playing tricks with your head. He's good at that." Claire gripped the rod, then plunged it into the sand, hoisting herself up.

I shook my head, unable to give myself the excuse that Ophidian made me do anything on the other side of that door. I knew what my heart wanted, and I had chosen my own path.

Claire sighed, running her hand through her hair before looking down at me. "You made a stupid decision, all right? We all do. But you wouldn't be here right now if you didn't fight back."

Her words made me pause as I remembered fighting against siti-Silas's grip, how I hadn't given up even when I couldn't find an escape.

"Look," she said, scratching at her white hair again. "I can't heal your hurt, but at least I can say this: you fought back. You chose to resist. If you didn't, you wouldn't have any skin left to show." Claire pointed to the scars on my arms, my face.

"There's no way to hide these marks," I muttered, pulling the sleeves of Lyle's sweater down as far as I could. "I failed."

Claire placed her hand on her hip and leaned over until she was almost nose-to-nose with me, allowing me to study her numerous freckles. "That's another choice you have to make. Are you going to let the Beast get the best of you? Are you going to let that snake get inside your head and mess with it? Or are you going to take charge—are *you* going to take control?" She let out a huff. "Not every choice is evil, Addie."

I stared at her blankly. How could I have any control over this? Over anything?

"You have that—and *that*—for a reason." She stood straight, pointing forcefully to the sword, then to the satchel where my heart beat softly. "Someone obviously thinks enough of you to have chosen you as the carrier of both of those things. You have more power than you think."

I frowned at her. This wasn't the first time I had heard that. Maybe there was more truth to it than I believed.

I grabbed the sword and held it up. The mark of the Mender stared back at me, daring me to take its power again. My heart quickened as I studied the emblem. It felt as though my heart and the sword were one, pulsing with the same life that flowed through me. I knew the break in my heart was still there, but, for a moment, it felt as though it had been healed, mended somehow.

Claire pointed the rod down at me, the wrinkle between her brows returning. "Are you going to be stupid and let that snake win, or are you going to toughen up and fight?"

I looked up at her with a new-found power surging through my veins. I had always thought I was alone, a burden to everyone else around me. I had always needed help from someone, whether it was Lyle, Nana, or Silas.

And because I couldn't take care of myself, the people I loved suffered.

Clenching my fingers around the hilt, I plunged the sword into the sand. I reached out and grasped Claire's rod, pulling myself up. A jolt of power surged through the rod and down my arm. It felt ten times as powerful as the sword.

A shimmering sheath of crystalline light escaped from the rod, traveling up my fingertips and coating my skin. It was warm, tingling, and soothing.

I glanced up at Claire, who watched with mouth agape. Like fine, sparkling dust, the sheath of light began to fade and was carried off in the wind.

I stared at the skin on my arm, stunned. It had been completely healed. All evidence of scarring the monster had created on my arm had vanished.

"Now, that's new," Claire whispered.

Clenching my hands, I stood with a new determination. I pulled the sword back out of the sand and looked to Claire. "Where's the next door?"

A devious grin spread across Claire's face. "That's my girl."

She pulled out her keys and swung them around until she grasped the one with the pig symbol. As soon as her hands touched the iron, an orange door appeared behind her.

I focused on the door, ready for whatever Ophidian had up his sleeve. He was no longer in control.

Claire placed the key in the lock. "Remember, Addie—"

I flicked my hand at her. "I know, I know. Don't be stupid." I waited for her snarky response, but none came. Instead, a voice I had longed to hear for seven years responded.

"Addie?" Lyle's voice crackled.

My heart stopped as every cell in my body froze. I slowly slid my eyes from the orange door toward the direction of the voice and let out a gasp. It was no longer Claire before me, but the bruised body of my brother.

CHAPTER 25

"*L*yle!" I cried, rushing toward him. I stopped short of embracing him. Bruises covered almost every inch of his exposed skin. A nasty gash on his cheek looked like it had tried to heal several times but kept getting reopened.

"Lyle," I whispered, my heart wrenching in pain as my eyes scanned him. I gently took his hand. "What happened?"

"Addie?" he repeated, a confused look coming to his face as he reached up to adjust his cracked spectacles.

"Yes, Lyle, it's me," I said, tears forming in my eyes as I gripped his hand a little harder. "I've come to get you out of here."

He squinted and adjusted his spectacles again, only he wasn't looking at me but past me. I glanced over my shoulder, but nothing was there.

"Lyle?" I asked, fear wrapping itself around my heart once more. "Lyle, can you hear me?"

He began to open his mouth to respond when he suddenly arched his back, a scream bursting from his lips instead.

"Lyle!" I cried as he fell to the ground, writhing in pain. My heart squeezed, panicked. What happened? Was he okay? My mind swirled with so many thoughts that I didn't know what to do.

My brother sobbed on the ground before his voice shifted from his deep, throaty cries to the soft, strained wails of another. I looked down at the hand I was gripping to find it was now covered in a fingerless glove.

"Claire?"

Claire's body shuddered as she fully transformed back into herself, the bruises and bleeding on Lyle's skin changing into Claire's copper tone.

"Ugh," she said as she tried to sit up, her movements unsure.

"Claire, what happened? Where's Lyle?"

"That one is always worse than possession," she grumbled, placing her hand to her head as she squeezed her eyes shut.

I wanted to burst out of my skin and continue asking her questions but waited until she opened her eyes once again.

"Wh—"

"Addie," she interjected, raising her hand toward me.

"Remember, Ophidian owns me. He can do whatever he likes. Although he hasn't used transformation in a while." She rubbed her head again before attempting to stand.

I helped her up as she groaned, stretching out her back, wincing with each movement.

As she twisted her upper torso from side to side, I couldn't believe Lyle had just stood there. "Was that actually Lyle? Can you feel what happened to him?"

Claire leaned to the side, issuing a loud crack from her back that resonated through the desert before she let out a sigh of relief. "Yes and yes."

"Claire," I began but stopped, reflecting on Lyle's state. He looked awful: beaten black and blue, and so thin, I hardly recognized him. An icy chill flooded my veins as my worst fear plagued my thoughts. "He's not—"

"He still has some time," Claire quickly reassured me, her voice somber as I sucked in a sharp breath. "But not much." Crouching, she picked up the lantern and rod with a grunt and walked toward the orange door.

Gripping the hilt of the sword, I followed her, knowing the only way I could get to Lyle was to defeat every last Choice.

"Make it quick," Claire said, all playfulness gone from her eyes.

"I will," I replied, giving her a firm nod.

The lock clicked, and the door burst open, allowing loud, jovial music and bright lights to pour out of it.

Smashing my hands over my ears, I ran toward the Fifth Choice.

The bright lights continued glaring all around me until my eyes finally adjusted. Like the previous Choice, a corridor greeted me. However, this one wasn't nearly as elegant as the previous one, as only gray stones composed its foundation. I clutched the hilt of the sword, not willing to be taken advantage of again. I didn't have time to play Ophidian's games. I needed to get to Lyle fast.

As I ran farther through the bare hallway, the music grew louder. A series of pipes accompanying a drumming beat vibrated throughout the walls.

The hallway opened into a large, rectangular room. Dark, wooden planks lay on the ground, shining like ice against the warm light beaming from above. A long, golden table surrounded by large, marble columns extended past my vision. The comforting scent of freshly baked bread directed my attention to what was on the table. Countless colorful bowls and plates of miraculous food rested upon it, waiting to be devoured.

A loud roar sounded, and I stopped, gripping the sword, only to realize the roar had come from my stomach. I placed my hand on my stomach, trying to calm my hunger. When was the last time I had eaten? I thought back to dinner at Nana's house, my heart squeezing at the memory of my loved ones.

My stomach roared again, and I winced. I wasn't sure how long I had been in Ophidian's Realm, but I knew it had been a while since I'd eaten anything. Lowering the sword, I inspected the table of food.

The brassy sounds of trumpets bounced through the room as cymbals chimed in between. Although the music was jovial and inviting, there didn't seem to be anyone around. I checked the perimeter once more before walking toward the golden table.

The food was immaculate. There were dishes in front of me that hadn't been in Barracks for years. Large platters of ruby-red lobsters, giant suckling pigs, and a turkey bigger than my body were laid out on the table.

Saliva collected in my mouth as my eyes feasted on the sight. Enchanting smells drifted into my nose, teasing me with delight. I began to take a step forward, but cautiously stopped myself. If this food was here, I knew something bad would come of it. Ophidian was trying to tempt me with another one of his tricks, but it wouldn't work this time. Not when I had so much at stake.

Holding the sword in defense, I walked further down the table. My stomach roared again. Luscious fruits sparkled in shades of deep purple and emerald green as the light danced across them. They looked so fresh and plump, tempting me to dive into them. The only type of produce we had in Barracks was what we grew ourselves or what could be traded from the everyday vendors. After Schism arrived, the frozen ground grew hardly anything at all, and the vendors always charged a hefty price.

My stomach growled, but I bit my lip, hoping that would be enough to control my hunger.

Continuing past the decadent fruits, I tried my best not to become enchanted by their beauty, knowing nothing good could come from them. I lowered the sword slightly, my shoulders relaxing, when the fruits finally disappeared and there was a break in the table. But a groan soon escaped my lips when I saw what came next.

Piles and piles of desserts were stacked one on top of the other. Chocolate crystals spilled from a sapphire bowl, pooling around the other luscious treats. Next to the bowl stood a five-tiered blue cake, decorated with intricate silver designs. Pink, sparkling glasses were filled with a golden liquid I was dying to taste.

I swallowed hard. I could handle living without some meat. I could even go without fruit. But sweets? There was no way I could avoid those. Especially . . .

My eyes grew wide and my thoughts stopped as a perfectly designed tower of the plumpest, juiciest cherry donuts appeared mere inches away from my hand.

My stomach roared louder than it had before. I was so hungry. I knew I shouldn't eat. But I was starving.

My mouth began to drool uncontrollably, my lips unable to hold the saliva in. My eyes focused on the delicious pastry as I extended my hand toward the plate. Just a bite, that would be all. One little bite. Plus, if I wanted to save Lyle, I needed my strength. It wouldn't hurt me. And it couldn't hurt anyone else. After all, no one was here.

My fingers were almost around the soft, golden crust when a plate clattered to the ground. I pulled my hand back, simultaneously whipping the sword in the direction of the sound. Just as I was about to charge, my legs froze, my mind unable to comprehend what I was seeing.

A plump arm extended from under the table, reaching for anything it could find, then pulled back, disappearing into the darkness.

I held the sword tightly and waited a few moments to see if the arm would return. The moment it reappeared, I rushed over just as it pulled down a tray of shining cherries. When the hand disappeared, I leaned down, hoping to make sense of what was going on. Before I could blink, the arm whipped out and grabbed the collar of Lyle's sweater, pulling me beneath the table.

I fell fast, landing hard on my backside. I didn't have time to stand before something soft and mushy was shoved into my mouth. I tried to spit it out, but my teeth had other plans. Chewing ravenously, my mouth devoured the sweet mush. I didn't know what it was, but it tasted amazing. I swallowed, only to be bombarded by another piece of food, this one hard and crisp. Its taste was completely different from the first, but just as delicious.

My stomach gurgled in delight, wanting more. I was about to shove my fist into it, when a hand gripped my chin, forcing my mouth open once more. A cool, wet liquid seared down my throat. It burned at first, bringing tears to my eyes. But after a few gulps, I relaxed, and my thoughts became fuzzy.

"That's it, girl," a breathy voice said. "Drink—drink it all."

My throat continued to burn from the liquid, but I didn't stop drinking until the bottle was pulled from my mouth and thrown to the floor, shattering into pieces.

With a break from feeding, I could finally see where I was. I tried to stand from under the table, blinking a few times to clear my head. Everything was fuzzy, but I could make out a very large room. And there were bodies. Lots of bodies.

An airy feeling swirled through my thoughts as everything began to slant. I raised one hand to my forehead and used the other for balance when another piece of food was pushed into my mouth. I half-choked on it as someone shoved it down my throat.

"Eat, girl," the breathy voice said forcefully. "Eat!"

As I chewed, my mind began to clear, and I remembered that Ophidian knew I needed food to survive and would purposefully make it more enticing. Quickly spitting the delectable mush out, I tried not to react as the scene in front of me came into focus. Elegant iron sconces hung on the stone walls of the enormous room, giving off just enough light for handfuls of figures to come into view. When the fog fully lifted from my thoughts, I took a step back as I saw clusters of people lying around, draped over one another and piled on plump pillows and cushions.

A chill ran up my spine as I remembered a similar scene from the first Choice. But this one was different. While those people were all sleeping, these were all eating, as if every piece of food they put in their mouths would be their last. Men and women were shoving food and drink down each other's throat, laughing wildly with each mouthful. With each burst of drunken laughter, bits of food shot from their mouths onto each other.

A tall, rotund male began to pour a dark-red liquid down the front of a scantily clothed, plump woman sprawled along a pile of purple pillows. I assumed he was too drunk to know where her mouth was, but once he started to lick the liquid off her, making her laugh hysterically, I realized he knew exactly what he was doing.

The odor of fermentation, various foods, and bad hygiene swirled in the air. Scrunching my nose, I tightened my fingers around the sword and began to back away. I needed to find a way out of here, and fast. A soft, sweaty surface hit my back, causing each one of the hairs on my neck to stand straight up.

Cautiously, I turned around to see another extremely large man with a wide smile on his face. Chunks of various food tumbled off his chin, latching onto his exposed stomach. He held up two bottles of the same dark liquid, shaking them with vigor.

"Why don't we give that a try?" he asked, wriggling his eyebrows.

"No," I said, backing away as I looked for an escape. "I think I'm okay."

"You can't be okay," he said, a look of genuine concern crossing over his face. "Look how thin you are! You must eat and drink! Eat and drink!"

I thought back to the beautiful, voluptuous woman from the previous Choice with Silas before blocking it out. She was only a monster, like siti Silas had been. She wasn't real.

And while I had always assumed being thinner had its perks, I still wasn't willing to give up dessert for it.

"I'm not thin," I retorted. "I'm just fine."

The power of the sword merged with my heart as if it knew we had little time to spare in this Choice. Its beating intensified as the glow of the blade began to match that of the bright light from the room.

"You are fine," the man said with a chuckle that made me want to vomit. "But you need to eat. You need to drink."

He began to walk toward me, and I knew it was time for me to act.

I raised the sword above my head, ready to strike, but the image of Silas came to my mind. The blood rushing down his chest, the shocked look in his eyes. I couldn't do it. I couldn't take the life of another human.

As I lowered the sword, the man in front of me began

to change. His eyes receded into tiny spheres, allowing his mouth to widen and disfigure. Fear gripped my heart as my fingers tightened around the hilt of the sword. The man's face continued to transform until there were rows upon rows of sharp teeth lining his mouth, waiting to devour me. In an instant, he dove at me, ready to feast.

This man was no longer human. I dodged the pointed teeth ready to sink into my skin, swinging the sword toward the monster. Its body immediately split into two equal halves. I blinked a few times, shocked at the accuracy and deadliness of the sword. I hadn't expected it to sever the monster in half. Panic rose in my throat, but I pushed it away, realizing that all the people around the room had stopped their eating and drinking, focusing their hungry attention on me.

Yet when I lowered the sword, I noticed they weren't focused on me, but on the man's body. I had only seconds to move before they started racing toward it like starved animals.

As soon as I was out of the way, the sound of teeth breaking through flesh filled the massive room. I held my hand over my mouth, literally holding back the vomit rising from my stomach.

Once I had it under control, I frantically searched for a way out. Although I caught Ophidian's temptation earlier this time, it didn't mean I wouldn't escape unscathed.

Looking up, I saw light streaming from the room above. A space, just wide enough for me to fit through, brought hope of an exit. My eyes traced down the high wall descending from my escape. It was at least forty feet high. I had no way to get back up there. The ravenous chomping quieted down, indicating that the crowd had dispersed to their original areas to continue eating and drinking, leaving a perfect view of the man's half-eaten body. I covered my mouth again, blocking the bile rising from my throat as pity lanced through my heart. Had this man realized this was how he would die when he traded his heart?

As I focused on my surroundings, looking for something to climb, my heart pulsated, prompting an idea. It was incredibly risky and left an unsettling feeling in my stomach, but as I looked around at the people gorging themselves, I knew their humanity had vanished long ago.

All their eyes began to transform into the same small, round balls as the creature had before. Their mouths overtook almost the entirety of their faces, and when they opened them, long, pointed tongues flicked in and out of thin lips. The tips of their pointed teeth shined against the dim lights. No, these people were no longer human, they were monsters.

With that thought, the unsettled feeling left my stomach, and I stood directly under the hole, allowing its light to beam down on me. Taking a deep breath, I let out a loud whistle. All eyes turned on me, and they were hungry.

CHAPTER 26

$\mathcal{I}$ grabbed a bottle of the dark liquid perched on a nearby table. Using the sword, I cut off the top, allowing a purple stream to seep out. Taking a breath, I poured it over my head, dousing my short curls and allowing the purple to stain Lyle's sweater. The scent of wine filled my nose as the gleam in the monsters' eyes changed from hunger to thirst. Their tongues rolled out of their mouths, dripping saliva on the floor. No more than a few seconds passed before they began racing toward me.

Planting my feet on the ground, I breathed in deeply once more, feeling the invigorating power of the sword entwine with my heart. I raised it high over my head and slashed the first creature that reached me. Its body instantly split in two, just as the one before.

Immediately, the monsters' focus shifted from me to

the body. Like a pack of wolves, the monsters descended upon it. I did my best to ignore their feeding frenzy as I slashed another body, causing more of the starved beasts to rush over.

Soon there were dozens of bodies heaped on one another, trying to get a bite of the meal below. Consumed by their devouring, the monsters didn't notice when I began to climb over their obese bodies toward the space.

The bright light shined through the opening like salvation. One more body, and I would be free of this madness and closer to saving Lyle. I reached my hand out and grabbed the ledge. As I pulled myself up, a sharp pain seared through my ankle, like hundreds of nails had punctured my flesh. I screamed before looking back at the monster chomping on my foot. I kicked my leg wildly, trying to shake the disgusting creature off. But it tightened its grip, leaving me no choice. Holding the ledge with one hand, I twisted my arm back, slicing the sword until I cut its throat. Its grip on me immediately loosened, and I kicked the monster down to the pile, pulling myself free from the chaos below.

The stench of rotting food rushed toward me as I pulled myself up, wincing as I put pressure on my mangled ankle. Hobbling away from the horrors below, I gagged and coughed before pinching my nose shut.

When I turned back toward the table, I gasped. The once beautiful food was a disaster. The succulent meats were green and squirming with maggots. The sparkling fruits were rotten, emitting a pungent, fermented scent. And the desserts were covered in ravenous rodents.

My heart pulsed with confirmation as the realization about the Choices entered my mind. Sleeping for eternity, wanting physical pleasure at the cost of compromise, and stuffing yourself with anything to feed a hunger that would never be fed. Every one of the Choices were temptations trying to lure me away from the path I was destined for, the one I had decided to take the moment I dove into Ophidian's Realm.

Energy pulsated through every vein in my body, filling me with a power I never knew existed. I wouldn't be enticed by pleasure or anger. I wouldn't be swayed by false happiness or laziness. I had been chosen. I would fight the darkness, and I would save my brother. My heart and the sword beat as one as I jogged parallel to the table. I'd never felt this alive before.

Doing my best not to injure my foot further, I slowed to a limping walk until I saw the orange door in the distance. Relief flooded my heart as soon as I saw Claire with her usual stance: rod gripped in one hand, the other hand on her hip with the lantern swinging between her fingertips. As I approached, she crinkled her nose with disgust.

"You reek." She placed the hand holding the lantern over her nose and mouth.

Taking in a deep breath to calm my racing heart, I held out my hands and smiled. "I think I smell all right."

Claire rolled her eyes. "You're a freak, but I'm glad you're a freak who's still alive."

I laughed, thankful that Claire was back to her old self. "I'm glad you're okay, too. I was worried there for a moment." I thought back to Claire turning into Lyle, both being simultaneously tormented by Ophidian. I needed to get to the final Choice and end his control over them both.

"You were worried about the cannibals? Yeah, I would be a little worried, too. Especially if I had decided to marinate myself for them," Claire scoffed, turning toward the orange door with the pig key in hand.

I shuddered at the thought of there being both those monsters and the siti behind one door. "What were those things?"

"They're called phagos. Another of Ophidian's disfigured creatures. While the siti feast on life, the phagos feast on you."

Another shudder ran down my spine, forcing me to physically wriggle it out. Claire let out a loud laugh at my response.

"Don't worry, Addie," she said as she turned back to the door. "I would patch you back up if they took a bite out of you."

"Speaking of which," I murmured, causing her to whip her head around. I gave her a weak smile as I motioned down to my bleeding ankle. The phagos had torn straight through her pants and my boot.

Sighing, Claire turned back around and placed the key in the lock. "Let's get out of here before we heal your foot." The lock clicked, and the door opened wide.

I smiled and followed her through the doorway, knowing that if anything else, somehow I had made a friend in the shadows.

But my smile soon faded as I saw what lurked behind the orange door. Tall trees of all widths wrapped around one another, creating the archway I had known for many years. I froze in place, my heart beating so softly, I thought it had died.

"Addie," Claire said, shining the lantern back at me. "What are you doing? Come on, you only have two doors left."

I swallowed and nodded. She was right. Lyle was dying, and I needed to keep going. Even if Schism was waiting to finish me off on the other side, even if Ophidian was ready to steal my heart, I couldn't give up now. Taking a breath, I walked across the threshold of the orange door and into the nightmare that had become my reality.

CHAPTER 27

The path beneath the archway was soft with brown soil, as if it had just been lain, waiting for our arrival. No foliage grew along the path except for the arched trees lining the perimeter. A dark, murky fog coated the air, obstructing our view, so we couldn't see farther than a few feet ahead.

Not wanting to wait any longer, Claire barreled through the doorway. I swallowed the fear accumulating in my stomach and followed, holding onto the sword so tightly, my fingers were sore. I tensed, waiting to hear the screams I had heard for so many years in my nightmare.

Claire cleared her throat and stopped abruptly. I jumped about a mile high, shrieking. My nerves had been on edge since we entered my nightmare. I was ready for Schism to pop out from behind any tree and take me to Ophidian.

Spinning around, Claire held the lantern inches from my face.

"What's the matter with you, Addie?" she asked as she pulled out the bottle holding the green salve. "The last time you were like this was when we were back at my place five Choices ago." She motioned for me to sit before she spread the healing salve on my ankle. "I was hopeful when I saw that you weren't doing that hand thing anymore. What's going on?" She held the lantern by my face.

Squinting, I pushed the light away. I couldn't confess to Claire how my nightmare had tormented me. I couldn't let her see how weak I really was. "Nothing."

Claire pursed her lips, her eyes shining with irritation as she stood. "Tell me now, or I'm leaving you here."

I was about to repeat that nothing was wrong, but I knew Claire would see right through it and leave me. Especially since I had to wait to move until my ankle was healed.

I looked down at my hands, knowing I hadn't been relying on them to release my fear, because I was overcoming it. I had gotten stronger since entering Ophidian's Realm, but I couldn't go through my nightmare alone.

"All right, all right." I held my hands up in surrender. "It's just that . . . I've been here before."

Her eyebrows furrowed, her eyes narrowing with skepticism. "You've been here before? How could you have been here before?"

Claire had no idea what had happened to Barracks. I'm not sure when she was taken, but I knew she had no idea of the effect Schism had created on our land.

"After Lyle traded his heart for a choice," I began, "I had a nightmare—the same nightmare I've been having for the past seven years."

Claire's eyes widened. "Your nightmare was about this place."

I nodded.

"What happens in your nightmare?"

I swallowed again, not liking the look in Claire's eyes. They weren't clouded over, like she was possessed, but filled with worry and dread. And if Claire was worried, I knew it couldn't be good.

"It starts when I'm walking through an archway of trees." I motioned to the trees above.

She nodded quickly. "What next?"

"Well, I begin to hear screaming, so I run toward the sound until I find a cave."

"And you go in."

My brows knitted together. "Yes."

"Oh, man," she said, pulling the lantern away as she ran her hand over her disheveled bun.

"What?" Dread, thick and heavy, filled my heart.

"It seems someone has been trying to tell you something," she said, her eyes darting all around.

"What do you mean? I don't know anyone who would want to warn me about this place. Unless, maybe Lyle—"

Claire shook her head. "Listen, Addie, I know you've been through a lot, but people don't just know about this place. Hardly anyone ever gets this far through the Seven Choices. And those who do don't give this forest a second glance. Somebody powerful was sending you a warning. Only a person with a special power can use that sort of magic."

"A warning about what?" I could feel my heart filling with fear. "And what do you mean 'a person with a special power can use that sort of magic'? What kind of magic?" The only magic I had ever known of was Schism's doors and their ability to send Traders here.

She peered into the forest. "Sending messages through dreams is not easily done. It takes an old magic, one that is only known by those who bare the mark of the Mender. I only know about it because of my role here. Unfortunately, it has long been forgotten across the realms. Since Ophidian gained half of the young blacksmith's pure heart, he's become better at luring people into his realm, leaving none left to bear the Mender's mark."

"But," I cut in, my mind spinning. "If what you're saying is true, then there's someone who still has the mark of the Mender."

"I guess." Claire shrugged. "But that means they had to have gone through the Seven Choices already and somehow survived. No one knows about Ofavemore."

I shuddered. "Do I want to know what that is?"

"Depends." Claire looked into the trees, searching.

"Ofavemore is, let's say, Ophidian's throne room. It's where he rules over this realm. What happens next in your nightmare?"

"As I walk farther into the cave, the screams grow louder, like when a storm is coming. The thunder and lightning are far away, then, within moments, they're right at your window."

Claire nodded.

"I begin to run toward the screams until the ground hardens under my feet. So, I reach down to feel it and pick up—"

"A black heart," Claire whispered, her eyes searching through the trees again.

"Yes, but—"

"Addie, listen to me," she whispered harshly, cutting me off. "Who else have you told about your nightmare?"

"My friend, Silas, knew I had the nightmare, but—"

Claire cut in again. "And he's already traded his heart?"

I shook my head. "He's like you. He doesn't have one."

She wrinkled her brow for a moment before she shook off whatever she's thinking. "Listen, I'm not supposed to say this, but you can't go through the last door. Someone was warning you about Oph—"

She stopped mid-sentence.

"About what?" I asked before Claire's eyes completely glazed over. My body tensed, the fear pouring in once more, knowing what was coming next.

"Adelaide," Ophidian's soothing voice said. "I must say I

am thoroughly impressed with your progress. Only two Choices left. Good for you."

"Leave Claire alone," I said, feeling the green salve dissipate from my skin. I scrambled to stand and held up the sword. A hiss came from her lips as the sword glowed brighter.

"Claire belongs to me. I can do whatever I like with her. And since she's been a disobedient wretch, trying to divulge all my secrets, I'll have to deal with her accordingly."

"No!" I exclaimed as Claire's body began to disappear. "No, please!"

"It's too late, Adelaide. I already gave you a chance to choose. This was your choice. Have fun with the consequences." Claire's body disintegrated, turning to ash until there was nothing left.

I stood frozen, not knowing what to do. Where had Ophidian taken Claire? How was I supposed to make it through the Choices without her? Was the same thing happening to Lyle, too?

I began to knit my fingers together when a sharp pain stabbed through the circle on my chest, the same pain that had nearly destroyed me before. I cried out and grabbed my chest and the satchel, knowing another crack had been made in my heart.

I knelt and held the satchel against my chest. Why did I lose everyone who came into my life? Destruction seemed to fall on anyone who tried to help me. Why couldn't someone stay with me? Why did I always have to be alone?

"You are not alone," the voice whispered.

I looked up from my crouched position. No one was there.

"You are not alone."

I focused on the voice. Though I hadn't heard it during the past few Choices, I knew that voice. It was the same voice that had told me to run since I had entered Schism's doors.

I stood and held the sword aloft. It felt more powerful than it had before, as if the voice had brought strength to us both. As I turned, an emerald green door appeared a few feet in front of me. I had to finish what I started.

I walked cautiously toward the next Choice, noticing a key with the head of a dog gleaming in the lock. The key began to turn on its own, clicking until the door unlocked. It creaked open with an eerie sound, sending chills up the back of my neck.

I held the sword in front of my body, staring into the dark abyss of the doorway. Then I heard them—the same words that began this torment.

"Run, Addie, run!"

So, I ran.

CHAPTER 28

I ran as fast and as hard as I could over the threshold, expecting the worst. This was the last door before the Final Choice—the one Claire was trying to warn me about. The one that caused Ophidian to take her away.

I clenched my teeth as I ran, trying not to think of what he could be doing to her and Lyle. I had to rescue my friend and brother from the darkness.

My legs became exhausted from the constant race, and I slowed down to a steady stride through the dark. The abyss extended longer than it had beyond the previous doors. Maybe the darkness was the only danger I'd have to face.

And then a faint glow shone in the distance.

I quickened my steps once more, tightening my grasp on the hilt of the sword. As I drew closer to the light, the glow divided itself into two, then four, then eight, rapidly multiplying before my eyes. The multiplying ceased when a large wall of white light stood a few feet in front of me. The individual lights swirled in all directions, moving and bouncing against each other until the particles began to form into a shape. The specks merged with one another until the shape became a mirrored image of me.

I yelped in surprise, holding the sword up to the image of myself. What was this? Did Ophidian make a doppelgänger of me to kill me?

I readied my stance, but my mirrored self in the light wall wasn't looking at me. She turned toward something I couldn't see. I placed the sword in the ring on the satchel, curious as to what was coming. A large smile spread across her face, and she darted away, fast as a blur, down the wall of light.

Curiosity piqued, I sprinted to catch up with her. As she slowed, I heaved, placing my hands on my knees and breathing a thank you to the Heavens that she—or I—had stopped running.

Regaining my breath, I looked up, and a gasp escaped my lips at what I saw. There I was, standing with a huge smile on my face, linking arms with a man with messy golden hair. Why was Silas in Ophidian's Realm again?

The odd feelings I had felt before my Heart Reign returned as I watched the image of Silas. The figure turned, causing me to remember the same scene from when I had stood outside the gates of Heart Reign. Seeing Silas's face twisted my stomach into several knots.

"Silas," I breathed, walking toward the wall.

He looked so real, like it was him and not the monster from the previous door. Reaching up, I stretched my hand toward the wall. But as soon as I did, my image twisted and changed into another's. It was a tall woman with long, blonde hair. I blinked twice. Wasn't that the same woman from the fourth Choice? I stared at her silver necklace with the yellow stone. Who was she, and why did she keep appearing?

I reached up once more, this time making contact with the wall. I cried out in pain, jerking my hand back as the wall seared my flesh with its light. My skin throbbed, and I clutched my hand to my chest.

"You can only look, but never touch," a wheezing voice said.

I grabbed for the sword, but my fingers screamed in pain from the burns. I bit back the agony, reaching with my left hand instead. I grunted, struggling to wrangle it free, but as soon as I did, I pointed it toward the source of the wheezing voice.

"Who's there?" I yelled into the abyss.

Silence. But within moments, joyful laughter danced from the wall behind me, and I turned back around. It was the blonde woman again, still embracing Silas. But this time, she was wearing a long, blue gown covered in intricate lace flowers. Was this the future? Or was this what was happening in Barracks right now?

I swallowed as I watched Silas pull her close, giving her the most tender of kisses before he held her hand up to his mouth, brushing his lips against it. A beautiful ring shimmered on her finger.

A lump grew in my throat. The sight sent new emotions through my heart that I'd never experienced before. The couple looked so happy. And Silas, he was *smiling*. His crooked grin was the most handsome thing I had ever seen.

With every choice, a fate is accepted, and another is left behind, a voice slithered through my mind, causing a chill to run down my spine.

"Who's there?" I whipped around again. This voice sounded like the voices from when I had first entered Ophidian's Realm.

More laughter came from behind me, and I turned back to the light wall, feeling the pain growing in my heart. Lyle bounded up beside Silas, clapping him on the shoulder with a huge grin. Linked to his arm was Claire, wearing a beautiful sunshine dress I never thought Claire would wear. Next to the blonde woman was Nana, looking years younger and a whole lot happier than she had been in a long time. And beside her stood a man I didn't recognize. His face was blurred, making it impossible for me to identify him.

Everyone was so happy. Everyone was so full of life.

Everyone was together, except for me. This dream was right at my fingertips, but I couldn't reach it. This dream wasn't mine. It was someone else's.

This is the fate you left behind when you made your choice, the voice cackled with cruel laughter.

I gripped the sword in my hand while the other still throbbed from being burned. The emptiness in my chest was filled with something hard and thick, demanding to be addressed. Didn't *I* deserve to not be alone? Didn't *I* deserve to be happy?

My eyes blurred, and I blinked. Little green dots flew through the air, whizzing all around the scene in front of me. I blinked hard once more, and they disappeared.

The scene on the wall changed again. No longer were Silas and the woman embracing one another on their wedding day. The mountainous scenery around them had been replaced with cream-colored walls, and they stood just inside the threshold of a bedroom.

I took a step closer to see around the happy couple. The bedroom was completely empty, except for a wooden crib. I frowned until the woman turned to the side with a hand on her stomach and a goofy grin on her face. Silas placed his hand on the woman's stomach as well, leaning in to give her a kiss.

A fate I never knew existed taunted me. My eyes blurred once more, and the green dots returned, flying faster through the air, clustering around my field of vision. I blinked hard, but they didn't go away this time.

Connecting with one another, the dots filed into my eyes until my vision was completely covered in green.

I looked back at the happy blonde woman with Silas, now shaded a deep emerald.

I hated her.

If I could trade places with her, if I could just be on the other side of that wall, then everything would be okay. Silas was there, Lyle was there, even Claire. Everyone I cared about was happy and healthy on the other side of that wall. *I* deserved to be happy, not her. *I* deserved to be with my family, not her. *I* deserved to not be alone. I just needed to switch places with her.

The idea locked into place, and I took a deep breath, striding quickly toward the wall. The green dots became heavier on my eyes, turning everything various shades of jade. No longer was the wall a bright white, but an emerald green, the same color as the door that led me here.

I knew it would burn if I touched it. I knew it would hurt. But I also knew that if I could switch places with that woman, I would finally have my dream. My family would be together, and I would never be alone again. Everything would be good.

Why would they even want you back? the voice slithered. *You were nothing but a burden, remember?*

My steps froze, and my outstretched hand paused in front of the light wall as the scene changed before me.

"So sad to think she ended up just like her grandmother," a voice from the past echoed throughout the chamber.

"It would probably have been better if she wasn't around. Her parents were known to be troublemakers," another voice said.

I swallowed as I watched Silas staring at my home. It looked more disheveled than when I had left Barracks. Every part of me prayed that I would open the door and let him in. But I didn't. Instead, he turned toward the blonde woman standing beside him.

"Things are better now," she said to him as she took his arm. "You're free to do whatever you like."

Silas clutched the woman's arm and smiled. "Yes, I've been waiting for this day for a long time."

"Silas," I whispered. A piercing pain jolted through my body as another crack embedded itself in my heart.

See? the voice returned. *They don't want the burden back.*

Before I could react, the scene changed again. No longer were Silas and the woman standing before me, but a mirrored image of myself. I took a step back. So did the image. Taking a breath, I stepped forward to where I was before and studied myself. My once beautiful hair was chopped and ragged, accentuating the grime that covered my face. Dark circles deepened under my ice blue eyes, making my appearance gaunt. Dried blood stained my neck, and the purple stains from the wine glowed brightly. I reached my hand up to my cheek. Is this really what I look like?

Yes, horrible, isn't it? the voice asked. I couldn't help but agree. *If you looked like her*—the blonde woman appeared next to my tattered appearance—*maybe Silas would have come to Heart Reign. Maybe he would have saved you from your fate. But instead, he let you go. He didn't want you. Just like Nana didn't want you. And Lyle. He left, too, didn't he? Nobody wants the leper named Adelaide Tye.*

"No," I said, feeling the tears burning in my eyes as my own words were thrown back at me. "No, that's not true."

It's not? The voice was closer, sliding around me, constricting my thoughts with its own. *Are you sure?*

I opened my mouth to respond again but stopped. I never had any proof that Lyle was still alive or that he would have wanted me to save him, anyway. He did leave me. My heart weighed down with agony at the thought. And Nana never tried to care for either of us when our parents died. She didn't want me, either. And Silas. It was true; Silas didn't come to Heart Reign. He didn't care what happened to me during the festival.

He just wanted it to be over with, remember? the voice crooned in my ear.

"Yes," I said, realizing everything it was saying was true. "Yes, you're right. No one wanted me. But they would want someone like her." I looked at the blonde woman standing tall, confident, and beautiful next to my image in the mirror. The green shade thickened over my eyes once more.

Yes, the voice said. *They would. And you can give that to them. You can be her. All you have to do is take her hand.*

I reached my burned hand toward the shimmering wall of light before me. The blonde woman did the same, a small smile forming on her lips as her hand extended beyond the light. Without hesitation, I reached toward the light wall. Smoke rose from my fingertips, but I pressed on. I wanted Lyle to come home and beat me at chess like he used to. Then Silas could come over, and the three of us could join Nana for dinner, all of us eating together at one table. We could talk about anything and everything: books, the market, the weather. We would laugh together, cry together—it didn't matter as long as we were together. But for that to happen, I needed to become someone they would love. My hand began to disintegrate, but the pain was nothing compared to the joy I felt when I considered being someone other than myself.

When I was inches away from the beautiful woman's fingertips, the joy began to subside, and the pain hit me like a boulder. I cried out as the fiery torment reached my forearm, the stench of my burning flesh and smoke from Lyle's sweater racing through my nose.

Only a little farther, the voice prodded.

It was now or never. Taking my stance, I readied myself to take the full plunge into the wall when my shoulders were grasped by a pair of sturdy hands, jerking me back and slamming me into the ground.

CHAPTER 29

$\mathcal{I}$ fell backwards, my spine hitting the stone floor. I groaned before the pain in my arm resurfaced, causing tears to barrel down my cheeks. I looked down at my arm and was greeted with a charred limb instead of flesh.

"What's wrong with you, girl?" the wheezing voice from before asked. "Having gotten this far, I'd think you would know a trick when you saw one."

My heart quickened. "Lyle?" I asked, looking around. Was that him? Hope sparked within me. He cared about me and wanted to come back. I tried to stand to get to him, but the pain in my arm was too great. Crying out, I stumbled back to the ground, clutching my burnt arm to my chest.

A pair of dark brown boots entered my line of sight. Tears streamed down my face from the pain in my arm.

The stranger crouched next to me. I looked up at him, only to see a pair of bright blue eyes rimmed with green staring down at me. I blinked a few times, finding a familiarity in those eyes. "Lyle, is that you?" My heart pulsed lightly. A grin began to form on my lips until I realized it wasn't Lyle. He hadn't come back.

Another shooting pain pierced my heart, and I knew it had cracked once more. I cried out, sobbing and clutching my arm. I couldn't care less if this stranger killed me right now. I just wanted to be rid of all the pain.

The man stood up, walked behind me, and pulled me into a sitting position, not acknowledging my cries. His hands were gentle but firm as they steadied my shuddering shoulders.

Coming back around, he handed me a piece of cloth and waited until I had finished crying. I was still in the Sixth Choice. The mirror wall was still before me, and the blonde woman still stood with her arm extended, waiting to take my life.

The man was right. I should have known it was a trick. Everything had been a trick up until this point, and I still fell for it. Gritting my teeth, I shook my head. After everything I'd been through, Ophidian still won, and I had failed.

"Now, now," the man said, seeing the turmoil on my face as he crouched down and began wrapping my arm. "Don't beat yourself up too bad. Not a day goes by where I don't wish to jump through that wall myself."

I felt nothing of his touch or the cloth. In fact, I felt nothing on my arm at all. All feeling was gone. Just like my hair, I had lost another piece of myself to Ophidian.

Looking up at the stranger, I noticed that his voice caused a deceptive perception of him. From the wheezing accompanying his words, I would have thought he was at least Nana's age. But looking at his smooth skin and light brown hair, the man was not a day over forty.

Wearing worn-out brown pants and a plaid shirt, he looked so . . . ordinary. Every person I had encountered in this realm so far had either been possessed with some motive to try to sway me to stay behind their door or turned into a monster that tried to kill me.

But this man saved me from walking through the light wall and killing myself. None of the other creatures or people so far had done that for me except for Claire, and look where that got her.

"Who are you?" I asked, narrowing my eyes at the suspiciously sane stranger.

"Names aren't important right now," he replied gruffly.

"Why are you here, then?" And why are you so normal, I wanted to add.

"Same as you," he said with a grunt that seemed familiar, too. "Just trying to make it through the Choices."

"Why haven't you?" I probed, still suspicious.

"Can't make it through the wall." He then rolled up the sleeves on his plaid shirt, letting out a rough breath.

I gasped at the sight of the burn scars covering his

hands and arms. No wonder he pulled me out. He was trying to save me from the pain he had already gone through. But why?

"Is there any way out?" I asked, my hope almost gone. Even if Lyle wanted to leave and never come back, he was still my brother. I wouldn't allow him to die at the hand of Ophidian.

He shook his head before letting out a phlegmy cough. "Not unless you stop wanting what you don't have. Which is impossible for me."

"What does it show you?" Considering everything I had gone through up to this point, I didn't care if I was being forward.

"Everything I gave up. My wife, my kid, my home. All for a choice. A really dumb choice."

I nodded thoughtfully. My choices didn't seem to be getting me any closer to happiness and what I wanted, either.

If this man had traded his heart for a choice, like all the others, shouldn't he have turned into a siti by now? Especially since it looked like he'd been stuck behind this door for a while.

Taking a deep breath, I decided against asking him outright about why he hadn't turned into a life-sucking monster.

"Trading a heart for a choice doesn't seem to be a smart decision for anyone," I murmured.

The man glared down at me, and I knew I'd hit a nerve. "I didn't trade my heart," he wheezed angrily.

I stared up at him. "Then how did you get here?"

"By my own dumb choice," he replied, running his hand through his hair. "My heart had already been sealed when I decided that it wasn't good enough."

I gave him a blank look. What was he talking about? Maybe I had misjudged him for being normal. He was probably a creature in disguise, like everyone else in this realm. But my curiosity got the better of me. "What do you mean, 'sealed'?"

"You know." He waved his hand in the air like I knew what he was talking about. When he realized I didn't, he let out a sigh. "So, it really has changed out there, hasn't it?"

I softened my expression, realizing we were both thoroughly confused. "I'm sorry, but I have no idea what you're talking about."

The man sighed again and started unbuttoning his shirt. Fearful of another lecherous display, I reached for my sword with my unburnt hand. There was no way I was going through that Choice again. Just as I was about to grab the hilt, the man walked toward the light wall.

"Look," he said as the emerald light shined on his bare chest.

There was nothing there at first. But as my eyes narrowed, the outline of a circle appeared on his chest. I placed my hand on my own, knowing that they were the same. As I looked closer, I could see that his circle had a line going through it diagonally as if marking out the circle. In the center of the line, another small line perpendicularly intersected the larger one.

"Sealed," he said. "Marked. Mended."

My eyes widened so much, they felt as if they were going to pop out of my skull. The mark of the Mender. The same mark on the sword. It was real.

CHAPTER 30

$\mathcal{I}$ knew the man saw the shock on my face, because he started to rebutton his shirt. "You've seen this mark before?"

I nodded, unable to speak. If the mark of the Mender was real, that meant—

"Yes," the man confirmed, finishing my thought. "He's real."

"But . . ." I began, but my head was so full of questions, I didn't know which would come out first.

"And I was a fool," he said, cutting me off. "He took me in, mended me, taught me his magic, and helped me with everything I had asked. And what did I do? I decided his way wasn't good enough and went to find another way."

"But," I repeated, my mind settling on one question. "How did you get in here if you didn't trade your heart?"

"I could ask you the same question." He motioned to the satchel. I grabbed the strap.

"Don't worry, I'm not going to take it." He held up his hands in surrender. "I didn't have to trade my heart. Ophidian thought it would be pleasant enough that one of the Mender's own would run to his darkness for help." The man let out another sigh. "I foolishly made it through the first five Choices, only to get stuck at the second to last one." He jerked his thumb back at the light wall.

Turning his head, he stared forlornly at the wall. "Every day, I want to cast myself into the fire, just to end my torment for the fool I was. For leaving my wife. For leaving the Mender." He looked back at me. "What's your name, anyway?"

"Addie."

"Addie," he murmured, staring at me with a look of fascination. He studied me closely, making me feel uncomfortable.

I stood and gripped the sword with my left hand, holding the hilt near my face. The mark of the Mender peered back at me. I narrowed my eyes. I knew the mark of the Mender was real; I couldn't deny it was on the sword or on the man's chest. But what about the Mender himself? If he was real, why hadn't he shown up yet? Why did I have to go through this alone?

"You are not alone," the voice said softly in my ear.

"You keep saying that," I muttered, still clutching the weapon. "But it sure doesn't feel like it." The voice didn't answer, but I figured as much. My heart beat softly, reminding me what was at stake. I didn't know how much time Lyle or Claire had left. I needed to get to the seventh Choice quickly.

"I think it's time to get out of here. What about you?" I asked the man.

"How?"

I didn't blame him for doubting me. I doubted me, too. The voice from earlier was right. I was a mess, and I knew I didn't look the part of the hero. My hair was chopped and scraggily, giving off the awful odor of dried wine from the orange door. I knew my neck still had dried blood and a cut from where siti-Silas had taken a bite. And now I had a useless hand and a broken heart. I was exhausted, hungry, and confused. It was only recently that I found the courage to leave my house, much less defeat an evil being. Why would anyone choose me to accomplish something as great as this?

Sighing, I looked back at the sword, then to the light wall. The beautiful woman was still there, waiting for my response. But this was who I was. I was broken and scared.

I clutched the sword and felt its power flow through me, as if telling me I was right. I was all those things, but it was okay. I needed to be scared and broken to be able to see my choice to the end.

Like a river rushing downhill, a surge of strength engulfed the cells in my body. The mark began to glow a bright orange, followed by the white glow of its blade. The air swirled around me, beckoning me into the sword's power.

The sword's power was great, and I struggled as I tried to grip it with one hand. I could feel the power pulsing through my veins in perfect rhythm with the pulsing of my heart.

Like an invisible force was pushing me forward, I walked toward the light wall. The man stared wide-eyed as I passed him, holding the sword in front of me.

The voice was silent, but the woman stood waiting. With her striking features and tall, shapely physique, she was dazzling in every way. There wasn't a person in the realms who wouldn't want her. She was perfect and everything I could ever hope to be.

The sword began to raise itself, and I let my hand go with it. The glow grew brighter against the light wall. The green began to fade from my eyes, purifying my vision of the lie before me. Perfection came with a price. One I couldn't pay.

I clenched my teeth and gripped the sword tightly as its power grew. It surged forward, piercing the light wall in the middle of the scene. I breathed hard as I watched the figure before me begin to crack. All her perfections were blemished by the shattering light. The fissures were small at first, but quickly transformed into huge canyons across the entirety of the wall. The sound of shattering glass disappeared into the void as I pulled the sword out and ran back.

"Come on!" I yelled to the man, who stared at the cracking light. When I destroyed my desires, I had probably destroyed his, too.

Although painful, I reached out and grabbed his arm as I ran by, pulling him away from the hopes that had tormented him since he first arrived in this Choice.

When I finally thought we had run far enough, an explosion of light and fire caught up to us from behind, pushing our bodies onto the cold, hard floor. My skull crashed against the ground, causing a large crack to vibrate through my ears. I started to think it was my heart, but my vision grew dimmer until . . .

Screaming. So much screaming.

CHAPTER 31

I woke with a jolt, my head whipping frantically back and forth. Everything was dark. As my eyes adjusted, I didn't see the man or the wall. Instead, trees formed, arching above me, sending me back into my nightmare.

My skin was no longer charred, and my sweater was fully intact. I pushed myself to stand. This had to be a dream.

A large cry broke me from my observations, sending my senses on alert. My body tensed before I slowly turned my head to see the trees parting before my eyes, allowing the cave to come into view.

"Ofavemore," I said, remembering Claire's name for this place.

I swallowed my fear and walked toward the scream. Sorrow, pain, and hatred filled each wail, tearing my heart apart. Each shrill scream for help and mercy made me want to run as far away as I could.

As I approached the cave, my hand glided toward the sword but found nothing but air. I jerked my head down to see that my satchel had disappeared as well. Panic rose in my throat. This could be my nightmare, but it could also be a trick Ophidian was using to take my heart, especially now that I was unarmed. I stood frozen for a moment, not knowing whether or not I should continue.

But before I could decide, my body was thrust forward into the cave of screams. I slammed into the cold metal bars of a cell. Groaning, I reached out and rubbed my head. The clanking and dragging of chains echoed against the walls, causing me to back away from the metal door.

"Addie?" a voice said.

Staring cautiously at the cell, I took a step forward and peered through the bars. That voice. It sounded like . . .

"Claire!" I yelled, grasping the bars. I stifled my gasp as her face came into view. Her bun had been pulled down, hair now laying in limp strands around her face and shoulders. Her left eye was completely closed with a blue and purple bruise decorating the skin around it. And on the right side of her face, three large gashes extended from her forehead to her cheek, as if someone had attempted to claw her eye out.

"Claire," I said again, softer. "What happened?"

"What? You don't like my new look?" She gave me a weak smile as she pointed to her face. Chains rattled from the shackles binding her wrists. I winced as blood slowly dripped down her arm. The shackles were purposely too tight.

I gripped the cell bars until my knuckles turned white,

trying to ignore the screams coming from farther inside the cave.

"This happened because of me, didn't it?"

Claire let out a snort. "Not everything's about you, Addie." Then she smiled. "Don't be stupid. Of course it happened because of you."

If I could feel my heart, I was sure it would be breaking again. "Claire, I'm—"

"Don't." She held up her shackled hand. "I don't need your apologies. If I had the chance, I would choose to help you again. Don't you understand? I chose to be here. Me. Not my mother. Not Ophidian. Me. And I don't want you to feel guilty because of my choice."

"But," I murmured, "look what Ophidian did to you."

Claire chuckled. "This? No. If Ophidian dealt with me, I wouldn't look this good. This was my fun time with one of his little projects."

The rage from the previous door, the red one, burned in my stomach. I took a deep breath to calm down. I had no way to avenge Claire, even if I wanted to.

"Still, I'm s—"

"Addie," Claire snapped. "What did I just tell you? Don't apologize, and don't be stupid."

I nodded as I pressed my face between the cell bars.

"Remember what I told you?" Claire said in a softer tone. "That you were chosen?"

I nodded again, bowing my head toward the floor. I knew she said not to feel guilty, but that was all I could feel.

"I was right."

I moved my eyes up to hers. "What?"

"I was right," she repeated. "You were chosen."

"I don't understand."

Claire scoffed. "The signs are all around you. Your heart, the sword, your ability to make it through the Choices."

"I just thought it was luck and your green stuff that kept me alive."

Snorting, Claire lifted her hand to her head, jangling the chains. "Oh, Addie. Luck is rolling away fast enough that your eye isn't gouged out. Luck is buying enough time to distract a monster and save your own life. I've seen luck. You don't have it."

I frowned. I had thought I was at least a little lucky in some of the Choices.

"Don't give me that look," she continued in a motherly tone. "You and I both know that something a lot stronger than luck is on your side."

I stared at her, my eyes wide with curiosity. "What is it?"

"Are you serious?" By the look on her face, I knew that if Claire hadn't been chained up, she would have slapped me.

I sighed. I knew what she was talking about. Or who she was talking about. But I couldn't admit it. It all seemed too unreal to be true.

I shook my head. "I don't know, Claire."

A low hum flew through my ears, and I immediately tensed. I quickly looked to Claire, not knowing who or what was coming down the corridor. Her face was stern as she nodded to the left, prompting me to find a large crevice in the cave wall where I could hide.

As soon as I slipped in, a dark figure passed by. A deathly aura permeated the air, squelching any notion of life. A dark mass, resembling a hooded being, floated through the tunnel.

The figure continued past me, then stopped at Claire's cell. I stuck my head out enough to see a solitary red eye centered on its face. It said nothing, only stared into the cell. Claire's screams arose from within, and I jumped out of the crevice. I had no defense, but I wouldn't allow that creature to destroy her.

"Leave her alone," I shouted over Claire's agonized howls.

The red eye snapped to me, leaving echoes of whimpers from the cell. The dark creature floated toward me, its red eye focusing on me. The lifeless atmosphere lay heavily on me as the creature hummed closer.

The master is waiting for you.

A cold chill swept through my body as the creature spoke in my thoughts. There was no feeling in the voice, no life. I took a step back; there was nowhere else to go. The red eye gleamed brightly in the dark cave before the creature floated past me, disappearing from sight.

I took a deep breath before rushing over to Claire. "What was that?"

Tucked into a ball, Claire's tear-stained face slowly lifted. "You don't want to know."

Anger rose in my stomach. How many times would Ophidian torment Claire?

Before I could ask further questions, the chains on her wrists began to shake. A white light shined in my peripheral vision, and I turned toward it. The light was moving fast, growing brighter, until it began to consume the cave.

"Claire!" I screamed, clutching her cell bars as the light consumed me as well.

"I'm all right, Addie," she yelled back. "Don't worry about me. Just run!"

I gripped the bars of her cell until the light fully encased my body, causing everything to burn brightly until it turned black.

"Hey," someone wheezed in my ear as they shoved my shoulder.

I opened an eye to see the man's ice-blue eyes staring at me once again. Groaning, I sat up and placed my hand to my head, breathing a sigh of relief. I was back.

Reaching down, my hand grazed the leather of the satchel. My heart was safe, beating soundly. I let out another sigh of relief when I saw the sword laying next to me. Its glow had disappeared, aside from the orange outline of the mark.

I extended my hand toward it, grabbing the golden hilt like I'd done many times before, but this time it felt different. This time it felt as if the sword was no longer a sword, but a part of me.

I felt the power of it blending with my heart, engraving its strength into my cells. A white light shot through my arm over my charred skin, causing it to tingle with a fiery sensation. I watched in amazement as my skin was healed of all burns.

"You are not alone, Addie."

I stared at the sword. I knew the voice came from it. But swords didn't talk. Even magical swords had their limits, right?

"You were never alone."

I gripped the sword tighter, not knowing whether I should talk back to it or not.

Before I could decide, something moved in the distance. The broken shards of the light wall began to rise from the floor, shifting and shaping, their color transforming from white to violet. The shards clinked against one another as they flew through the air. Like pieces of a puzzle, the shattered light molded together, creating the shape of a door.

The man let out a gasp. "The seventh Choice." He gave me a look of surprise. "You did it."

Standing, I placed the sword through the metal circle on the satchel. I had done it. But at the same time, I hadn't. Not entirely. For the first time, I began to believe what the voice said. I wasn't alone.

Although it never felt like it, I had always had someone there for me. First Lyle, then Silas, now Claire. Regardless of what the last Choice had said, I knew they cared about me. Without them, I wouldn't have made it through the Seven Choices. They loved me when I was alone. They saved me when no one else cared. The beating in my heart pumped harder. Now it was my turn to return the favor.

Taking a deep breath, I looked over at the man. I had no idea what his backstory was, or why he was here. But I did know that his path had crossed with mine for a reason. Because of that, I was determined to do whatever I could to get him out of this hell.

Giving him a smirk, I said, "I had help."

I began walking toward the violet door. A key with the head of a lion rested in the lock, waiting to be turned. I remembered seeing this key when Claire had first described her bondage to Ophidian.

"The last Choice," I said. I was almost there. I prayed Lyle could hold on just a little longer.

Grabbing the metal key, I twisted it until the door clicked, opening inward. I glanced over my shoulder to where the man was still standing.

"Are you ready to get out of here?" I asked.

Without any hesitation, he gave me a nod. A smile filled my face. I wouldn't allow whatever rested in the last Choice to have any power over me.

I stared back into the gray mist swirling through the violet door, ready for whatever Ophidian had waiting.

"Then let's run."

CHAPTER 32

My heart beat simultaneously with the pounding of my footsteps as I ran through the gray mist. I glanced behind me every so often to check and see if the man was still with me. For an older guy, he kept up pretty well.

We sprinted until my eyes landed on what I had been waiting for. Reaching over, I removed the sword from the satchel's ring. The sound of the blade caressing the metal loop brought tingles over my skin as I lifted the sword toward the archway of trees. This nightmare had haunted me long enough. It was time for it to end.

As I moved forward, I felt a gentle hand on my shoulder. Glancing back, I was met by the man's wearisome eyes.

"What?"

He shook his head. "There's no way to kill Ophidian. He's too powerful."

I shared a small smile with him. "Good thing I'm not here to kill him, then."

Ophidian was never my goal. There was only one person I was here for, and I would bring him back.

Turning toward the trees, I breathed in the cool air and closed my eyes, allowing the power resonating from the sword to run up my arm, through my body, and into my heart. I had overcome six Choices. I would overcome the last. Opening my eyes, I looked at the man.

"Then why are you here?" the man asked, rubbing his chin as he studied the forest around us.

"To save my brother."

I took off in a sprint before he could say another word. I hoped he would stay outside Ofavemore and be safe. This was one Choice I knew I must face alone.

The thumping of my heart and the power of the sword filled me with life. The harder I ran, the more I felt it flowing through me.

I breezed past the trees, watching, waiting for what I knew would come next.

Sooner than I expected, an agonizing scream bellowed ahead of me. I raced toward it, gripping the sword. The trees began to separate before my eyes, revealing the darkness of the cave I had traveled to many times before. My steps slowed as I cautiously approached the source of my fears.

My shoulders tightened at the piercing screams. I had heard them countless times before, but nothing compared to the present sound. Gripping the hilt, I refused to succumb to my fear. I had made it this far; nothing would stop me from finding Lyle. The hope and strength that had sprouted in my heart bloomed, prohibiting any terror or doubt that attempted to grow.

The sword glowed a faint white, lighting my way as I stepped into the cave. My nightmare was accurate in what I had heard, but the details of the cave made it difficult to focus. I strained to see through the dark abyss beyond the light of the sword. The sharp odors of sulfur and musk filled my lungs. Monitoring my breathing, I continued to walk, my boots gliding silently across the dirt floor, effectively concealing my presence.

White marks, etched into the gray walls, glowed as I passed by. A shudder ran through me as I recognized the same marks that had branded Claire's face in my vision.

A gut-wrenching cry, echoing from the end of the cave, stole through my thoughts. I turned, trying to find the person who had screamed, but the rapid vibrations against the stone walls made it impossible to locate the source.

Once the screaming subsided, I let out a deep breath. Whatever was in this Choice was worse than anything else I had faced.

But I didn't have to face this Choice alone. I knew someone, or something, had continued to encourage me through each Choice. I knew someone had sent me this sword. Whether it was true or not, I finally thought I could believe that if there was darkness, there had to be light.

The sword shone brighter than freshly fallen snow, as if it had heard my internal proclamation. I had to shield my eyes as it pulsated with light against the weary shadows.

When my eyes adjusted, the light illuminated the entire length of the cave. The screaming continued once again, piercing my heart, but I kept on until the light of the blade revealed openings in the cave walls. As I shifted the blade, the light reflected off the iron bars of a prison cell. The rods were thick, prohibiting anyone from going in or out. Holding the light to the cell door, I peered in, hoping to find Claire.

But as I leaned closer, I didn't see Claire, but a man wearing pants and two ties with no shirt underneath. As he cowered in the corner, bloodied and bruised, I recognized him as the balding man, who offered his leather shoes for the bottle of happiness in the second Choice. He rocked back and forth, muttering under his breath, "Need happiness. Want happiness."

The vision the bottle of happiness had shown me—of Lyle living in Barracks unscathed—flitted through my mind, but I pushed it away. Nothing was more valuable than a human life. Still, had it not been for the voice, I would have been no better off than this man; it could have easily been me in that cell. With a heavy heart, I moved on. If I could give this man happiness, I would.

I continued through the cave to the next cell. I knew Claire had to be in one of them. As I peered into the cell, a hand swiped at the sword before I could yank it back. The fingers were instantly severed on the blazing metal. Wails sounded from the cell, and I made sure I was at a safe distance before I looked again. I didn't recognize the face, but I was confident the woman had come from the fifth Choice.

Her cheeks were plump, and her body was covered in remnants of food, thickly smashed in her hair and smeared down her face. But what paused me were the rows of pointed teeth that grew in her mouth. She jerked forward and chomped the air, and I jumped back. I tried to look closer, but she chomped again, giving me a harsh growl. Taking the hint, I continued my search for Claire.

Walking a few more paces, I investigated another cell and gasped. A creature, mid-transformation, with dark, leathery skin like the siti, looked out at me.

"Adelaide," the rusted voice of Governor Willow wheezed out.

A cold feeling of dread and suspicion arose in my heart as I raised the blade to illuminate the cell. I hid my shock; from the waist down, Governor Willow's body had been transformed into a siti, but the leathery, gray skin continued to creep upward.

"Governor Willow?"

"Adelaide, " he repeated as the leather skin began to inch down his arms. "Ophidian said he would take the vendors away." He let out a cry as his arms began to extend into the sickly length of a siti's. I winced and looked away. After the cracks from his bones stretching ended, he said, "But he was the one who sent them to Barracks. He gave them all the magical items in exchange for hearts."

"What?" I asked, closing in on the bars again.

"He wants your heart, Adelaide," the governor wheezed. "Your brother's wasn't pure, but yours—" The words were cut off by another ear-splitting cry from his mouth, sounding more like a moan than the first.

Governor Willow panted after the pain passed. "Your heart will complete his mission. He told me to get him the pure heart, and he would take care of the rest."

His words swirled through my mind. Was that why Lyle had traded his heart to Schism? Had Governor Willow somehow enticed him into trading it? But when it wasn't pure, Ophidian took pleasure in allowing Lyle to be destroyed, anyway?

I gritted my teeth at the man before me. He had to have known about Nana's pure heart, back in the day. Why else would he have targeted our family?

Governor Willow's fingertips grew into the long, black claws of the siti. "I will complete the task he gave me." He raised his hand. "I will give him your heart."

I jerked back as he swiped a claw through the cell bars,

then raised the glowing blade in defense. Leathery skin crept up the governor's torso, covering what little human skin he had left. His limbs had fully lengthened to the elongated state of the life-sucking creatures, black claws protruding from each hand. As if a final farewell, the creature let out a moan before a single cord began threading over his lips, causing the governor of Barracks to be fully replaced by a monster.

He tried to swipe at me once more, but I was already barreling down the tunnel. Like animals to the slaughter, Lyle and I had both been intended as sacrifices to Ophidian.

The vendors had been coming for hearts in Barracks for so long, no one could remember how the tradition of Heart Reign had begun. Anger rose within me as I scoffed, realizing Ophidian was the one who had initiated heart trading. And Governor Willow was the fool I had always thought he was.

I swallowed the tension in my throat, clenching my jaw as I remembered the extra guards that only I had at Heart Reign. I had run straight into the governor, who had just happened to be heading to Doctor Magnum's office right when I was leaving with my newly extracted heart. He knew Ophidian wanted my heart and was going to give it to him. Fury rose within me, but I had to let it go. For now. My purpose here was to save Lyle and Claire. I wouldn't allow myself to become distracted.

Deciding to pass the next few cells as the inhabitants

moaned, I settled on one further down the cave. The light of the sword reflected off a head of white hair, flooding my heart with relief as I rushed closer and gripped the cell bars.

"Claire," I whispered, not knowing who or what was close enough to hear.

The downcast head moved slightly, but still hung from its neck like a weight.

"Claire!" I said with a little more force.

The head lifted to reveal Claire's face, beaten and bruised as I had seen before. I gulped, trying to control the despair and fury in my heart.

"Addie?" she whispered, sitting up, her chains shaking as she brushed the black strand of hair from her cheek. An irritated look crossed her face. I sighed. She was okay.

"Are you really here this time?" She narrowed her eyes. "Or are you going to vanish in a puff of smoke like before?"

I suppressed a laugh, allowing a smile. Claire could be falling off the edge of a cliff and still have enough strength to complain about how the cliff wasn't high enough to kill her.

"Yes, I'm really here this time."

"Well, good." She snorted. "It's about time. Ophidian's going nuts."

"What do you mean?"

For once, Claire didn't tell me to not be stupid. Her face paled, her eyes bulging as she looked past me. "I know he's making them. Hundreds. Thousands. I hear their screams until they're silenced forever."

I pressed my face against the iron rods. "Making what?"

Her face drained of all color as she looked at me with wide eyes. "Terrible creatures at least three humans tall. Their bodies are cloaked in black mist, except for the one spot on their faces that's a single red eye. They never blink and are always watching. They're a thousand times worse than the siti. In one glance, a malum can take your heart and corrupt it, making you turn against all you know is good. They're like the siti, because they crave life. But they won't stand and wait for you to defend yourself. The malum destroy you from the inside out." Claire leaned her head against the wall of her cell and closed her eyes. "You would beg to be attacked by the siti if you came face-to-face with a malum."

I took slow, deep breaths to calm my racing heart. A malum. That's what I had seen in the vision before. But how was Ophidian making them? My mind immediately thought back to all the people in the cells. Why were they here? There was only one reason why Ophidian had all these people locked in cells: they were ingredients for his new monsters. I had to get Claire out of here.

"He must be using the people from the Choices to create them," I said. "But how does he transform one into the other?" Maybe if we could stop the process, we could stop any more malum from being created.

Claire shook her head, rattling her chains. "I don't know. I just hear the screams. They've tormented me day and night. This must be the reason why he wanted me to get people through the Choices, Addie. Why he allowed me to leave this realm." Distraught, she gripped her hands over her knees and began to rock back and forth.

"We need to leave, now," I said, crouching down, still holding the iron bars.

"Addie, if Ophidian finds you, you're dead. He's already irate that you've made it this far. He knows you're here for Lyle, and he'll do whatever he can to stop you. Leave me and find your brother."

I shook my head and laughed. Claire narrowed her eyes.

"Don't be stupid." I stood up and pointed the sword at the cell bars. "We're going together."

I rotated the sword behind me. With all the strength I could muster, I swung it into the cell bars. The iron dissipated into the musk of the cave.

Claire stared wide-eyed at her freedom. "Whoa."

I gave her a smug smile as I held the sword aloft again and carefully sliced through her bonds, releasing her from her chains.

"Oh, wipe that stupid grin off your face," she growled, rubbing the blood off her wrists. "You owed me, anyway."

Nodding in agreement, I offered her my hand and helped her from her cell. The tormented screams had stopped. Hopefully, no one had heard us.

"We need to be careful," Claire whispered as we moved through the cave. "Ophidian has eyes everywhere. He probably already knows you're here."

Nodding again, I followed her into the abyss until the walls widened into a large cavern. As we drew closer, a faint dripping echoed from above. I looked up and watched the steady droplets fall from the stone ceiling to the ground, collecting on the earth below. From a pool in the ground, the droplets slid toward the rushing water, which beat against the sides of the cave. A river? I hadn't seen any signs of water since I had entered Ophidian's Realm.

Claire crouched and crawled on her hands and knees. I did the same.

We crawled behind a pile of large boulders surrounding the perimeter of the cavern. As I reached my hand out to move forward, I noticed the glow of the sword had become dimmer. I prayed to the Heavens that it was because it wanted to keep us hidden, not because it had lost strength.

We continued moving until we found a break in the line of boulders, allowing a path to cut through. Claire placed her arm in front of me, alerting me to stop.

The sound of chains dragging along the ground echoed around us. Claire gave a nod before we flattened our bodies on the ground, hiding ourselves from view. Soon enough, I spied the face that I had come to curse for the past seven years.

Schism strolled into view, arrogant as always, wearing a vicious grin on his face. In his hand, a rusted metal chain extended back into a tunnel similar to the one we had come from. As he passed us, I saw that his other hand had been replaced by ebony stone. A smug satisfaction came over me, knowing I was the one who had sliced it off.

He growled savagely as he yanked hard on the chain. "Cease your struggling!"

Schism pulled the chain as he walked closer and closer to the center of the cavern. I started to move, but Claire placed her hand on my shoulder, stopping me again. When I looked back to her, she nodded in the direction of the chain.

A long line of people filed in, each bound to the next, held by horribly rusted chains. I stared as they dragged by. Some were men, some were women. Some were fully human. Some had already begun to transform into monsters. Many had missing arms or hopped on one leg, reminding me of what Claire had said about those who made it through Ira's Vindicae.

As the line went on, the variety of shapes and sizes of people continued to appear. Some had pale skin that amplified their cuts and bruises. Others' skin was flawless, but crazed looks swarmed over their faces as their heads jerked back and forth. Had Ophidian really captured all of them? I couldn't see why they would come here on their own.

The line soon came to an abrupt halt in front of us.

"Move!" Schism yelled, pulling on the chain.

The bodies flew forward, but the chain strained and pulled back into the tunnel.

"Fracious, can you not control our guests?" an irritated voice asked.

I shuddered, remembering the sound of that voice. For the first time, I was hearing it straight from the mouth of the Beast himself.

"Of course I can, my liege," Schism replied in a way that was hardly convincing. "It's probably that boy from Barracks again."

My heart jumped. The boy from Barracks. Could it really be him?

"Take care of it," Ophidian muttered, clearly annoyed.

Claire and I shifted our bodies farther into the darkness as Schism's feet stomped dangerously close to our hiding place and back toward the tunnel. I held my breath in anticipation, praying for the face I hadn't seen in seven years.

Schism's footsteps resonated off the cave walls as he wrapped his pale fingers tightly around the chain. With a clenched jaw, he yanked the chain as hard as he could. A body flew from the tunnel and landed right in front of the boulder we were hiding behind.

I stifled a cry. After all these years, after all this time, Lyle was still alive.

CHAPTER 33

I was ready to reach out to Lyle when Schism's foot slammed into his spine, planting him into the ground with a sickening crack.

"You're lucky my master has deemed you fit for Aeternam Scientia, or you would be mine to devour."

Claire's grip tightened on my forearm. I couldn't tell if she was trying to hold me back or herself.

Glued to the scene playing out inches from us, we watched as Lyle reared his head and spat at Schism's leg. I couldn't stop my heart from swelling with pride.

Schism let out a loud roar, black claws extending from his fingertips.

"Fracious," Ophidian warned like a mother disciplining her child. "We need him alive."

Schism's claw swung toward Lyle's face, and Lyle jerked away. A degrading laugh erupted from Schism's throat as he retracted his claws. He dug his heel deeper into Lyle's spine, delivering a disgusting crunch that made me wince.

Lyle cried out, causing his broken spectacles to slide down his nose. It took everything within me not to rush over to him.

Lifting his foot, Schism jabbed his toe into Lyle's ribs before strolling away, dragging my brother's limp body with him.

"If you're quite through trying my patience, I would like to get on with the ceremony," Ophidian's voice sneered.

Claire and I exchanged a look before quietly crawling to where two boulders were almost touching, creating a small crevice for us to look through.

The cavern had a vast dome with the potential to house thousands of creatures. Stalactites of various sizes descended from the ceiling, dripping droplets of black liquid onto the red, clay floor. The droplets formed puddles that flowed into one another, creating a steady stream that fed into the rushing river behind the boulders on the far side of the cavern.

I squinted into the distance, hoping that the stream led to an exit. In the center of the cavern stood a large, black mound. I couldn't see what it was made of from so far away, but my heart knew. Hundreds of thousands of black hearts were piled on top of one another. Black hearts that used to be red and alive. What had happened to their owners?

Upon the mound of black hearts rested a throne of skulls, each one representing the previous owner, who must have suffered immensely before their death. On it sat the Beast, adorned in flowing, dark robes, giving off the appearance of royalty. A pompous smirk played upon his thin lips as he twirled a set of keys around his index finger.

I glanced over at Claire. The scowl on her face confirmed what I was thinking.

"Welcome." Ophidian arose from his throne and extended his arms toward the chained people in a welcoming gesture.

It was unbelievable how deceptive his appearance was. Besides the glimmer of his blackened robes and deathly pale skin, his face could be described as nothing other than beautiful. If it wasn't for his snake-like eyes and the identical serpent tattoos curling from his neck to his temples, I would have been completely enthralled.

Ophidian smiled widely as he looked at his guests. "Welcome to the seventh Choice of the Seven Choices. You should all be proud. These past few days, months, or even years have been tough on all of you. I know some of you have had a harder time choosing than others."

Ophidian descended the mound of black hearts with his hands clasped behind his back, the heads of the snake tattoos slithering around his yellow eyes with each step.

The hearts tumbled out from under his feet, rolling and colliding with one another until they reached the hard, red clay below.

He stalked toward the line of chained people, growling at Schism as he passed. Schism placed his ebony hand across his chest and bowed so low, I thought he would snap in half. Ophidian didn't give him another glance.

The man in the very front cast his eyes downward, as if averting his gaze would make him invisible. Though Ophidian noticed him, the Beast didn't look entirely interested.

Farther down, a petite woman shook so hard that the rattling of her chains echoed throughout the cavern. When Ophidian passed her, he gave her a dashing smile, causing her to shake more. He let out a heinous laugh, breathy and quick, before patting the woman on the head. If it weren't for the chains linking her to the person in front and behind her, I was positive she would have bolted.

Ophidian continued down the line until he reached a tall, lanky man. The man was neither old nor young. He had jet-black hair with pale skin and red freckles. Next to the Beast, the man looked like a child. But unlike the other quivering people, he stood proudly.

"Isn't that right, Lucas? You had some difficulty leaving the fourth Choice, did you not?"

The man named Lucas gave Ophidian an arrogant

smirk and shrugged his chained shoulders. "What can I say? The ladies love me."

I looked over to Claire, whose face was so contorted in disgust, I thought she would vomit.

"But you left it of your own accord?" Ophidian inquired.

I blinked a few times, looking back to Claire for further explanation. She gave a quick shrug and focused back on the man.

"Yeah," Lucas said, nonchalantly. "The ladies will always love me, but if I know everything, I could have them *and* all the power in the realms."

Ophidian nodded thoughtfully. "Very good, Lucas. Your heart is right where it should be."

Continuing down the line, Ophidian grazed a few more people with his slender fingers, as if inspecting their quality of life. But it wasn't until he reached the end of the line that I held my breath.

"Ah, here he is. The young man who has been causing so many problems in my realm." Ophidian spread his arms toward Lyle with the same grin he had used before, the serpents on his brow coiling to his jaw bone.

Lyle may have been losing his mind, but his expressions hadn't changed at all. Very rarely had he become angry with me, but when he had, he would give me the exact look he was giving Ophidian. Beneath the broken glass, his eyes had lost their beautiful sparkle and thirst for life, beaten until nothing was left but cold metal.

Claire grabbed my wrist. I knew she was just as worried as I was.

Ophidian circled him like a vulture, but Lyle's glare never wavered from Ophidian's beautiful face.

"Yes," the Beast sneered again. "The boy from Barracks. When you first traded your heart, I was convinced you would never make it past the doors. Little did I know, you would make it all the way to the Final Choice."

"I didn't make it here on my own," Lyle said coldly. He let out a gasp and grabbed his back, but then straightened his spectacles and his stance until he stood tall.

I stared, fixated on Lyle. His voice had changed, too. It was deep and hollow. Claire's grip tightened on my wrist as we watched the exchange.

"Yes, yes." Ophidian swatted his hand toward Lyle in annoyance. "But you have no idea who helped you, do you?"

For the first time in seven years, I saw a glimmer of the Lyle I knew. His hard look softened, the blue in his eyes becoming lighter, as he attempted to reposition his spectacles by tilting his head back. By the way he furrowed his brows, I could tell he was trying to remember.

"I know there was someone," he said in a distant tone. "She was so kind."

Claire was starting to turn my fingers blue. I gently shook my hand, making her aware of her strength. She loosened her grip but remained latched to me for support.

She clearly couldn't stand Lyle being out there alone any more than I could.

"Yes. Well, we have a special treat for her. As well as your sister."

Lyle's eyes widened to the size of moons, his spectacles sliding to the tip of his nose.

"Addie," he whispered, seeming to lose all hatred and contempt. "She's here? No. NO!" he screamed. "Why is she here?"

I bit back a cry as another crack split through my heart. Reaching for my chest and the satchel, I held back the pain and tears that so desperately wanted to break loose.

I couldn't bear to see Lyle in this state. He was so brilliant and intelligent; now he was reduced to nothing. What was worse was how quickly he jumped to defend and protect me, like things had never changed. He still cared.

Tired of Lyle's antics, Ophidian raised his hand and backhanded him across the cheek. Lyle's spectacles flew from his face, glass raining down as they shattered upon impact. But Lyle refused to fall. A large, red spot emerged on his cheek.

"Just like you, she *chose* to be here."

"Please," Lyle murmured, desperation lacing his words. "Please. She doesn't know. She doesn't know anything."

"Ah, and there is the problem," Ophidian shouted, lifting his hands into the air. He walked toward the front of the line. "Each and every one of you has made it this far because you want one thing: knowledge."

An uneasy feeling crept up the back of my neck as I remembered Claire's story about her mother.

"You want to know," Ophidian continued, "how things happen, what they mean, and most commonly, why they happen. Isn't that right, boy from Barracks?"

I drew in a deep breath, remembering Lyle's thirst for knowledge. How he loved to research and study something until he knew all he could about it. Was that how Ophidian lured him here?

"I don't want to know!" Lyle yelled from the back of the line. All those chained in front of him turned toward him, their faces stricken with fear.

"It's too late!" Ophidian growled, his voice deepening, echoing off the walls. "You've made your choice."

He marched back toward Lyle. Suddenly, I felt the growing fear that if I didn't act now, I'd lose him forever.

Heaving the sword, I moved away from the boulder. Claire's hand clasped my shoulder, forcing me to pause. Then I saw what she was gawking at. The small, shaking woman from before had stepped out of line.

With her separated from the rest, I was able to get a closer look at her. Her hair was cropped short to her chin, the same length as mine, but was a shade of obsidian. A slight wave covered half her face. Her creamy complexion was flawless, neither blemished nor bruised by the Choices she had endured.

"My lord," she said in a voice that was more confident than I expected, considering how petrified she looked.

Ophidian whipped his head around, his pupils slits and his teeth bared as he let out a throaty growl. His tattoos spiraled into springs, amplifying his irritation at the interruption.

"The boy is an imbecile and knows nothing of Aeternam Scientia." She bowed low, beckoning Ophidian closer.

His shoulders straightened, the snakes on his cheeks smoothing from their coiled state as she spoke.

"If you find me worthy, I would be honored to receive your knowledge," she continued.

Ophidian's demeanor instantly changed. His lips twisted into a grin as his eyes gleamed with delight at his new specimen. The inky serpents on his pale skin straightened, smoothly slithering toward Ophidian's brow once more. The once-evil overlord had transformed into a gracious friend.

"Oh, my dear." He gave the woman another gentle pat. "I always knew you'd be the one."

I looked to Claire to see if she was just as confused as I was, but her face held no trace of confusion. Her muscles were strained as she concentrated on the woman. Hearing Ophidian's footsteps crunch along the black hearts, I returned my attention to him.

Once he had settled back onto his throne, Ophidian snapped his fingers, causing black smoke to escape from his fingertips. The smoke infiltrated every space of the mound of hearts, oozing from the crevices. Before long, the smoke receded, carrying two dying hearts with it.

Ophidian kept his hand opened, allowing the black smoke to drop the hearts into his palm. His long fingers clutched them tightly as he strode back down the mound.

Standing in front of the once-shaking woman, he held out the hearts. One was a dull gray, while the other was pure obsidian. Ophidian looked down at the hearts, a hunger in his yellow eyes.

"Which one of these, do you believe, is more powerful?"

The woman stared at the two hearts before nodding at the black one, causing Ophidian to grin widely. "Very good. A black heart is not easily formed. You must believe you deserve the answer to any question, no matter the consequence. You will do whatever it takes to know. Do you agree?"

The woman nodded her head quickly, her eyes fixed on the black heart.

"Whereas this heart only has one purpose." Ophidian squeezed the gray heart between his long fingers. A dull, red light poured from it, streaming from the heart into Ophidian's chest. The Beast sucked in a deep breath, a look of ecstasy on his face, as the power of the dying heart entered his body.

My stomach squeezed as I watched him unfurl his fingers to reveal the withered remains of the powerless heart. Ophidian tossed the useless heart to the ground, returning his attention to the woman who had chosen the black heart.

"Do you, Diana Magnum, choose to trade your heart for Aeternam Scientia: the knowledge beyond all that is known?"

I stifled a gasp when Ophidian said the woman's name, suddenly understanding why Claire was so focused. That was the woman who had traded her away. That was her mother.

Without any hesitation, Claire's mother nodded again, causing a demonic grin to spread across Ophidian's face. He extended his fingers, and long, black claws slid out from the nail beds. In one swipe, she was cut free from her chains.

As soon as Claire's mother stepped away from the broken metal, Ophidian sliced a gash in her chest and slammed the black heart into it, causing her to scream a horrible shriek. I pulled my hand away from Claire to shield my ears from the noise.

She screamed more and more as the blackness of the heart spread over her body, tightening around her like rope. Soon she was completely covered. Her limbs began to fade, followed by the unpleasant sound of bones shattering. A black cloak formed from her broken body, encasing it entirely, until her screams were silenced forever. I stared in horror as all her humanity was erased.

Ophidian smiled, taking in the creature in front of

him. Lifting one of his clawed fingers, he poked it where he had placed the black heart. As if placing a key in a lock, a finalized click clattered within the cloak, causing a singular red eye to form in the center of the creature's face.

CHAPTER 34

he blood drained from my face as terror seized my heart. I couldn't believe that anyone would voluntarily want this.

Glancing over, I could see Claire's face was just as pale as I'm sure mine was. I reached out and grabbed her hand, expecting her to shove me away, but she didn't. Bowing her head, she cupped my hand in both of hers.

I didn't know much about my parents, only what Lyle had told me and shown me from their journals and letters to one another and the few details Nana had given me. I didn't even know how they died. But I couldn't imagine watching my mother condemn herself to life as a malum.

"My lord, choose me next!" one of the half-siti men screamed, trying to wrench himself away from his chained companions.

"You're pathetic," Lucas sneered, shoving the man out

of the way. "If the master is going to choose anyone next, it'll be me." He pushed the man aside again, causing the other prisoners chained to him to stumble back.

"Why would he choose you? You're nothing but an idiotic child!" a voice shouted from the back. Murmurs of agreement rose out of the long line of people, and soon they were all shouting—some at Lucas to stand aside, or at Ophidian, begging him to choose them next for Eternal Knowledge.

I clutched the sword in my hand as the man who had spoken out first forced his way toward Ophidian. The shouting of the chained people ceased as they watched Ophidian assess the man. Some of their faces fell with disappointment as Ophidian snapped his gaunt fingers, retrieving the man's black heart, deeming him worthy of the prize. As soon as it dropped into his palm, Ophidian sliced, then shoved it into the man's chest, repeating the same process as before.

Ear-splitting screams and bone-crunching cracks filled the cavern, sending my head spinning. How could they be so willing to give up everything? Was knowing all the answers worth the price of humanity?

I looked over to see Claire curled in a ball once more, plugging her ears with her fingers, her face contorted in anguish. With each new malum created, she curled farther within herself.

My heart was beating hard inside the satchel, but not with the fear I expected. A light shone in my periphery, and I looked to see the sword glowing brightly once more. The power laced itself through my veins, warning me that my time to act was coming soon.

Swallowing hard, I peered through the space between the boulders, stifling a gasp. All the people who were once chained were no more. Their shackles and chains were laying in heaps on the clay floor. The hair lifted on the nape of my neck as I watched countless malum line the cavern walls.

The stench of decay filled the air as I searched for the one person I came here for.

Not everyone who had been chained had traded their heart for Eternal Knowledge. There was still one line of chain left. I followed the rusted links to the defiant, hardened face of my older brother. He looked minuscule against the hundreds of malum.

A wave of relief flooded over me. There was still a chance I could save him. But how was I supposed to save Lyle from evil incarnate and his life-hungry demons?

"You are not alone," the sword whispered, vibrating slightly in my hand.

I glanced down and saw the mark of the Mender glowing back at me, not bright orange like before, but a dark red. I didn't have to think long before I knew what I needed to do.

Closing my eyes, I took a deep breath. Was I crazy for doing what I was about to do? Yes. Was it stupid? Yes. Was I going to die? Probably.

But was it worth it?

My eyes flew open, locking onto Lyle. He was my brother, and I loved him more than I feared Ophidian's wrath. If I could give Lyle another chance to choose, I would. Grasping the sword tighter, I rose from my crouched position.

Claire slightly uncurled from her fetal position, shaking her head at me. I shot her a smile and pressed my index finger to my lips. There was no reason why Ophidian needed to know we were both here. She shook her head even faster, but I was already halfway to the exposed path.

The sword and my heart pulsated as one as I marched toward Death himself. For the first time since this adventure began, the voice didn't tell me to run. Rather, it seemed to be telling me to stay. To fight. To win.

My feet landed on the path, and I stared down the huddle of malum surrounding my brother. A new feeling crept through my veins. I looked down to see that the glow of the sword had spread from the blade to the hilt, and then up my arm. It was hot and cold at the same time. Wild, yet tame. Complex, but utterly simple. I took my stance as the glow continued to spread from my arm to my entire body. Once it reached the tips of my toes, my heart let out a solitary beat.

The ground shook beneath me, but I stood tall.

The malum paused their movements, turning their hooded faces toward me. Their red eyes scanned my glowing body, itching to devoid me of this power. I knew they hoped to seek out my heart and corrupt it. But the glow around my body was thick, a barrier protecting me from their penetrating gaze and an immunity keeping me from their wrath.

My eyes fixed on the path ahead, and I raised the blade. "Step away."

A powerful voice had erupted from my lips, commanding the attention of all around me. Not a demonic and possessed voice like Ophidian's, but dynamic, strong, and confident.

The malum glowered at me, their red eyes never wavering as they floated in the air. My fingers tightened around the sword, my heart fearless of the battle ahead.

Releasing the inner warrior I never knew I had, I unleashed an earth-shaking cry and charged toward them without an ounce of fear in my heart.

The stalactites hanging from the cavern ceiling began to fall, shattering into pieces as they crashed on the red ground. But I didn't stop. I swung the sword back and sliced through the first malum I reached.

Its sword-length, black claws swiped at me, inches from slicing off my head. The clang of the sword against the metal claws rung throughout the cavern, stunning the malum long enough for me to retract the blade and slice it through its middle. A horrible noise rose from the monster as it collapsed in a mass on the ground.

A dark, thick liquid escaped from the hole I had

created, bubbling over the floor, causing the clay to disintegrate.

My heart beat steadily as I pulled the sword back once more, driving it into the malum's red eye. It let out a horrid screech before contorting on the ground. As moved across the clay, the malum liquified, creating a giant hole where it had once been. The sound of rushing water escaped from the hole, and I peered down, watching as the black water receded beneath the cavern's foundation.

A slow, exaggerated clapping from the Beast returned my focus to the group of malum. I lifted the sword again, ready to strike. But the obedient creations separated, allowing the malicious face of Ophidian to appear. His lips curled with disgust, and his cold snake eyes never wavered from my face.

Against the darkness of the malum, Ophidian looked like a beautiful creature of light. Though pale, his skin was smooth, a stark contrast against the decrepit beings surrounding him. His cropped hair gleamed against the light of the sword, lush and thick with health. But as with Schism, I knew the monster he was. I kept the sword high and my stance defensive as he approached.

Touching his palms together, Ophidian ceased his clapping, a cynical smile replacing his scowl as he gave a mock bow. "Well done." The snake tattoos flicked their tails toward me, mimicking the motion of their master.

My heart continued to beat steadily with the pulsations of the sword, but my stomach clenched with disgust from his approval.

"I've never seen anyone take down one of my children so quickly before," he growled, straightening to his towering height.

I didn't react as his eyes analyzed my glowing body.

"I see your help has not left you," he muttered, wrinkling his nose before a wide grin spread across his face. "However, your new power will make this all the more fun."

Ophidian snapped his fingers as he had before, sending black smoke from his hands. It retreated behind me, pulling on the last segment of the chain.

The links tightened and loosened as the smoke struggled to maintain its grip. Once it secured its captive and delivered him into Ophidian's hand, he gave it a hard tug, forcing Lyle to fly forward and fall prostrate in front of me.

Lyle groaned loudly as he landed, then shook his head and looked up. He squinted before his bright blue eyes grew wide in awe.

"Addie?" he whispered. "Wh—how?"

I only had a moment to look at him before Ophidian yanked the chain back with a powerful force. He snapped his fingers again, cocooning Lyle in a thick, black film. Lyle's face contorted as the breath departed from his lungs, and his head hung limp as he was fully consumed by the smoke.

I whipped my attention back to Ophidian as my heart picked up speed. "Let him go."

A wicked grin spread across Ophidian's face. "I would love to, Adelaide. But you see, your dear brother traded his heart for a choice, and until he makes his Final Choice, his heart stays with me. Interestingly enough—" he clasped his hands behind his back while the malum created a wider circle around him as he paced "—this is not the first time your brother has sought the knowledge he so desperately desires."

I flinched back slightly at this new information. I tried to conceal my surprise before the Beast could notice, but by the grin on Ophidian's lips, I knew it was too late.

"Ah, so he was right. You don't know."

"I don't know what?" I gripped the sword and pointed it at Ophidian, not about to be distracted again.

"Anything, apparently," Ophidian scoffed. "But I won't bore you with the details. Let's make this a little more fun, shall we?"

I kept the sword level with his chest, unwilling to be swayed by his taunts.

"Oh, come now, Adelaide. You've made it through almost all of my Seven Choices. Don't you want to see it through to the end?"

My heart beat as the sword pulsated. I knew Ophidian was going to vie for my heart one last time. And just like the young blacksmith, I knew I would be expected to sacrifice something dear to me.

I nodded my head so slightly that only the Beast would see.

"Excellent," he growled before a demonic grin passed over his face as he turned back toward the black mound. Behind him, the dark smoke lifted and carried Lyle like a captive animal.

The pack of malum divided in two as I followed. I still held the sword high, not trusting Ophidian to keep them at bay.

The final malum floated into formation around the mound of hearts. I would have thought it would be smaller, considering all the black hearts Ophidian had used to create the malum, but it appeared unchanged.

Ophidian grinned. "The question *why* is always spinning through the minds of humans. They are obsessed with the unknown and that which they cannot understand." He turned and settled onto his throne of skulls, crossing one leg over the other. Schism flanked his right side, squaring his muscular shoulders as he placed his ebony fist across his chest in salute. "I give them peace in offering Aeternam Scientia. Now they know everything."

I kept my face stoic, but my mind raced back to the process of gaining Eternal Knowledge. All those people gave up their lives just to find out the answers to their questions. I shook my head. Some things weren't worth knowing.

But how could Lyle have resisted Ophidian for so long? He loved knowledge, and he loved giving it to others, too. When I was young, Lyle would let me pick out any story I wanted and read to me before bed. He never prevented me from picking a story too childish or suggested something different if I picked a book too mature.

"How about we make a trade?" Ophidian asked, tenting his fingers as he interrupted my thoughts. The serpents surrounding his eyes curled tightly around his eyes before loosening.

"What kind of trade?" My voice teemed with power, causing the black hearts to rattle as I spoke.

Ophidian shrugged. "A simple one, really. You give me half of your heart, and I give you your brother."

I pointed the sword at the Beast. Although I already knew the answer, I asked anyway. "Why only half?"

Ophidian growled, his eyes shifting to black. He extended his long claws and punctured his chest. Black liquid, similar to the malum's, oozed out. Pulling his claws out of his chest, he unfurled his fingers to reveal a disfigured heart.

The right half of the heart was red and vibrant but outlined in a dark gray. The left half of the heart was black like coal. They had been fused together, but their beating wasn't synchronized.

My mind fled back to how Ophidian had sucked the power from the gray heart, rendering it powerless. He had to be using the power of the dying hearts to sustain his own disfigured one.

With another growl, Ophidian clutched the heart and slammed it back into his chest. His eyes reverted to their snakelike stare, ready to feed.

"Do we have a trade?"

I stared back at Ophidian. He wasn't the same as when I saw him in the young blacksmith's vision. There, he had been old and decrepit, barely hanging onto life. Here, he was young and vibrant, looking like he could live for centuries. I realized then that the power of the young blacksmith's heart had preserved him for this long. If I were to give Ophidian half my heart, it would assist him in achieving his goal of immortality.

But if I didn't take his trade, what would happen to Lyle? I'd come all this way, and I wasn't going to lose him now. My mind raced as I tried to piece together a countertrade to propose.

"No more trades!" a voice from behind me yelled.

Amid the sea of malum, Claire stood tall with her chin held high and her eyes blazing. To my surprise, the man from the sixth Choice was with her. His plaid shirt was torn and his face bore several cuts and scratches, but his eyes were just as defiant as Lyle's.

"Isn't this sweet?" Ophidian growled through clenched teeth. "My own slave and the fallen follower of my sworn enemy have come to defy me."

"Leave her alone, Ophidian. She's protected by the Mender. You can't harm her," the man proclaimed.

I looked down at the sword and my matching glowing

skin. The mark of the Mender was still burning a deep red upon the gilded hilt. The Mender *was* protecting me. But why did he choose me? I had always denied his power and existence.

"You're right, Betrayer," Ophidian snapped, grinning as the man winced. "Though I can't touch her, she can choose to give her protection away, just like you did."

Ophidian snarled, then flung his hand at the man, causing him to fly into a boulder. The crack of his skull against the stone sent my nerves on edge.

"And you." Ophidian turned to Claire. "I own you. You cannot defy me."

Snapping his fingers, the black smoke rushed from his fingertips and encased Claire. She tried to dodge the smoke, but it soon covered her body, sucking the breath from her lungs. Another cloud rose up on the other side of Ophidian, directly opposite of Lyle.

"My, how interesting things have gotten, haven't they, Adelaide? "Here I offer you a trade, yet you decide on something entirely different."

I swallowed hard, chastising myself for not acting sooner.

"Your brother for half of your heart, or I will destroy this filth." He motioned to Claire. "From the inside out."

I stared in disbelief. I couldn't let Claire suffer because of me anymore. And I'd been longing to find Lyle for so long. But if I gave up half of my heart to Ophidian, what would happen to me? I felt as if I was standing back in

Barracks once more, looking at Schism's two red doors at the edge of Wintertide. I knew nothing of what lay behind either one, but I had to make a choice.

I squeezed the sword tightly, praying it had some words of wisdom. In a soft voice, it said, *You are not alone.* And I knew my answer.

Taking a deep breath, I looked Ophidian straight in the eye and nodded. "Deal."

CHAPTER 35

"*A*ddie, get out of here! Run!" Claire screamed, but her voice was distorted by the smoke swirling around her. I kept my eyes focused on the snake before me. His smile widened to reveal sharp, gray teeth, as if he could already feel the power of my heart beating within his chest.

Taking a step toward Ophidian, I watched him rise from his throne. I grasped the sword, feeling its power flow through me.

"Before I give you half of my heart, I need to see that my brother and Claire are unharmed."

Ophidian grinned again, snapping his fingers. One of the black clouds immediately dissipated, causing Claire to fall to the ground.

As soon as she landed, Claire gasped for breath before digging her heels into the ground and rushing toward me with all her strength. Schism, however, grabbed her arm with his ebony hand, ceasing her escape. Seeing she wasn't physically hurt, I looked toward Lyle. Ophidian followed my line of sight and snapped again, causing the cloud to fade and the chains to fall around Lyle.

Lyle crumpled to the ground. His chest heaved as he sucked in gasps of air. His eyes were wide, desperately drinking in all around him. As he tried to stand back up, he looked up at me, his gaze darting to my face.

"Addie. But . . . why?" he whispered.

I gave him a small smile before turning back to Ophidian. His mouth had grown wider, displaying multiple rows of sharp teeth. I could see where he had gotten his template for the phagos. His pale skin turned translucent, revealing a dark layer of grayish-green flesh beneath. His eyes bulged, displaying further attributes of a snake: bright, yellow, and deadly. The black serpents surrounding his eyes lengthened, sliding from the sides of his face and receding beneath his translucent shirt.

Taking a deep breath, I grabbed the satchel by my side and lifted the strap over my head. I carefully opened the pouch and removed the tattered, white cloth. A hue of red surrounded the dirtied strips, as if they could barely contain what was inside.

I swallowed hard and unwrapped my heart. It was no longer cracked and dulled by the evil of Ophidian's Realm, but was still alive with life, beating with a new power I'd never felt before.

Every gaze latched onto my heart as its red light illuminated the musty cavern. Claire, Ophidian, Lyle, Schism, and the malum—all watched and waited to see what would happen next. Heat radiated from my heart's pulsations. I placed my heart in one hand and grasped the sword with the other.

"You want half," I said in my powerful voice, raising the sword above my head. "I'll give you half."

Ophidian's face changed, the gleam in his greedy eyes dissolving into a cold, hard glare as I brought the sword down, splitting my heart in two. I screamed from the pain, causing the mound of black hearts to shake apart until each one lay on the cavern floor.

The malum screeched in response, hovering before flying around the room, creating a swirling mass of black chaos. Claire stumbled across the black hearts and landed a few feet away from me. Lyle rolled down as well, landing on the other side.

Clutching the empty cavity in my chest, I stared at my heart, broken in two even halves. I looked over to the two people who either made a poor choice or none at all. Before anything could attack me, I carried both pieces over to Lyle. His eyes were still shut from the force of his fall. My breath caught at the sight of his battered and bruised face. He had done so much to care for me; it was time for me to look after him. With the tip of the sword, I sliced through his chest, causing a mixture of red and black blood to ooze out. Swallowing hard, I clasped one half of my heart and plunged it into Lyle's chest. If he had at least half a heart, there was no way Ophidian could give him a black one. Hopefully.

The wound immediately closed up, covering the beating organ. Lyle's eyes flew open, and he looked at me in shock.

"Addie," he gasped, eyes still wide before he squinted them to focus. "What did you do?" He placed his hand over the place where my half heart was beating. "Why would you trade your heart to save me?"

I shook my head quickly, remembering Nana's choice from her journal. "Love's not a trade, Lyle. It's a gift."

Lyle reached out and held me close. "I'm so sorry. I'm so sorry for everything."

I hugged him back, then released him. "You need to get out of here. Now."

"Not without you." His voice was stern.

I huffed as he reverted to his overprotective ways. "Stay hidden."

Rushing back through the black hordes, I swung the sword at the creatures soaring above until I found Claire. Her body was still limp at the base of the throne.

As I ran toward her, a large, black hand reached out and grabbed me by the neck.

"You've done quite enough, little Addie." Schism's voice slithered as his eyes shifted to red, his skin blackening into the monster he truly was. "Now be a good little girl and give me your heart."

I grasped at the cold, stone fingers as I was lifted from the ground. My feet flailed, kicking at the surrounding air as oxygen escaped my lungs. Gasping, I tried to swing at him with the sword, but I could only manage a small nick on his cheek, causing Schism to laugh at the poor attempt. The power of the sword drained from my body, growing fainter with half of my heart missing.

Schism's fingers tightened around my throat before I jerked the sword back, scraping the blade across his blood-red eyes. With a horrible cry, he released his grip on me, and I fell to the ground.

A loud crack vibrated through my body. Horror weighed on me as pain shot from my leg. Looking down, I found below the knee, my leg had flipped in a way that wasn't normal.

I wanted to scream, but my head spun from the tremendous pain. Nausea built in my stomach, threatening to escape. Tears streamed down my face, blurring my vision. I almost missed the other half of my heart resting just a few feet away from Schism's feet. I didn't have time to dwell on my pain. I had to save Claire.

Biting my tongue, I grabbed my fallen sword and hoisted myself up as much as I could. There was enough power in the magical weapon to dull the pain. I could finish what I started.

I held the sword in one trembling hand, willing to face Schism until the bitter end. I had expected to find him already flying back to Ophidian with the other half of my heart in his hand. But he simply stood there, staring at it as he had before.

The half heart beat steadily in front of him, continuously giving off the red hue.

While Schism was hypnotized by its power, I continued to crawl toward him, pain flaring through my leg. If anyone was going to slay this monster, it would be me.

Each pull I made across the clay ground felt as if my body was being ripped apart. I gritted my teeth and continued moving. The frantic malum were still flying chaotically. The tips of their floating bodies were sharp, cutting into my flesh as they rushed by.

Below Schism, I raised the sword high to strike. He broke his attention from my heart and growled.

Wiping the blood from a gash in my forehead, I heaved myself forward.

Unsheathing his long, black claws, Schism wasted no time in bearing down upon me.

I gripped the sword with both hands and met him head-on. The sound of the sword against his claws reverberated through the cavern, and everything stopped. The malum ceased their flight, silencing their deafening screeches. The only sound heard was the beating of my half heart.

All eyes were transfixed on the half heart as I battled Schism. Their stares weighed on me as my power further weakened, the agony from my leg growing more intense as the power and protection of the sword drained away.

Gritting my teeth, I shoved Schism back, swinging wildly. He laughed again. I tried to rise but felt a new searing pain in my leg. Crying out, I crumpled to the ground.

Retracting his claws from my broken leg, Schism lifted his foot and pressed down on my mangled limb. As I screamed louder, sobbing, he pressed harder.

"Scream, little Addie. It will be the last sound you ever make." His claws grew longer as he leaned in close to my face. "You see, once a heart no longer has a body to belong to, anyone can have it."

The tips of his claws began to push into my chest, slowly, painfully. I tried to bite my lip and stop my screaming, but I couldn't. Schism's eyes grew hungrier and his grin wider as he attempted to further drain my body of blood, leaving my heart no live body to return to.

How could I have come all this way just to die at the hand of the monster who started it all?

CHAPTER 36

$\mathcal{I}$ swallowed hard and sank deeper into myself, numbing my mind to the pain. I said a silent prayer to the Heavens, asking them to care for all those I loved when I was gone.

As I was about to surrender, a bright light shone in my periphery. Schism's attention was quickly drawn away from me and toward the ball of white light hurling toward him. It slammed into his face, knocking his claws free from my skin.

Unable to move, I felt a set of strong, wiry arms encase me. I tried to push them away before the familiar beating of my heart pounded next to my ear. Looking up, I found Lyle staring down at me. He brushed a strand of my short hair out of my face.

"Hang on, Addie," he said, clutching me close.

I nestled into his chest, remembering the comfort he had always given me. The white light shone again. When I turned toward it, I let out a gasp. In the midst of the hovering malum, the man from the sixth Choice stood alone against Schism.

As the man stepped forward, white light poured from his palms, thrusting into the creature of darkness. Schism snarled and flew higher. The man moved forward, this time hitting one of Schism's wings. Screeching loudly, Schism descended, his wing disintegrating into dust.

My body was failing, but my mind was still working fast. I looked up at Lyle, whose attention was locked on the battle between the man and Schism. I tugged at his shirt until he looked down at me.

"My heart," I murmured, my voice a fraction of what it had been. My skin had stopped glowing, too, fading to a translucent blue. "Go get it—and Claire."

Lyle's eyebrows furrowed.

"The girl with white hair."

He nodded before grabbing the sword and running over to Claire. The glow of the sword began to shine again, and I wondered whether it recognized the power of my heart within Lyle.

Pain flooded my body, but mostly my chest. I placed my hand on it, then brought my hand to my eyes, watching the bright red liquid drip from my fingertips.

A hollow breath escaped from my lips as Lyle returned

with Claire in his arms and the other half of my heart clutched in his hand. He gently laid Claire next to me before running back to retrieve the sword and waiting for further instructions.

My hand reached out, shaking and pale. With a pained look, he dropped the other half of my heart into my palm. I managed to sit up slightly, causing pain to erupt from every nerve in my leg.

With my half heart in hand, I wrapped my fingers around the sword's hilt and crawled toward Claire before Lyle reached out and grabbed my wrist.

"What are you doing? You need that."

I shook my head, lacking the strength to argue with him, and brushed his hand away.

"Addie," Lyle said protectively. "We don't even know who she is. Why would you save her? What's going to happen to you?"

I looked at him sternly, remembering how Claire had said he had begun forgetting things. I guessed half of a pure heart could only heal so much of his mind.

"I know who she is," I said, but it came out barely above a whisper. "She's saved my life, and yours. She deserves another chance to make her own choice."

Before he could argue with me, I gently pierced Claire's skin with the tip of the sword and pushed the half heart into the empty cavity in her chest. Her blood didn't flow out of her like Lyle's had. Instead, it stayed securely in place, welcoming the beating heart. A loud gasp poured from her lips as she sat up.

I fell back, my head thumping on the hard ground, missing the protection the sword gave my body. I don't know how it works, but I *do* know it protected me. A guttural wail escaped my lips, and my hands shook uncontrollably. The burning heat of my blood escaped my body until my fingertips cooled, and all feeling was lost. The numbing glided its way up my arms. Was this what it was like to die?

Looking up at the domed ceiling, I watched the malum stare down at me with their red eyes. I blinked up at them, not caring whether they fed off my life anymore. I had nothing left to give.

Claire and Lyle knelt over me, blocking the malum from sight.

"You were stupid again," Claire said, tears brimming in her eyes. "I told you not to be stupid."

"You said you never got to choose," I said weakly. "Now you get the chance."

"Is there anything to save her?" Lyle asked frantically, looking at Claire.

Claire shook her head, tears tumbling down her face. Bright streaks of light erupted from behind her. The man from the sixth Choice was still fighting strong. I wondered who he was to be fighting for us so loyally.

"Listen," I said softly, "Get out of here. Go now."

"No!" they both said.

"We're not leaving you, Addie," Lyle added as he picked me up again.

I let out a sharp cry, and he quickly lowered me back to the ground.

"I've made my trade," I managed to say with a weak smile. "I would rather choose to give someone I love another chance at a choice than live through my own."

"Addie," Lyle whispered, bowing his head so his forehead touched mine.

I reached out and grabbed his hand, then reached for Claire's. I couldn't feel their skin or the life it was giving off, but I knew that they were there.

"Enough!"

I turned slightly to see Ophidian rising from his skull throne. Had he been watching this whole time, as if we were a form of entertainment for him? The malum scurried from above and fell back behind Ophidian.

"Fracious, I asked you to retrieve the heart. Did you?" Ophidian's voice was cold and hard, shooting like daggers.

"My lord—" Schism started, but his sentence was cut off by a gut-wrenching noise.

"Disgusting fool," Ophidian sneered. "Your touch would only taint my prize."

All were silent, with only the sound of the rushing river echoing through the air. The stillness was soon broken by Ophidian's steps vibrating against the clay floor as he walked toward us. I looked back to the ceiling, now malum-less. My toes were beginning to cool, and I expected the numbing to completely consume me when a warm touch ignited my ankle.

I glanced down to see the man from the sixth Choice, covered in black and red blood, holding a finger up to his lips, a determined look on his face. He moved his hands in a back and forth motion, causing a bright light to appear from his palms. It tingled across my skin as it traveled up my body, covering Claire and Lyle with it.

Ophidian continued his steady, long strides toward us, and I wondered why no one else had noticed how close he was. Lyle's head was still bowed, and Claire squeezed her eyes shut, her mouth moving, the words inaudible.

Ophidian's snake eyes stared straight at me, analyzing my body as his tattoos coiled frantically around his features. He let out a snarl, swiping at a nearby malum before stalking back to his throne. I sucked in a breath as Schism came into view. Not only was his other clawed hand dismembered, but a large crater was left where his face had been. I blinked, trying desperately to convince myself that what I was seeing was true.

"The Bellata is no more," Ophidian said to a malum on his right. "Ready the siti. We must find the boy and the slave who possess her heart."

Except Lyle and Claire were right beside me. I looked to the man, who was still at my feet, moving his hands.

When we made eye contact, he gave me a quick wink, his eyes crinkling at the corners as he smirked.

I wished that I could thank him, but I knew my body was failing fast.

As I sucked in one final breath, my mind wandered back to a cold place where I had left another piece of my heart to a kind boy with golden hair.

CHAPTER 37

*D*eep moaning closed in. I squeezed my eyes shut and tried to move my arms and legs, but my senses pulled away from me. It was as if my body was floating in one direction and my mind in another.

High-pitched shrieks bounced from stalactite to stalactite. I tried to turn my neck but felt nothing again. I thought my eyes were open, but I could only see darkness.

As I shifted my gaze, a figure began to form. White light encased the body, but as it drew nearer, the white quickly turned into an ash-gray that spewed out around the figure.

As it came closer, something small began to move in my mind, as if a worm had been unleashed inside my brain, trying to wriggle its way into my thoughts. I tried to scream, but no noise came out.

After the slithering departed from my mind, the figure

got so close, I could feel its cold breath. Leaning close, the lifeless voice of the Beast whispered, "Don't think that Magister's trick fooled me. I know you're still alive. Be wary of the times to come. Everyone you love will suffer because of your choices. The fight is not over, Adelaide. It has only begun."

The bitter cold that had surrounded me with the figure's approach left in a fury, leaving me hollow and bare.

Soon hushed whispers surrounded me.

"We need to go now," an older man's voice said.

"Where? How can we get out of here?" a young man's voice retorted. "She's dying."

A bright orb of light shone in front of me. I wasn't dead, not yet. The light pulsated gently.

"I know where we can go," the older man said firmly.

The bright light glowed slightly brighter and began to move back and forth. It looked so warm and comforting, and I was so tired and worn. I hadn't felt comfort in a long time.

"Follow me," a female voice murmured.

"I'm not letting either one of you go anywhere with her," the young man said with even more of a bite in his voice. "Not until you tell me who you are."

Who were these people?

"I've saved your life and hers hundreds of times," the female voice said forcefully. She sounded very upset.

"Now she's dying. I suggest you shut up and let me help her."

The bright light faded into the distance, and the conversation disappeared. My body and mind split further apart. Surging forward, I pushed my thoughts ahead, trying to follow the light. But the closer I got, the more it faded into the distance. I pushed harder until I felt myself being pulled toward it.

A strong arm braced my back, and another lifted my legs under my knees. Was this light my consciousness? I focused everything on the orb.

The sound of rushing water captured my attention. I looked all around the dark abyss, waiting for the water to pour in, but nothing came.

As I reached my hand toward the light, tight arms circled my waist, squeezing me close to a warm body. But when I looked behind me, no one was there. Pulling my hand away from the light, the strength of the arms disappeared, leaving me cold once more. I reached out again, and the voices returned.

"Let's go!" the older man yelled above the roaring water.

The arms holding me tensed. The beating had returned, this time on my back, pulsating hard and fast.

"Trust me," the female voice said.

I didn't have time to wonder why I should trust her before I felt my stomach fly up to my throat as the rest of my body was hurled in the opposite direction. As I intertwined myself with the light, I could feel the spray of water hit my face, my hair flying in different directions.

I pulled back again, and the feeling faded, allowing my mind to finally grasp what was happening. Another choice was laid out in front of me. Would I choose to return to my realm, become one with my body again and face the cold figure who had threatened me? Or walk away from it all, farther and farther, until the light was but a distant memory, and I could allow myself the peace of the surrounding darkness?

The light continued to pulse brightly as I stared into it. It would be so much easier if this choice could be made for me. Someone else could tell me what to do, and I wouldn't have to worry.

"That's not how it works, unfortunately," a soft voice said.

Like before, I glanced around, but no one was there. I turned back to the light. Its glow shifted slightly. I couldn't help thinking there was something I was meant to do. I didn't feel like my life was finished yet, but it would be so much easier to end it now.

Except there was someone I was meant to find. Someone I had made a promise to. What would they think if I decided to quit and die on them? The glow of the light brightened and dulled as I argued with myself.

"Sometimes a feeling is more truthful than a thought," the voice from before said.

My mind and body were split, making my feelings

hard to understand. But buried deep within, I somehow knew I still had life within me.

Staring back at the light, I pushed myself toward the glowing orb until we were intertwined as one.

I let out a gasp as the freezing, black water soaked through my clothes, cutting through my body like a knife. The pain in my leg seared, setting my nerves on fire as my leg whipped back against the force of the rushing tide. My arms reached out, flailing against the current as the arms holding me tightened.

"Addie!" the young man's voice yelled in my ear.

I cringed, pushing away from him, only to be pulled back. I opened my eyes to see that it wasn't an enemy, but Lyle.

His eyes focused in concentration as we were carried by the black river. Swallowing hard, I shifted my body until I was facing him. Tears streamed down my face as I wrapped my arms around his neck and held him close. I didn't think I would ever see him again. Although it hurt to feel, I was glad I could.

His arms tightened around me once more as the rushing water began to slow into a steady current, pushing us through the dark walls of the cave.

"I'm glad you didn't die on me," Lyle said in my ear.

I laughed and sobbed. If only he knew.

The current dragged us through the cave, where it led to another large cavern. Green moss covered the tops of the rocks that lay on the edge, creating a stairway leading out of the dark water. My eyes squinted as a bright light protruded from an opening above the rocks.

When we arrived at the mossy stairs, a stream of white hair and a bloodied face greeted me with a smile. Detaching myself from Lyle, I reached out and grabbed Claire's hand, and she hoisted me up and enveloped me in a hug.

"Stupid, stupid girl," she whispered in my ear.

I let out a small laugh and hugged her back, happy to hear her words of encouragement once more. I was so thankful to be back with Claire and Lyle that I forgot everything that had happened earlier. Until I tried to take a step.

I cried out in pain, my knees buckling beneath me as I collided with the mossy steps. The pain in my leg resurfaced, causing more tears to drip from my eyes. As Claire and Lyle rushed over, the emptiness in my chest and satchel gnawed at me, and I was aware of what was missing. The cool feeling of death began to creep on me once more.

"Come on!" Claire shouted to Lyle, cupping her hands under my arms.

Lyle gently scooped me up, cradling me in his arms. The familiar beating of my heart within him was strong and warm against my cold skin.

The rhythmic steps of Lyle's feet pounding up the stones lulled me back into the darkness. Maybe I was only meant to come back to say goodbye.

I shut my eyes as the bright light from the cave cascaded across my face. I had been in darkness for so long, I had forgotten what it was like to be surrounded by light.

"How is she?" a deep, concerned voice asked. It sounded so familiar, like something from a dream.

Warm, petite hands gripped both of mine and squeezed them tightly.

"She doesn't have much time," a gentle, female voice said.

It didn't sound like Claire's harsh and pointed tone. It was much too light, as if white, fluffy clouds were formed when the woman spoke.

"Come," the first voice spoke again, and I could feel myself moving forward.

I struggled to take in another shaky breath, feeling Lyle's arms tighten around me as I rocked back and forth with his steps.

In a matter of moments, I felt myself leaving Lyle's arms. My back connected with a hard surface, reminding me of the marble slab in Doctor Magnum's office.

My body temperature had dropped, and my limbs were shivering. I knew it wouldn't be long until the numbness returned once more.

Glass or instruments clattered around me as I strained to open my eyes. I cracked one open enough to see a man's back. He was tall with dark brown hair that had been pulled away from his broad shoulders. His thick hands were working on something I couldn't see. But the weight of my eyelids became overwhelming, and I shut them.

"Can you help her?" I heard Lyle say. His voice sounded distant.

"Of course," the man said. "But it is not yet the right time."

"She doesn't have time!" Lyle yelled.

I wanted to sit up and tell him that everything was all right. He didn't need to worry about me. But my muscles refused to move. With no life left in my limbs, I was a corpse, clinging to a few last breaths.

"Sana," the man said calmly. "Please show this young man to where he'll be staying."

A rustle of feet danced across the floor. The light, fluffy voice whispered something soft. Stomping steps mixed with the light steps as they filed from the room.

"I know you're still in there, Addie," the man said, his voice as calm and gentle as before. "You chose to come back. Otherwise, you'd still be in the void of your indecision."

How did he know that?

The light footsteps returned to the room where I was lying. "The brother has been placed in his quarters," the soft voice said.

"And the heartless?" the man asked, his hands pausing in movement.

"She, too," the light voice responded. "Although she is no longer."

The man hummed, as if he hadn't expected that answer. But what did it mean?

"Very good, Sana. I need to work now. Please retrieve my mallet and chisel."

The fluttery steps bounced away and returned within moments. Something heavy thudded on the marble slab next to me. The voice dismissed Sana from the room, leaving us alone once more.

A few minutes passed before the solid steps of the man came nearer. "The time is right, Addie. I can save you, but I need your permission. Are you ready?" His voice was still gentle but carried a hint of concern.

I didn't know how or why, but I managed a slight nod. Before I could change my mind, a hard pounding blasted across my chest, and I let out a scream as everything went dark.

CHAPTER 38

a hot pounding pumped throughout my body, like a burning fire waiting to be released. Footsteps rushed around: solid ones, light ones, hard ones, ones I couldn't identify. I didn't know where I was or what was happening. All I could feel was my chest radiating with heat.

"Sana, the herbs. Now." The fluttering feet flew with haste around the room.

Soon something leafy pressed against my chest. Simultaneously, something hard and smooth was pressed to my forehead.

"Hold on, Addie. We're almost done," the voice said.

A sharp pain seared its way through my chest. I could feel the flesh ripping in two. I cried out, arching my back in response. Cool metal left my skin and returned, pounding harder. I cried out again as hot tears streamed down my face. I tried to open my eyes but couldn't.

"Sana."

The light steps came closer, and more flat, leafy things were placed on my chest. The leaves immediately cooled my body. Something wet and sticky seeped from them, trickling around the heated parts of my chest.

My breathing evened out as the cool leaves worked their way around my skin. Cool air hit me as someone lifted the sheet covering my legs.

"Retrieve the linkslock from my garden, Sana. There's more work to be done."

The steps fluttered away, then returned in seconds.

I prayed that linkslock was some kind of magical herb that would fix my leg and knock me out for good.

The man carefully removed my boot, and I winced at the pain. The tearing of fabric came next. I hoped Claire didn't want those pants back. Gentle yet calloused hands worked their way around my foot.

I could *feel* the callouses on the man's hands. My skin felt alive again.

The hands gripped my knee and heel, then snapped my leg straight. I screamed with everything I had. Heavy footsteps rushed from a hallway. The fluttery steps intercepted them.

"What's he doing to her?" Lyle yelled.

The fluttery steps and light voice of Sana, I presumed, said something soothing as my eyes shut.

A hard thump vibrated through my veins, causing a red light to flash through my mind. It happened again; the red light pulsated with a mixture of yellow and orange. The thump pounded again, this time quicker than the last. The red light continued to flash with each thump until it reached a steady, rhythmic beat.

My eyes shot open at the sound. This was impossible.

Another thump.

This beating. It shouldn't be happening. Where was it coming from?

I lifted my hand to my chest, expecting to feel the cold void that had been there this entire time. Soft palpitations vibrated against my fingertips. Something was in there. Something alive.

I sat up, tossing the tangle of sheets to my legs. Silver leaves fell from my flesh, tumbling to the ground as I rushed out of the bed.

Running to a mirror a few feet away, I carefully pulled my shirt down enough to find the source of the beating. A thin red line crossed through the white circle on my chest, right above the thumping. I ran my fingers down the line, still not believing what I felt.

"Don't worry," a gentle voice said from behind me. "Time heals all wounds."

I tensed at the voice, recognizing it from before. "What did you do?" I whispered, frightened.

A soft chuckle answered. "I did what you asked. I gave you a new heart."

My eyes widened in the mirror as I attempted to process his response. With my hand still on the steady beating, I turned around. "That's impossible."

A tall, sturdy man sat in a wooden chair, one leg crossed over the other. His oval, olive-toned face was covered in a thick, brown beard that matched his long, wavy hair, which was pulled back with a piece of string.

He studied me with dark eyes, holding me frozen in front of him. Though his disposition seemed kind, I couldn't help but be frightened of him.

It was impossible to get a new heart. Once you traded your own, it was gone for good. You didn't get a second chance. I knew that when I gave my heart to Lyle and Claire. I never expected a second chance.

But as I felt the steady beats coming from inside me, I began to wonder what was fact and what was fiction.

The man uncrossed his legs and stood, giving me a better view of him. He was dressed in brown slacks that were held up by dark suspenders stretched over a crisp, white shirt. Brushing his hands on his thighs, he looked at me with satisfaction.

"Impossible? No." He walked closer until he was only a few feet away. "Extremely uncommon? Yes." He let out a laugh before his face saddened. "Especially with how the realms are faring now."

I fidgeted with the hem of Lyle's sweater, thankful to have some comfort in this strange place. I took a deep breath. "I didn't ask for a new heart."

The bed creaked from the weight of the man as he sat on it. "No, not verbally, anyway."

I looked at him through the curtain of my short hair. "Then how?"

Reaching over, he grabbed his chisel and began twirling it within his steady fingers. "Love is an interesting thing. It makes people jump from the highest mountains, believing they can fly. Or it convinces them to hide in the darkest caves, assuring them they never will. But what you did was something extraordinary. Something I haven't seen in many millennia."

"What?"

A soft smile alighted on the man's face. "You loved, dear child. With all your heart. Not many people are willing to do that. Not only did your love save one person, but two. Because you overcame your fears and willingly gave your heart, a new one could be formed."

Biting my lower lip, I grasped the hem of Lyle's sweater once more. "I still don't understand."

The man laughed again and stood, placing his chisel on the bed. "In time, you will. You are still very young and have much to endure in the coming days."

I was about to ask what he meant when he held his hand out to me.

"Come," he said. "There are those who wish to see you."

Closing my mouth, I grasped his calloused hand and followed.

CHAPTER 39

*A*s we crossed the threshold of the door to the small operating room, I gasped. This was not what I was expecting to see on the other side.

A long hallway made of gigantic trees stretched before us. Their light branches bent over one another, creating a ceiling with small gaps to allow golden sunlight to pass through.

Everything else was just as magnificent, bright, and beautiful as a summer's day. I stared in awe as the light glittered through the air. I hadn't seen light this pure since I was a child.

As we passed through, tiny buds bloomed on vines spiraling across the branches. Enchanted, I stared as a little blue bud sprouted into a yellow blossom with thick petals that waved as we walked by. I wanted to stay and study it, but the man gently nudged me along.

A long vine cascaded from the ceiling, wrapping itself around my wrist. I gasped and tried to struggle away, but the man gave my hand a small pat and motioned toward the vine.

I looked down to see tiny leaves growing from the vine and dancing across the top of my hand. The foliage rotated with vigor, prompting a smile from me as I gazed upon them. The leaves moved left and right before swaying in, then out, dancing to a melody I wished I could hear. Suddenly, they came together in the center of my hand and sprouted into a beautiful pink flower. Just when I thought the show was over, the flower gave off a soft lullaby, swaying to the notes as it sang.

The man laughed. "They seem to like you."

I stared back at the flower. "How do you know?"

He gave me the same soft smile. "They're showing off."

"Flowers don't usually sing and dance here?"

He laughed again. "Oh, they do. But never so eloquent-ly. Usually, they're off tune, each singing to a different melody. It's quite a mess."

A smile came to my lips as I imagined the little leaves flailing about.

As the man led me along, the flower ended its song and folded one of its petals, gesturing to me as if it were blowing a kiss. A tiny tingle landed on my cheek before we continued down the magical corridor.

The archway of trees split into four different corri-dors as we reached its end. I hesitated, not knowing if this was another choice. I was so tired of having to choose.

The man pulled me along as if he knew what I was thinking. "No need to worry. I'll show you which way to go."

Relieved, I followed him down the second hallway. The trees in this archway were covered in a light green moss, sprouting delicate purple flowers. As we walked through, tiny white butterflies escaped the moss and greeted us with quiet hums. I stared at them, infatuated.

"They're saying hello," the man said.

A small white butterfly landed on a lock of my hair.

"Hello," I whispered.

The little butterfly scurried off, frightened by my booming voice. Within a few moments, it returned, landing on the same lock of hair. I listened to its series of hums and looked to the man for translation.

He let out a soft chuckle. "He says, 'You are very beautiful, but would look better with wings.'"

I couldn't help but laugh at the butterfly's compliment.

As we made our way down the corridor, the butterflies hummed once more, saying their goodbyes before flying back to their homes in the moss.

We came to a stop in front of a peaked wooden door. Intricate carvings of vines and leaves lined the perimeter, leaving space for a strange symbol in the middle: a circle with a thin X crossed through it. The ends of the X extended past the circumference of the circle. I studied the symbol, trying to remember if I had seen it somewhere.

Before I had a chance to file through my mind, the man gave the door a nod, and it opened without so much as a touch to a handle or lock, unlike the ones in Ophidian's Realm.

Walking in first, he looked over his shoulder as I lingered outside. "Not all doors lead to darkness."

Nodding, I grasped his hand and followed him through. The room immediately lit up as we entered, revealing a round area walled in by the same pale trees. Vines spiraled their way around the trunks, sprouting white, purple, and pink flowers as they ascended. The trees slightly arched at the top, creating a tall ceiling with their green leafy branches.

Letting go of the man's hand, I looked around, trying to take in as much as I could. The ground began to sprout warm, green grass, creating a verdant rug beneath our feet. It tickled the underside of my toes, reminding me that I'd lost my boots somewhere along the way.

A few feet ahead, a thin tree sprouted from the lush grass. I watched closely as three more trees shot up near it, winding themselves around one another, creating four posts of a bed. Small, yellow flowers appeared from the branches above and began to weave themselves into a lush blanket.

The magic continued its work around us. A chandelier of branches and buds hung itself from the ceiling. Another tree sprang up from the far corner of the room, bending over backwards into a rounded table.

At the sound of rushing water, I turned, gasping at the sight. A sparkling waterfall flowed behind the bed, descending into a small stream that babbled around the perimeter of the room.

"This room has been waiting a long time," the man said quietly.

"For what?" I asked, still mesmerized.

The man didn't answer, turning toward the door instead.

"Ah, they're here." He gave the door another nod, and it swung open. He looked to me before saying, "Your brother has a very powerful magic within him that he does not yet know of. With it, he was able to warn you of what lay within Ophidian's Realm." He gave me another smile. "Nightmares are only shadows before the light."

I looked at him with wide eyes before I was bombarded by two sets of arms holding me close. The soft click of the door was the only signal that the man had left.

"We were so worried," Claire said in my ear.

I could feel Lyle nodding in agreement. It took a few moments for me to pry them off.

They were both thoroughly clean. So clean, in fact, that their skin sparkled in the sunlight. Lyle had been scrubbed of the filth from Ophidian's Realm and was dressed similarly to the man who had saved my life, minus the suspenders. He even had a new pair of spectacles.

I glanced at Claire to see her wounds from the malum were completely healed. Her eyes were both open and bright, no longer bruised. Her skin no longer bore the claw marks from Ophidian's vicious creatures. She was also dressed in a long, cream-colored gown embroidered with dark green leaves on the hem. The leaves curled and waved before laying back on the fabric. Her hair was woven into delicate braids, making the brown and white strands look immaculate.

Looking down, I frowned at my attire. I was wearing Lyle's sweater, which was somehow still intact. But the lower half was a mess. The black pants were full of tears and red clay, with one leg completely cut off from the knee down.

I opened my mouth to speak when a tree sprouted up behind me, creating an elegant chair from its soft leaves and branches. Two more sprung up behind Claire and Lyle. We all jumped and gasped before chuckling. With grins, Claire and I sat in our chairs while Lyle inspected his. Tilting his spectacles up and down, he examined the seat until he was convinced it was really there.

Slowly easing himself down, Lyle relaxed. Satisfied, he nodded before looking at me. "Are you all right? I mean, he didn't hurt you, right?" He balled his hand into a tight fist.

Claire frowned before giving him a small nudge, causing Lyle to relax his whitened knuckles. I smirked, remembering that Claire and Lyle had known each other in Barracks before the Seven Choices. But *how* well had they known each other? I decided to question them later.

"We heard the screaming," she said. "We didn't know what to do."

"Well, it did hurt," I replied frankly. Lyle's lips turned downward, and Claire let out a laugh. "But" —I placed my hand over the beating heart in my chest— "He saved me. He gave me another chance."

Claire shrugged. "Well, that's what he does."

I furrowed my brows, giving her a look of confusion. She looked at me, then back at Lyle. A message passed between them that I couldn't decipher.

"Addie . . ." Lyle began softly. "You don't know who that was?"

I gave them a blank look.

Claire scoffed before shaking her head. "Addie, that was the Mender."

"What?" My mind traveled back in time. The mallet and chisel. The pounding on my chest. The magic surrounding me in this place. The peace that had cradled my new heart, diminishing any thought of fear or worry. I smiled, realizing what I had missed all along.

Claire let out a sigh. "He was right in front of you, and you didn't even know it."

I placed my hand over my beating heart. "I think I knew it was him. I was just too scared to admit it."

"Why?" Lyle asked. As he leaned forward, a cluster of dark curls fell across his forehead. Like Claire, he didn't know what had happened the past seven years. How Barracks had changed. How I had changed.

Giving him an empathetic smile, I said, "It renounces everything I know. With one realization, everything I've learned is gone in a moment."

"Wouldn't you rather know fact than believe in a fairytale?" a gentle voice asked from the door.

All three of us turned to see a small, chestnut-colored woman, barely the height of my shoulder, looking at us with a kind smile. She practically floated into the room, her footsteps were so light.

Another tree sprouted into a chair for her as she joined us. She placed her hand on the tree, causing white orchids to sprout all around it, then gave a nod. Swaying her head, she pushed her long, ebony hair over her shoulder and sat down. The blue fabric of her gown shimmered, unleashing sparkles into the air as she shifted her feet beneath her, elegantly crossing them.

"Sometimes the fairytales are easier to believe," I said quietly.

The woman gave a small smile. Placing her hand on the chair, she beckoned the twigs upward, and they braided her long hair. We all sat, awestruck, and watched the branches do their work.

"That may be true," she said in her light voice, her dark green eyes staring at me. "But many fairytales derive from fact."

Before I could reply, she hopped down from the chair,

her long braid cascading down her back, and stretched her hand toward me. "Come. We have much to do."

I glanced back at Claire and Lyle, who were still staring at the woman's braid. Knowing I had to make the decision on my own, I placed my hand in hers and immediately felt small tingles on my palm.

"My name is Sana," she said, then nodded at the door to the bedroom.

Like it had for the Mender, the door swung open. I remembered the man, or the Mender, saying her name earlier.

"You were there when . . ." I trailed off, placing my other hand over my palpitating new heart.

Sana nodded as we walked down the mossy hallway. The butterflies greeted me once more, planting small kisses all over my face. I let out a laugh as Sana's angelic giggle joined mine. I looked over to see the butterflies wrapping around her head, forming a crown.

"I'm a healer," she said, holding her hand out for one of the butterflies to land on. It bounced around her palm, dancing to an unheard tune. "I help Eman in all of his mendings."

"Eman?" I felt the familiarity of the name on my lips. "I thought he was just the Mender."

Sana laughed again, sounding like a little silver bell. "Mending is what he does. Eman is who he is. But he answers to each one the same."

I nodded, then followed her as we said goodbye to the

butterflies. Walking along, we returned to where the first hallway divided into four. Instead of taking me down the main corridor again, Sana turned down the one adjacent to the moss-covered one.

My mouth dropped open as I gawked at the difference between this hallway and the last. The trees were still arched as they had been before, but every few feet, the branches parted into peaked windows.

I gazed out the first window with wonder. A beautiful starry night stared back at me. The intricate balls of fire twinkled like diamonds against the soft black blanketing the sky. Feeling the slight pull of Sana's hand, I reluctantly walked away.

The next window held even more wonder. Soft waves of crystalline water flowed against the glass, trickling down to the edge of the frame. Small, yellow fish with purple spots swam into view. They darted up and down, then left and right, as if unable to decide which direction to go.

"What is all this?" I asked Sana, trying to take in everything from the other side of the window before I was pulled away again.

"Fene Luxus, or the Windows of Light. Some are from the Twelve Lands of Decim; others are from different realms. Eman often walks this hall to remind himself of why he mends."

I looked at her, waiting for an explanation.

Sana gave me a small smile before continuing.

"Mending hearts is not an easy task. It takes a toll on the one who is being mended as well as the mender. With every mending, a part of the mender is placed within the heart. It's what protects us from the darkness."

Maybe that was how I could hear Eman's voice in my head. But I hadn't always had a mended heart, and I'd been hearing him for a while. I wanted to ask Sana about it when a sullen look passed over her otherwise joyful face.

"There used to be many heartmenders within the realms."

"What happened?"

Sana let out a sigh and patted my hand with her free one. "There is much time to learn. Not everything needs to be known in one day."

I held back an irritated grunt and nodded politely. Sana seemed very sweet, and she had helped Eman put me back together again. But I wished everyone would stop being so cryptic and explain at least one thing I didn't know.

As if hearing my thoughts, Sana patted my hand again. "All in good time, Bellata."

I knitted my fingers together. I had heard that name before, but couldn't remember where. As I tried to concentrate, my gazed floated in the direction of the next window.

A cascade of trees stood tall, each one supporting the next as they grew from one another. The light shone through their leaves, glowing down upon a castle, more regal than anything I had read about. Rather than stone, the fortress was made from the trunks of the towering trees.

Releasing Sana's hand, I walked toward the window to get a better look at the breathtaking view.

Intricate corridors and archways created by branches swirled their way throughout the castle, forming small windows, where light poured through. Waterfalls descended from openings in the bark, creating a moat around the base of the trees. The water sparkled as it fell into different pools. I could almost taste its crispness on my lips.

"What is this place?" I whispered.

"We're in Ramni, the home for the wounded. That's Lignum, the home of the Rexus."

I frowned. First the Mender, now the Rexus? Who were all these people, and why hadn't I ever heard of them?

Sana looked over at the window with the same sullen face. "It's said that the Rexus will join forces with the Mender and defeat the Beast once and for all."

"Well," I began. "We know who the Mender is. Who's the Rexus?"

Sana shook her head, allowing some of the small flowers in her braid to come loose and float to the ground. "The Rexus is king over all the realms. He will return and bring peace. Unfortunately, a darkness descended upon this realm many millennia ago, stealing all other knowledge about the Rexus."

"You didn't write your knowledge down anywhere else?"

Sana gave me an empathetic look, reminding me of Claire in Ophidian's Realm—how she knew everything, and I was stupid.

"Our knowledge is not written but given," Sana stated.

I stretched my lips into a thin line.

Sana, noticing my irritation, let out a laugh. "My, you do emit strong emotions, just like he said." She took my hand again, and we continued walking down the hallway. "There is a place located within this realm where all knowledge of all the realms is placed. We don't know why or how, but the knowledge appears there. Sometimes in books, other times in scrolls. But one day, a book went missing. It was the only book we had on the prophecy of the Rexus."

I nodded, not having to ask who took the book. There was only one clothed in darkness I knew of who would want to prevent his own demise.

"What are you going to do?"

Sana let out a small sigh. "Wait."

"For what?"

"For the Rexus."

"But you don't know who he is." I tilted my head, making sure I understood.

"But we do know his mark," she said with a triumphant smile.

I thought back to the mark on the sword. That was the mark of the Mender, the same mark I now wore on my chest. But what was the mark of the Rexus?

"Only one man has been prophesied to bear the mark of the Rexus."

Sana lifted her hand and began drawing in the air. Small puffs of white escaped from her fingertips, creating a circle with a thin X through it.

"But," I said, staring at the symbol, "that was the mark on the door to the room Eman led me to."

"Yes, it was." A smirk came to her face. "Interesting, isn't it?"

I was about to hold Sana up by her tiny little arms and demand she tell me what was going on, when the sound of falling water trickled from ahead. Sana pulled me along until the hallway opened into a giant room.

Large, white trees surrounded us in an open circle. Their branches spread wide, creating a domed ceiling with their silver leaves. Through the spaces between the trees, beautifully clear water sparkled down into a shining pool.

"This is the Pool of Liqua. It will restore your body and mind to the state they were in before the Seven Choices."

I turned back to her. "Will I forget everything that happened?" Ophidian's Realm was horrible, but I never wanted to forget the strength I found there. Or the friends I had made.

Sana shook her head. "The darkness of Ophidian cannot be easily undone. I'm afraid you will remember all of it, but you will have peace in due time." Before I could ask any further questions, she gave me a small bow and tread to the hallway of the Windows of Light.

I frowned at her exit, thoughts and questions about this new realm still swirling around in my mind. I was ready to follow her down the corridor when the trickle of the pool behind me caught my ear once more. When I turned, the sparkling water beckoned me into its healing waves.

CHAPTER 40

*A*fter I had bathed in the pool, I dried off and dressed before entering the corridor of the Windows of Light once more. I studied Lignum in the distance. If the identity of the Rexus wasn't known, who was living there now? Or was it only a vacant castle, hiding away until the day its master came?

Fluttering footsteps approached, and I whirled around to see Sana standing with an armful of scrolls.

"I see you've enjoyed the pool."

I gave a nod and a smile, pressing my hands against the soft fabric of the tan dress that had been left at the edge of the water. Like Claire's gown, it had dark green leaves along the hem. I looked down, seeing the tips of my repaired boots peeking out from beneath the beautiful hem. "Yes, it was wonderful. Thank you."

"Did it answer any of your questions?"

My head shot up, and I frowned at her and shook my head. Was it supposed to?

Letting out a small sigh, she smiled again. "Oh, well, I'm sure all will be answered soon. Come, there is someone who wishes to speak with you."

My heart beat quicker, not with fear, but excitement from the thought of meeting another magical person from this realm.

Sana turned toward the hallway leading to the door with the mark of the Rexus.

I frowned at the door. "I still don't understand how this is my room."

Giving me a knowing grin, the healer nodded at the door, and it opened. The sound of the beautiful waterfall babbled throughout the spacious room, and I longed to walk inside. But before I did, I looked over at Sana.

"Unless . . ." My eyes grew wide.

"You are many things, Bellata. But you are not the Rexus," the gentle voice of Eman said with a chuckle as he stepped up beside Sana, a tattered brown text in his grip.

I frowned once more, slightly insulted. How could he know if I was the Rexus or not? He didn't even know who the Rexus was. Eman laughed heartily, and I could feel my cheeks redden.

"Thank you for your help, Sana," he said, bowing to the healer. Sana flushed slightly before returning the bow, mumbling about a new herb she needed to plant.

I gave her a quick nod of thanks before Eman glided over the threshold, motioning for me to follow.

My jovial steps soon ceased as I looked at the chairs Lyle and Claire had been sitting in. Their vacancy sent a sad pulse to my heart. I hadn't seen Lyle in seven years. Now that he was saved, I'd barely had a chance to talk to him.

Eman came toward me with an understanding smile before nodding toward the door. With a soft click, it closed behind me, and the heartmender extended his hand.

"Come, there is much you need to learn in such little time."

Reaching out, I grasped his rough hand and followed him to the base of the waterfall. I gasped when my sword materialized in the warm soil surrounding the pool of the falls.

Releasing my hand, the heartmender grasped the hilt and traced lines into the dirt floor with the tip of the blade. Careful not to disturb him, I tiptoed closer and saw a large circle with a thin X running through it like the mark of the Rexus. The only difference I saw was that one of the lines of the X was thicker than the other. He looked up at me and smiled before thrusting the sword into the ground. Not sure how to respond, I stared back at him.

"Come." He held out his hand once more.

I swallowed hard, hoping this wasn't a trap. As I stepped into the circle, the fluid from the waterfall traveled toward us, filling the deep grooves in the dirt. I stared down in awe as the water transformed from clear crystal to cerulean blue to a dark green, then a pale yellow, and finally a deep red.

Eman placed his hand on my shoulder, handing me the worn book he had been holding. Its binding was old and frail, as if the book had been used many times. I ran my fingers along the strange script burned into the front cover.

Scienta non sit nis en fide ver sit

"What does that mean?" I asked, not recognizing the language.

"'Knowledge is not but true belief,'" Eman replied.

I stared down at the phrase. Knowledge. The thing that had drawn us here: the constant desire to know everything. My mind flashed with images of Ophidian and the promise of Aeternam Scientia, as well as the cost. I shuddered at the thought. Yet the phrase before me felt different, like it wasn't pointing to Eternal Knowledge, but something else entirely.

"You can open it now," Eman said gently, motioning toward the book.

Biting my lip, I placed the book flat against my palms. I shifted its weight to one of my hands as the other peeled open the cover. Of its own volition, the brown cover jerked from my touch, landing on the cross section of the

X. The pages flipped furiously, as if a strong wind blew them. I shrank back, but Eman held me firm. When he snapped his fingers, the pages stopped.

A chill rushed down my spine as I remembered how Ophidian had used the same command for his black smoke.

Eman directed my attention to the pages. Written in a beautiful calligraphy, the book seemed to begin in the middle of a story rather than the beginning.

In the darkest of times, a Warrior will rise among them. Braided with the Sword and the Mallet, the Staff will complete the trio of almes, rendering light over dark.

I quirked a brow at the text, turning my gaze toward Eman. "Almes?"

Eman stared down at the pages as well. "An alme is a magical weapon, one that only those baring my mark can wield."

"Are there only three?"

Eman smiled. "There are only three that are powerful enough to defeat the darkness of Ophidian. But they must be used together." Leaning out of the circle, the heartmender pulled the sword from the ground. "This is one of the three almes. It was made by a very dear friend of mine, one who is not so different from you. Though it is not your own, it will assist you until your alme reveals itself to you."

My lips parted, but no words came out. What had the

book said? I read the writing again. A sword, a mallet, and a staff? I looked up at the sword that had come to me in Ophidian's Realm. If the sword was the young black-smith's, the only question now was: who was the young blacksmith?

A small gust of wind retreated from the book's pages again until the pages lay flat once more. A dark line scrawled across the page. However, instead of writing words, this one drew images. I leaned forward, recognizing the curved outline of one of the shapes.

"That's Barracks," I said quietly.

Surrounded by a sea of trees of Wintertide, then barri-caded by the tall Shalley Mountains, my home appeared before my eyes. Wintertide looked far thicker than I remembered, and the Shalley Mountains seemed to cast a shadow over our frigid land, warning others not to come near. I swallowed hard, realizing just how isolated we really were from the other Lands.

I parted my lips, another question forming, when the dark line continued across the pages. Straight and curved lines drew themselves, some intersecting with one another, some only connecting with themselves.

"Are these . . ." I murmured once the final line had finished.

Eman beckoned to the book, and it lifted from the ground, levitating a few inches from my face.

"The Twelve Lands were not always as you know them to be now, ravaged by bloodlust and greed," he said in a serious tone. "They used to trade with one another in harmony."

I was about to object, saying that we still traded with the other Lands, but the map caused me to pause. Everything I had learned about the other Lands was from Headmaster Clive, who had also told me that Ophidian wasn't real. I pursed my lips, realizing his knowledge about the other Lands was probably false as well.

Eman held up his hand. "Trading hearts was not customary many millennia ago."

"What happened?"

As the question left my lips, darkness filled one of the Twelve Lands on the page, breaking it away from the rest. Eman traced his finger along the dark lands, as if stroking a child.

"Darkness from another realm came, carrying the myth that a heart was only as valuable as its owner deemed it."

I looked to the dark island once known as Regno, floating alone within Patet, the ocean that surrounded the Twelve Lands.

"In Barracks, the myth evolved into what you know as Heart Reign. But in other Lands, the myth evolved into war and plagues."

I shuddered. "But isn't it true?"

"Yes, you are correct."

"About which part?"

"All of it." He gave me a solemn look. "The Traders, as

you call them, have the power to choose the value of their hearts. That is also the power of the myth: convincing a person that their heart is not valuable. If a heart is invaluable, it's a burden to its owner. And no one wants a burden."

I tried to break eye contact with him, hoping to hide the shame I felt for believing I was a burden to everyone around me. His brown eyes turned hard before softening once more.

"You've never been a burden, Addie. To anyone. And you have never been alone."

I swallowed the hard lump rising in my throat, finally accepting that it was Eman all along who had been speaking to me in Ophidian's Realm. He was the one who had encouraged me to run when I wanted to quit. He was the one who had told me I wasn't alone. Now I finally knew he was right. Eman had been trying to help me survive the Seven Choices the entire time.

Unsure of whether I was allowed to hug the powerful heartmender or not, I reached forward and wrapped my arms around his waist anyway. Eman's strong arms returned the favor.

"You are stronger than you believe," he said, releasing me. "That is why your journey is just beginning."

CHAPTER 41

"What?" I asked, wiping away the small trickle of tears that rolled down my cheeks.

Grasping the levitating book in his hand, Eman pushed it toward me. My eyes landed on the shadowed island. The darkness had begun spreading in splotches toward the other Lands.

I moved my gaze to Barracks to see that, while the other Lands had patches of darkness within them, Barracks was covered in a gray hue, stretching from one end to the other.

"There used to be a time when all hearts were mended." Eman looked above my head, lost in thought. "The Lands of Decim were lush, and the people loved. Everything was perfect."

He sighed. "I knew something was wrong when small

battles broke out in Regno. I gathered the other Elders to try to convince them to send additional Magisters there, but they refused, saying I wasn't wise enough to know such things." Eman ran his fingers along the dark island again. "Look where their knowledge got them."

I breathed quietly, trying to not interrupt.

"Ophidian struck swiftly and efficiently, creating monsters that were intelligent as well as deadly."

"The malum." I had thought the malum were a new creation of Ophidian's, something he had recently discovered. But, once again, I had been fooled by the Beast; he had been using them for centuries.

Eman nodded, his lips stretching into a tight line. "The malum have all knowledge of your realm, this realm, and Ophidian's Realm. They are a deadly force that won't hesitate to destroy anything. I fear for what will happen if Ophidian begins creating his other creatures." Shaking his head, he closed the book. The water near our feet trickled back to the waterfall, erasing the symbol he had drawn. "Only the bonding of the Twelve Magisters and the leadership of the Rexus can destroy Ophidian's darkness. There is a Magister for each Land of Decim who has sworn to protect their land from darkness. They have known this day would come and have begun preparing for battle. Without them, darkness will overtake all the realms, starting with Decim."

My mind spun with all the new information, and I

took a step back. Magisters? Rexus? Battle? My new heart started beating harder.

"But where do I fit into all of this? I'm just a girl from Barracks. I didn't ask for a pure heart."

Eman extended the book toward me with a serious face, and I knew to take it. "You weren't given your pure heart. You created it. Did you ever wonder why only you noticed Schism's deception? Or the cold that covered Barracks when he arrived?"

Before I could ask what he meant, a flash of memories spiraled through my mind: my younger self, trying to stop Lyle from trading his heart to Schism; meeting Silas by my favorite birch tree along Wintertide; reading to Nana on a cold night by the fire; laughing as Silas and I played chess; finding Lyle's sweater in my house. And each and every one of the Choices I had overcome. I blinked, trying to understand what it all meant.

"When you could have run from the pain, you embraced it and changed it into something better. Everyone has a choice. Where many chose to hate, you chose to love. Where many chose to run from their fears, you chose to overcome them."

I clutched the book to my chest, feeling the strong, steady palpitations of my new heart. "That's why I could still feel without my heart?"

Eman nodded. "The power you wield is stronger than any I have seen in centuries. Even with help, hardly any have survived through half of Ophidian's Choices.

"Because you were willing to sacrifice your heart, you were given the same gift: a chance at another choice." Taking a step forward, he presented the sword to me. "Here is the next choice. Once you take this sword, you make an iuram, a binding oath only broken by death, to bring the Twelve Magisters together. You and only you can complete this task."

Feeling the weight of the realms on my shoulders, I looked down. The blade of the sword glowed a faint orange, a color I hadn't seen on it before. I didn't have to grasp the hilt to feel its power. It was as if my heart was reaching out to it, and the sword reached back with a familiarity I wanted to explore.

I didn't waver on this choice. I didn't know what would happen, but I knew what my heart felt. Accepting it, I grabbed the hilt. A white light folded itself around my hand and the hilt of the sword, and, as I handed the book back to Eman, I knew I had destined myself to another journey.

The thought of the young blacksmith rose in my thoughts. I had made a promise to try to help him, too. Once this was all over, I would.

The white light disappeared as the orange glow escaped the sword and traveled up my fingertips, causing me to feel stronger than ever before.

Eman watched me closely before walking to the door, holding the book at his side. "Come, there is much to do for your departure."

a large pond, shimmering and shining in the golden sunlight, rippled before us. Bright purple water lilies danced on its surface as its waves gently rocked them back and forth. Tall weeping willows and long, smooth grass surrounded the perimeter, making the scenery the definition of peaceful.

Beyond the pond, ancient stone steps covered in delicate moss and hanging ferns ascended until they reached a landing that split into three rising directions: one left, one right, and one up the center. At the top of the stairs, on the landing, stood four figures. Worry gripped my heart, as I couldn't ignore those who waited.

Without hesitation, Eman continued toward the pond. When I faltered, he turned around with his soft smile and motioned for me to follow. But I paused instead.

"Eman," I started, then stopped, looking down at the mystical sword as I tried to find the right words to say. "I don't know where I'm going or what I'm doing."

The heartmender took the satchel he was carrying and handed it to me with a gleam in his eyes. "You will encounter much on your journey, but you are well prepared."

Raising my brows, I took the satchel and opened it to find various jars filled with herbs and salves. Tucked beside them was the tattered book he had shown me. I pursed my lips.

"This is all I need?"

Eman grinned, reaching forward to secure the flap over the satchel. "Yes."

"That's it?"

He nudged the bag toward me once more with an amused smirk. "That's it."

Reluctantly, I took the satchel and put the strap over my head so that it ran across my chest as Eman turned back to the pond.

Round, gray stones rose up from its waters, creating a path for us to walk on. While the heartmender glided smoothly across the stones, I struggled to keep my balance on the slick surfaces, praying I wouldn't fall.

As I hopped off the final stone, Eman extended his hand, catching me before I tripped. He offered me his kind smile.

"Thank you," I said, standing straight. "For everything."

He didn't respond, only studied me before continuing on.

We ascended the steps until we reached the landing. Four sets of eyes watched me, and I turned toward them, gripping the strap of the satchel hard. Sana was first, wearing a small smile and carrying a bundle of clothes. I instantly recognized Lyle's sweater and yearned to feel its security once more.

"I thought you would need these when you traveled back to your realm," she said softly. Walking to me, her feet fluttered across the stone, creating the pitter-patter I had gotten used to. Her bright green eyes filled with tears as she passed me the sweater and black pants. Latching her petite arms around my neck, she whispered, "I believe in you, Bellata."

I clasped one arm around her small waist, then released her. She sniffled once before standing next to Eman, who wrapped one arm around her shoulders.

"Are you coming with me?" I asked the heartmender.

A solemn look passed over his face as he shook his head. "I can't leave Ramni when Ophidian's forces are running rampant throughout the realms."

"Throughout the realms?" I repeated, knowing Ophidian would try to find the halves of my heart, which now belonged to Lyle and Claire. My new heart quivered in my chest at the thought of the Beast scouring Barracks to find them. What if he found Nana and Silas, too?

"Addie, do you believe you can do this?" Eman asked, interrupting my thoughts.

"What?"

He wrapped his large, calloused hands around my small ones, which gripped the sword. "Do you truly believe you can do this? Unite the Twelve Magisters against Ophidian?"

My eyes met his with uncertainty before I understood what he was saying. The script in the book stood clearly in my mind: *Knowledge is but true belief.* If I believed I could do this, then I knew I wouldn't fail. But that was the problem. I wasn't sure if I believed in myself.

Before I could either shake my head or nod, I felt the palpitations of my new heart grow stronger. Each pump felt like my heart was filling my veins with something new, something powerful. I looked down to see my hands begin to glow around the hilt of the sword, shining the same orange as the sword had.

"Trust your heart, Addie. It already knows your power. You only need to believe in it."

Eman released me from his grasp with a firm nod before leading me to Claire.

Though her gown was elegant and her hair done beautifully, the scowl on Claire's face assured me she wasn't happy. She crossed her arms, furrowing her brows as she walked toward me.

"So," I said. "I guess you're not coming with me."

She snorted. "Not by my choice."

I looked over my shoulder at Eman.

"Though you saved her with your heart, we still don't know who possesses Claire's original heart. Without it securely within her, Ophidian can easily take her once more if she leaves Ramni."

I nodded. "Protect those who are here?"

He gave a small smile and tightened his arm around Sana's shoulders.

Looking back at Claire, I sighed. "Who's going to patch me up when you're not there?"

Claire tried to scoff, but a smirk interrupted her expression as a tear gathered at the corner of her eye. "If you die, I'll never forgive you."

I laughed.

"Plus," she continued, "I asked the Mender to make you some of your favorite green salve. It's in the orange container."

I rifled through the satchel until I found the bright orange bottle. I squeezed it tightly before placing it carefully back inside. "Thank you."

Claire uncrossed her arms and pulled me into a hug.

"Please don't be stupid, Addie," she whispered before releasing me.

I gave her a nod, trying to hold back the tears welling in my own eyes. Claire took a step back, leading my gaze to the next figure in line.

Cleaned and fed, Lyle almost looked like his old self again. But as he met my eyes, I could still see the darkness lurking inside him. Ophidian still had his heart.

"Not coming?" I asked with a playful smile and a tug on the satchel.

Lyle shook his head, his brown curls bouncing. Then, in one fluid motion, he rushed to me, scooping me up. His arms were weak but warm. I held him close, hugging him as tightly as I could.

After a few moments, we released each other, and Lyle straightened his spectacles before gathering my hands in his own. He squeezed them, allowing his gaze to shift to mine, as if he was trying to decide what to say. I gave him a weak smile and began to pull free from his grasp. I didn't want this to be more difficult than it had to be. He quickly clamped down harder on my hands.

"Addie, I'm so sorry," he said, hanging his head.

Seeing Lyle so humbled and broken was more than I could bear. Giving his hands a squeeze, I murmured, "It's okay, Lyle. I found you. And Eman will take care of you until I return." I began to pull away again.

"Wait!" he yelled as he snapped his head up, making everyone jump. His spectacles slid to the edge of his nose from the force. "There's, there's a book. A book I found."

"What?"

Lyle hung his head once more, running a hand through his hair.

"It said something." He pushed his palms onto his forehead. "Something important. I can't remember." He hit his head, grunting, until Claire grabbed both of his hands, pinning them to his sides.

My new heart filled with sorrow as I watched Claire lock her arms around Lyle, trying to stop him from hurting himself. He struggled ferociously within her grasp, telling her to let go of him, but she held strong.

"*They are more connected now,*" the voice said in my head.

I glanced at Eman, who was watching the scene as well.

"*Not only was she his light in the darkness, they also share a piece of you,*" his voice continued. "*They still have a long way to go.*"

Turning back, I saw Lyle standing still, watching Claire study him intently before she straightened his spectacles.

Once he was calm, Lyle walked slowly toward me. "I'm going to try to remember, Addie."

"It's okay if you don't," I said, holding back more tears. "Not right away, at least."

"There is one thing I do remember," he said, placing his hand on his head. I watched Claire tense up, ready to restrain him again, but Lyle simply scratched his temple and lowered his hand. "Before I traded my heart, I was looking for something."

"What?"

Lyle shook his head. "It wasn't a thing, but information. Something about our parents." His eyes grew wide with remembrance and horror. "Addie, he killed them. I know he did it," he whimpered. "They didn't just die; they were murdered."

Tears began to stream down his face as he plummeted to the ground, pounding the stone in frustration. Before anyone could react, I dropped to my knees and wrapped my arms around him, remembering the note with our father's handwriting: *Take care of her.* Lyle had been taking care of me by trying to find out what had happened to our parents.

It was devastating to see my confident, intelligent, fearless brother reduced to this broken being. I soon felt two arms around Lyle and me, and I looked up to see Claire holding both of us. Before long, a large, rough hand

and a small, smooth one grasped my shoulders as I held my sobbing brother.

Once he quieted, sunk into our arms. I released Lyle to Claire, mulling over Lyle's revelation. I had always thought the death of our parents was a little suspicious. Whenever I had asked about it, everyone was always vague, saying they were in a better place now. But they never said what had happened.

Logging that information away for later, I placed a kiss on Lyle's shaking head before I turned back to the final figure.

"Addie," Eman said, walking over to me. "You were wondering about who the Magisters are." He motioned to the final figure. "So, I decided to allow one to go with you."

My breath caught in my throat as I looked upon the man from the sixth Choice. He gave me a weak smile before looking hesitantly at Eman. Eman gave him a firm nod before proceeding.

"This is James. He is one of the Twelve Magisters. Among them, he is known as Dimitte. He will assist you on your journey to find the other eleven, each bearing the same mark as his."

I gave James an approving glance as I remembered the extra line through his mark and the way he had protected us from Ophidian back in Ofavemore.

Eman walked up to him and placed his hand on James' shoulder. "Although he chose the darkness before, all that matters is that he chose the light again."

I gave a nod in agreement, feeling a greater familiarity about the man as I smiled. I was thankful that I wouldn't be beginning my next journey alone.

"You'll return here," Eman assured me. "I don't know when. Time flows differently between the realms, but I know we will meet again soon."

"How will I get back here?"

"A door will always open," Eman said, looking down at me. "But you must choose to knock." He walked past me and waited on the bottom step of the central staircase.

Preparing my new heart, I walked over to Lyle and Claire. Lyle was seated on the ground, his hands clutching his knees, his brow furrowed in concentration. It pained me to see him in such a state. I hoped, in time, that my heart would help him heal from the darkness within.

"Take care of him," I said to Claire.

Looking up, she gave me a partial smile. "Don't be stupid. Of course, I will. Even if he never remembers me."

I bit my lip and turned away before more tears spilled down my cheeks. Taking a few steps toward Sana, I gave her another nod of thanks before turning back to Eman and James, who stood waiting for me.

With one last glance, I rushed toward them before I could change my mind. James gave me a sad smile while Eman motioned me up the stairs. A large, peaked door made of white wood appeared at the top of the central staircase.

As my feet pounded against each step, my heart

thumped a little softer, feeling the weight of all that had happened in Ophidian's Realm, the anticipation of what was to come next, and the pain of once more leaving what I loved behind.

I gripped my satchel's strap as I took the final step onto the landing before reaching the frosted door. Eman and James stood on either side of me.

"Don't fret, Bellata. All will be well soon." Eman gave me a sincere smile.

"Bellata," I murmured. "What does that mean?"

"'Warrior'," James replied with a firm nod. "It means 'warrior'."

I frowned at the definition as Eman reached forward and knocked on the door. In a matter of moments, it swung open, revealing a shimmer of white and gold light streaked with lines of blue and pink.

"Not all doors lead to darkness," Eman repeated as he looked at the swirling lights.

James shot a thankful nod to Eman before proceeding through the door. I was about to follow when I felt a rough hand on my shoulder. Turning back, I saw Eman holding a small purple bag tied shut with a golden cord.

"This will help you on your journey," he said, handing me the bag.

"What is it?" I stared curiously as the little bag was placed in my palm. It was light and somehow familiar.

"You'll know what to do with it when the right time comes."

I frowned again at yet another one of his cryptic statements, and he laughed.

"You'll be fine. And remember" —he patted his chest where his own heart lay— "you are not alone."

I gave him a nod, confident that this would not be the last time we would meet.

Taking a deep breath, I turned toward the glowing light. After all the doors of darkness I had traveled through, it should be easy to pass through this one. Yet, knowing Governor Willow was the one who had been behind everything in Barracks, and that the vendors had really been working for Ophidian, I didn't know what was waiting for me on the other side.

I placed the purple bag inside the satchel and ignored the fears attempting to scare me from my next journey. Clutching the strap draped across my chest, I walked into the light.

AUTHOR'S NOTE

Though the events within *Heartmender* are fiction, the symbolism behind them is very real to teens and adults alike. The reader (you!) enters Addie's realm, where the human heart is the main form of currency. Throughout the story, we learn that the heart is the essence of what makes a human *human*, and without it, they are nothing but an empty shell. In relation to modern society, every day, we are bombarded with different ideals (wealth, power, vanity, etc.) that insist on convincing us of their truth. Many accept these ideals as truth and "trade" themselves away to them. Yet, like in *Heartmender*, over time the trade leaves the individual hollow and unable to live the life God planned for them.

The central conflict of Addie's journey is to save her brother, Lyle, who traded his heart for an unknown choice during his Heart Reign. She later discovers that the unknown choice leads to Ophidian's Realm, where she must battle through each of the Seven Choices to find Lyle. Heart Reign (the unknown choice) and the Seven Choices symbolize humanity's free will. Each citizen of Barracks may choose to trade their heart for whatever they desire. But Schism tempts them with an unknown choice, something that the citizens of Barracks have never experienced before. Once they choose the first choice, they are thrown into seven more Choices. At the end of each Choice, they must decide whether they want to stay in the current Choice, or continue on to the next choice. Similarly, we are given choices throughout our daily lives and must decide which doors we are going to walk through or keep shut.

When Addie first enters Ophidian's Realm, she is guided by a light that only shines a few feet before her. This light represents our steps in our journey with Christ. Though we wish for miles of light to show us the way, more often than not, we are only given a few feet and must trust that we will gain more clarity as we continue moving forward. This is also represented by Claire's lantern throughout the Choices.

As Addie approaches each of the Choices, many readers might acknowledge that each door she faces depicts one of the seven deadly sins. Beginning with slothfulness, or laziness, the doors are represented by a color and an animal on its corresponding key:

· Slothfulness, sky-blue, goat

· Greed, yellow, frog

· Wrath, red, bear

· Lust, royal blue, snake

· Gluttony, orange, pig

· Envy, green, dog

· Pride, violet, lion

Each one of these seven deadly sins is amplified to their worst level to depict their severity.

Throughout Addie's battle through the Seven Choices, she hears the phrase, "Run, Addie, run," over and over again. Each time, it is meant as a warning for Addie not to stay where she is, but to keep going and flee from the temptation, or Choice, she is in. In some instances, it is yelled, whereas in others, it is only whispered. These warnings symbolize how God speaks to us throughout our lives. Sometimes His voice is a loud shout, and other times, it is a soft whisper. Regardless, we should always be listening.

Once she is through the Final Choice, Addie learns that each Trader who has made it through the Choice must make the Final Choice of accepting Eternal Knowledge from Ophidian. But, in choosing Eternal Knowledge, each Trader becomes a monster known as the malum. Knowledge was chosen to be the theme of pride for the Seventh Choice because that was man's first downfall. Eve desired to know everything that God knew, which was how Satan convinced her to take fruit from the tree of the knowledge of good and evil. Since then, humanity has always desired to gain more knowledge so that they may reach a "god-like" status and be in control. Those who accept Ophidian's Eternal Knowledge turn into malum, which symbolizes that we, as humans, are unable to handle vast amounts of knowledge of the spiritual realm. Like Adam and Eve realizing they were naked and would eventually die, the acceptance of Ophidian's Eternal Knowledge does the same. But instead of dying, some people become a terrifying monster controlled by Ophidian.

When Addie awakens in Ramni, the realm of healing, she learns that while Ophidian's abuse of knowledge is evil, knowledge, in itself, is not. Some believe that having knowledge is "bad," but it is not our intelligence or knowledge that is our downfall, but how and why we use it that defines our character.

One of the most important themes throughout *Heartmender* is Addie's constant race throughout the Seven Choices. This over-arching symbolism is also an allegory for the race we run throughout our own lives. Sometimes in life, we are like Addie at Heart Reign: ready to run into the unknown, no matter the consequences. Other times, we are like Addie within the Choices: confused, tired, and ready to give up. Regardless of what point you are at in your own life, there is always hope. Hebrews 12:1 states: "Therefore we also, since we are surrounded by so great a cloud of witnesses, let us lay aside every weight, and the sin which so easily ensnares us, and let us run with endurance the race that is set before us." Like Addie's race, there will be fears, monsters, and obstacles in our lives. But, as we read at the end of *Heartmender*, the darkness only lasts so long before the light. In Addie's realm, that light is the Mender. In ours, it is Jesus Christ. Whether you are running your race confidently and swiftly, or you are stumbling with each step, trying to catch your breath, remember that it doesn't matter how you begin your race, but how you finish it.

ACKNOWLEDGMENTS

I would first and foremost like to thank Jesus Christ, my Savior, for this amazing opportunity I never saw coming. I am so thankful for this story and the many blessings He has given me!

A big thanks to my family, who have always lifted me up so I can reach the stars: Momma (Nana), for instilling a love for reading in me at a young age. Daddy (Paw Paw), for always funding my dreams and cheering me on. Lauren, for drawing my first map of the Twelve Lands of Decim when all I gave you was a lined piece of paper with some triangles labeled "mountains." And Steph and Jake for always hanging out with me when I would write.

David, even though I had finished an early (and very rough) draft of *Heartmender* before we met, you still read and loved it in our early dating days. You are not only an amazing husband and father but my best friend who I can nerd out with and have no fear of judgment. Thank you for never clipping my wings and always encouraging me to soar.

Matthew, thank you for making me a mommy, for

keeping me on my toes, and for helping me to become more efficient than I ever thought I could be.

Thank you to the Burton clan for your encouragement, excitement, and support.

My college squad! Thank you for reading numerous drafts and still loving everyone. I couldn't have made it this far without your encouragement, love, and support.

Lydia, thank you for instantly falling in love with my characters and their stories. I so appreciate all your editing help!

My twelfth grade English teacher, Mrs. Zeek, you were the first teacher who taught me how to write and how to do it well. I will never forget your dedication to your students and their education.

A final thanks to everyone else in my life who has loved, supported, encouraged, and prayed for me throughout this journey. I couldn't have done it without you!

ABOUT THE AUTHOR

V. Romas Burton grew up bouncing up and down the East Coast, where she wrote her first story about magical ponies at age seven. Years later, after studying government and earning an M.A. in Theological Studies, V. Romas Burton realized something even bigger was calling out to her-stories that contained great adventures and encouraging messages. Because she couldn't find exactly what she was looking for, V. Romas Burton decided to write her own great adventure. When she's not writing, she spends time reading as many books as she can, watching YouTube videos, and taking care of her adorable son. *Heartmender* is her debut novel. You can visit her online at www.vromasburton.com

HEARTBREAKER

CHAPTER 1

The cold breeze slapped me in the face, and I welcomed it as an old friend. Goosebumps popped from my arms, which were thinly covered by the fabric of the tan dress I had received by the Pool of Liqua. I let out a shiver as the wind beat against my exposed neck, blowing my short locks from their braids.

Home. I could hardly wait to find Nana and Silas and tell them everything that had happened. I could practically see them as I looked around, expecting their blank faces to greet me. But as I scanned the horizon, my heart dropped at the unfamiliar sight.

The field was covered with dark, dirty ice. While there had always been ice around Barracks, it had never been filthy. A thick, dark coating covered the trees as well. The sky was darker, dense with charcoal clouds. Worry rose in my chest. This was not the Barracks I had left.

Leaving the warmth of the white door, I stepped onto the mud-streaked ice, my foot sliding a bit from its fickle foundation. Frowning at my surroundings, I unwrapped Lyle's sweater from the bundle and pulled it over my head. The warmth of it cocooned my skin in remembrance of what I had been through and how I had changed for the better.

With the satchel secured under the sweater, I placed the additional shirt and pants Sana had given me within the satchel and looked to James, who was staring out at the landscape of Barracks. His eyes were soft, drinking in the icy land, and the downturn of his lips deepened.

"It wasn't always like this," I said.

"I know," he replied gruffly, letting out a raspy cough before cutting his eyes to me. "It was my home, too."

"Oh." I had wondered which Land he was the Magister of.

"We should probably take a look around," he continued as he adjusted the pack on his shoulder. He started trudging through the thick snow.

I nodded before following. The layer of ice on top of the snow crunched beneath our feet, echoing against the eerie silence.

James' head turned from left to right every few steps he took, analyzing the state of his former home. Barracks was probably still a fruitful land of happiness and warmth when he was last here. Unfortunately, that Land was long gone.

Taking a few strides, I caught up to him. He breathed in deeply, allowing the air to trickle slowly from his mouth. I was curious about this strange, quiet man who had agreed to accompany me on an unknown journey.

"So, a Magister?" I asked, hoping to relax the harsh line of his brow as he looked ahead.

James grunted as he shook his head, keeping his ice-blue eyes focused forward. The market was just coming into view. "It's a position of honor bestowed upon those who have mastered the way of the Mender." He tapped his chest, where the mark of the Mender was carved.

"Is that what that extra line means? That you're a Magister?"

He nodded. "Eman is an ancient creature, knowledge-able in the oldest of magics. When darkness first descended from Regno, he chose one Magister from each of the Lands to protect and defend them. I was the Magister for Barracks."

I sucked in a breath as we stepped into the thick mud the filthy ice had changed into. I wasn't sure whether to ask how Ophidian had entered Barracks so easily. Luckily, James explained without much prompting.

"It was my job. And I failed." He whispered these words so quietly, I could barely hear them.

My new heart beat with empathy for James, knowing that he had been carrying that burden for many years. Swallowing hard, I stopped and turned toward him.

"Yes, you did." He winced at my words. "But that's in

the past now," I said, remembering what Eman had said before. "Everything that happened in the past can't be changed. What matters is what we do now." Pulling out the sword, I held it out to him in imitation of Eman, offering the hilt. "Are you willing to help me bring the Twelve Magisters together to stop Ophidian?"

I had been filled with fear and anxiety for years, allowing everything in the past to torment me. The sorrow and pain I had felt would always be with me, but I would no longer allow it to control me. I wouldn't be fighting the coming battle alone, and neither would James.

He studied me carefully, rubbing his hand over his chin before reaching toward the hilt. As soon as his large fingers encased my own, a line of cool, white light wrapped around our hands, twisting in on itself until an intricate knot was formed. As soon as it was tied, the light dissipated from the air, sprinkling to the ice below.

"An iuram," James said with fascination, looking down at our hands. "It's been many years since I've seen one made."

"Eman showed me," I replied, remembering how the heartmender had offered me the choice in uniting the Twelve Magisters to defeat Ophidian.

"It is a powerful oath," James continued, flexing his fingers. "Not many can bind another to an iuram without the use of strong magic."

He looked at me the same way Eman had, as if seeing

something more than what was there. As the final light faded, we broke apart.

"I am bound to my oath to you, Bellata," James said, bowing on one knee. "I will fight with you until the end."

I bent my fingers a few times, still feeling the power rushing straight through them to my heart. I nodded, unsure of how else to respond. James stood and brushed the grime off his slacks before we continued to the market.

A fierce wind erupted, spewing debris against our already-frozen faces. We both held up our arms to shield our faces. Hunching forward, we fought against the strength of it as we marched through the slick terrain. I didn't remember the air being so thick or strong.

As we reached the opening of the market, my eyes widened despite the wind, studying the scene. It was nothing like the vivacious place it had been before. Displays were knocked over, broken beyond repair, with holes tearing through their fabric roofs. Countless items were sprawled, tattered and broken, along the street.

The air smelled of ice, but a repulsive stench lurked beneath it. I wrinkled my nose and continued.

"What happened?"

James shook his head, his eyes narrowed, as he continued to scan the market.

I took a step to investigate when something soft squished beneath my foot. Red mush from rotten fruit stained the filthy ground crimson as a horrid smell secreted from its opened skin. Scrunching my nose in disgust, I wiped the mess off my boot in a nearby snowbank. The destroyed displays and rotting food were disturbing enough, but where was everyone?

A door slammed at the far end of the market, and my heart jumped. Maybe I could find someone to tell me what had happened. I rushed toward the sound, careful to avoid the wooden remains of the displays scattered throughout the path. The door slammed again, and my gaze landed upon Doctor Magnum's office. My mind swirled with the memories of when I was last here. I placed my hand over my new heart, assuring it that it would never be extracted like my last one.

Maneuvering around a large display that had once held valuable paints, I made my way to the slamming door. Disappointment weighed on me as I placed my hand on the door and found the culprit to be nothing but the wind.

Walking into the familiar office, I shut the door behind me. The patients' chairs were either destroyed or missing entirely. Strands of shredded newspaper lay all over the floor, muddied and crumpled. I let out a sad sigh, remembering how tidy Doctor Magnum had kept everything. At least the sterile smell of the office kept out the putrid scents from outside.

I was about to leave when a glint of color beneath a sheet of newspaper caught my eye. Grabbing the hilt of the sword, I dragged its tip along the page and gasped.

Large, blotched letters scrawled across it: RUN. The end of the *n* whipped to the right, as if the person writing it had been dragged away before he could finish. An unsettled feeling fell on my heart, and I shivered.

"Addie!" James called from outside the office.

"In here!" I yelled, still staring at the word.

Crouching down, I ran my finger along the letters. They had been dry for a while, but I knew this dull red-brown wasn't cherry filling. The feeling in my stomach grew into a nauseating knot in my throat that I forced myself to swallow.

James's footsteps stopped behind me as he looked over my shoulder. A grunt came from his throat before I heard his footsteps retreat outside.

I narrowed my eyes at the letters and traced them once more. "What happened, Doctor Magnum?"

Moving more of the newspapers out of the way, I found my answer. Five long claw marks were etched into the hard floor. Fear gripped my heart, and I swallowed hard, realizing what had happened.

Standing abruptly, I walked out of Doctor Magnum's office to find James. With his back turned to me, he stared in the direction of Nana's house.

"James," I said, causing him to turn around. "Ophidian was here. Or, at least, the siti were."

James nodded thoughtfully before turning back toward Wintertide. I followed his line of sight, confusion threading through my heart. Had he known Nana?

"Is there someone you'd like to see?" I asked, the intrigue of the Magister growing with each second he didn't answer.

"There's someone I've been wanting to see for a long time," he replied with a grunt. Adjusting his pack once more, James marched through the broken displays of Heart Reign toward my grandmother's house.

Excitement bubbled in my chest as I bounded through the debris to catch up with him. My mind reached back to the memory of Nana's journal and the man who had brought her extracted heart back. Could James be him?

The ice cracked beneath our feet as we stopped in front of Nana's old house. It looked older and more worn than I remembered. Patches of shingles from the roof had fallen to the ground, and the shutters were askew or missing completely. I held back my worry, praying that what I thought wasn't true.

James froze, his eyes wide. He opened his mouth, but no words came out, not even a cough or a wheeze.

I placed my hand on his shoulder before sliding past him and up the wooden stairs, enjoying the familiarity of their creaking. I soon heard more creaking coming from behind me as James followed.

Once we reached the porch, we both stared at the wooden door. Giant claw marks had sliced through it, leaving five long gouges in the wood.

Holding the sword high, I tested the knob. The door slowly swung in, sending all my senses on edge.

The floorboards creaked beneath my feet as I walked through Nana's house. It was vacant, as if no one had been here in ages. The furniture was in disarray: chairs, tables, bookshelves all broken or shredded. Claw marks had punctured everything. All the windows were broken, leaving shards of glass scattered over the floor. My new heart ached at the sight of the destruction. If this was what the siti had done to the house, what had they done to Nana and Silas?

James began to wander through the rooms as if in a daze, picking up things and turning them right side up. I decided to let him be.

Still gripping the sword, I was about to check the kitchen when a rustling came from Nana's living room. I sucked in a quick breath, fear tensing my muscles. I knew James had stopped moving, along with the rustling. As light as I could, I tiptoed toward the living room.

My breathing became soft, my pulse racing faster. The only sound was the saliva running down my throat as I swallowed my nerves. The rustling sounded once more, only to stop again when I did. I'd learned how the siti attacked. This was no siti.

Bracing myself against the nearest wall, I closed my eyes and listened to all that was around me. Ophidian could have created any number of creatures to stay in Barracks. Eman had said he could make more.

Or I could be paranoid, and it could be a small animal looking for food. Either way, I was going to find out.

Taking a deep breath, I tightened my grip on the hilt once more. In one solid move, I jumped out from behind the wall with sword held high, only to hear the clanging of metal against metal.

Opening my eyes, I watched as the sword clashed against Nana's long, iron fire poker. My eyes followed the line of the iron to the hand holding it, then up the arm to the ferocious face staring back at me. I let out a gasp as the hand released the poker, sending it to the ground with a clang.

"Addie?" Silas asked, his face softening from anger to disbelief.

Before I could respond, two strong arms wrapped around me so tightly, I could barely breathe. The sword dropped from my grip as my body turned rigid against his. Could he really be real?

Silas released me from his grasp before his rough hand cupped my face. I was frozen, unable to move. I didn't realize what my reaction was until I saw his furrowed brows.

"Addie," he breathed again, lowering his hand as he studied me.

I stared up at him, unblinking, as confusion and turmoil ran through my heart.

Steady Silas looked at me with a crooked smile on his lips: the beautiful, crooked smile I had seen in Ophidian's Realm. But it wasn't real there.

"I thought I lost you," he said softly when I said nothing.

My heart was torn between the Choices and right now. Too many emotions and thoughts swirled within me. It was better not to speak. I shook my head, sending my short curls sprawling.

His crooked smile morphed into a frown, but he didn't move from his position. "What happened to your hair?"

I tried to speak again but failed, choosing to look away instead. I couldn't tell Silas of the shame I felt from Ophidian's Realm. From every door I had received a mark, a scar of what had happened there. Though not all of them could be physically seen, they were all still fresh and easily torn open. I had cut my hair to be rid of my greed, but the burns on my skin, although healed, were still aflame beneath my flesh, reminding me of the horrid blue door.

"I know it looks bad," I finally said, refusing to look at him as the memories of the beautiful blonde woman he had been with whipped through my mind.

Silas took a small step forward. "No, it looks beautiful. You always look beautiful."

My heart beat faster at his words, softening against the torturous memories. What was happening? Was this all a dream, another trick? Silas would never say things like that.

I began to conjure some sort of response when Silas leaned forward and slowly reached for my hand. I didn't help or stop him but allowed him to bring my hand to his lips. I expected a burning sensation to singe my flesh, but it didn't. Instead, a soft, warm flutter danced on my skin and went straight to my heart, enveloping it with comfort and peace.

For a moment, the memories fled, allowing me to look at Silas as he released my hand. His tall stature and strong muscles. His handsome face and tousled hair. I let out a small gasp as I finally noticed the three red lines etched into his skin from his forehead to his neck. I knew these scratches were from the siti. But how Silas managed to still be alive, I had no idea.

I frowned as I looked up at him. "Silas, what happened?"

He began to open his mouth in response when wheels rolled along the old wooden floor.

"Addie?" a withered voice asked.

I spun around, my eyes locking onto Nana. My heart wanted to crack at the sight of her, because it was my fault. Nana's thin white hair was thinner than it had ever been, displaying the pale skin of her scalp. Her arms and legs were corpselike, looking as if they would break with one movement.

A fresh batch of tears welled up in my eyes and rolled down my cheeks as I rushed toward her. She extended her arms with a weak smile, beckoning me closer.

"I'm so sorry, Nana," I cried as I fell to the ground, clutching her old, tattered skirt.

"Shhh, child. There's nothing to apologize for." She stroked my hair, sending waves of comfort through my body. It was as if the curse of Barracks was lifting, allowing people to feel again.

Everything that had happened rushed through my head at once, but the only thing I could get through my lips was, "I found Lyle."

Nana let out a gasp. Before I could explain, soft steps against the creaking wood entered the room. I looked over my shoulder to see James standing in the doorway. He fiddled with the hem of his shirt, as if he were scared to come closer. A cry of shock, pain, and relief came from Nana's mouth, causing me to jump up in surprise as she began to weep at the sight of him. My head whipped from Nana to James as he rushed to her, plummeting to his knees before taking her hands in his.

"Anna." He kissed her old hands. "Will you ever forgive me?"

Nana was too overcome by emotion to respond but gave a nod, and James wrapped his arms tightly around her.

I opened my mouth to ask a question, but closed it, unable to form the right words. Was James the man from Nana's journal? He had to be.

"Addie," James said gruffly, standing from his position beside Nana's chair. Though his voice was hoarse, his eyes were lit with something new and alive. "Eman thought it best not to give you too much information at once."

"But," Nana cut in softly, taking James' thick hand in her own frail one. "James is my husband, your grandfather."

I blinked a few times, looking from James to Nana, then back to James. There had always been something familiar about him. "How long have you known?"

"Since the first time I saw you in the sixth Choice. I hoped it wasn't true. I hoped that one of my kin hadn't been sucked in by Ophdian's lies. But after I saw how you defeated the Choice and stood up to the Beast, I hoped it was true. Eman confirmed it when we arrived in Ramni."

I thought back to when James had saved me from the light wall in the sixth Choice, then again when he battled Schism and cloaked us from Ophidian when we were fleeing. My grandfather, all this time. My heart beat steadily in my chest, accepting James fully and without question. The pieces of my family were starting to come together again.

I smiled widely and walked over to James, giving him a hug. "Does this mean I can call you Paw Paw now?"

His body went stiff beneath my hug, and he coughed twice. "James is fine."

Releasing him from my grasp, I chuckled. "Sounds good."

A hand lightly touched my shoulder, and I looked back at Silas. He gave me a quick nod toward the kitchen. Looking back at Nana and James, Nana gave me a delicate smile of encouragement. I tilted my head to the side. First

Silas, now Nana. I'm not sure how many more beautiful smiles I could admire today.

Stooping down, I picked up the sword before crossing the room and following Silas into the kitchen.

His back was to me as he gripped the edge of the sink. A line of tension ran through his broad shoulders, and I swallowed, unsure of what he was going to say. His shoulders rose and fell before he turned to face me. Those warm brown eyes swirled with questions as they darted over my face. His Adam's apple bobbed before he spoke.

"It's been so long, Addie," he said quietly. "I thought …" he ran a hand through his golden locks. I noticed how much longer they had grown, and how they matched the light blond hairs growing on his jawline. How had I not noticed before? "I thought you were dead."

I gripped the hilt of the sword, dreading the question I needed to ask. "How long?"

"Over a year."

"What?" I found the nearest unbroken chair and fell into it before I could faint. A *year*? It felt like days. How could I have been gone for over a year? My mind raced back to the ruins of the market. Something must have happened as soon as I left.

"You didn't know?" Silas asked, sitting across from me just like he used to.

I shook my head. Eman was right. Time did flow differently between our realms. A lot differently.

I looked back at him, feeling my new heart give me

strength. "I had to go. I had to know what happened to Lyle. I had to see if there was a way to save him."

Silas looked away, balling his hand into a fist on the table. "And you did?" he asked. "You found Lyle?" I nodded. He looked back at me with furrowed brows. "Where is he?"

I took a deep breath. "With Em—" I stopped, realizing Silas wouldn't recognize the name. "With the Mender. He's real, Silas. Just like the stories said. Everything, the good and the evil. It's all real."

A look of relief covered his face. He began to reach out to me, but he stopped on seeing me tense at his movement. Pulling back his hand, he asked, "Is he safe?"

I nodded, remembering Lyle's unraveling before I left Ramni. "He's safe. The Mender will take care of him."

"What about you?" He stared at me intensely. "Who's going to take care of you?"

I gave a small smile. "I'm not alone, so I'll be okay."

Silas looked at me in confusion, then smiled. My heart warmed at the sight. I was starting to love his smile.

"Plus" —I held up the sword— "I've learned I'm a pretty good swordswoman."

Silas laughed, and my heart beat with adoration. His laughter was deep and soothing, full of life and joy. I couldn't help but laugh as well. But when he looked at the sword, his smile faded into the stern line it had often been. He held out his hand, and I placed the sword in it, curious about his sudden change. As soon as the hilt touched his skin, a small, white glow pulsated from the blade.

I studied the sword, my heart beating faster at the reaction. "Silas, what is it?"

Silas grasped the golden hilt and studied it. "I don't know. I feel like I've seen this sword before. Like from a dream."

I bit my lip when I felt a thump against my leg. I jumped in surprise, but Silas didn't seem to notice, still entranced by the sword. The thump happened again, and I looked down to see the satchel moving.

With my new heart matching the pounding within the satchel, I lifted the flap and rested my hand on the tiny purple bag. I waited a moment longer, and the thump vibrated against my fingertips.

Grasping the bag, I pulled it out of the satchel as Eman's words reverberated in my mind: *You will know what to do with it when the right time comes.* The thumping increased as I thought this through.

"Silas," I said, staring at the little purple bag. He pulled his attention away from the sword and focused it on me. "I think this is for you."

A confused look passed across his face as I placed the bag in his hand. I watched intently as he pulled the gold cord, opening the pleats along the top. His eyes grew wide at what he saw inside. I leaned forward, bursting with suspense.

"Addie," he whispered, not taking his eyes off whatever was in the bag. "How did you find this?"

I was about to reach for the bag myself when he placed his hand in the bag, pulling out its contents.

"What is it?" I asked, trying to contain my overflowing curiosity.

Extending his arm across the table, Silas opened his palm for me to see what he was holding. I gasped and stared in disbelief.

Beating steadily against his palm lay the severed half of a bright red heart.

Look out for *Heartbreaker*, second book in the Heartmender series!